AT THE PALACES OF KNOSSOS

Nikos Kazantzakis

AT THE PALACES OF KNOSSOS

A Novel

translated by Themi and Theodora Vasils
edited by Theodora Vasils

Ohio University Press
Athens

Library of Congress Cataloging-in-Publication Data

Kazantzakis, Nikos, 1883-1957.
  At the palaces of Knossos.

  An abridged translation of: Sta palatia tēs Knōsou.
  Summary: With the help of the princess Ariadne and other
friends in the palace at Crete, Theseus enters the Labyrinth and
slays the hideous Minotaur, thus spearheading the resistance of the
Athenian people against King Minos.
  1. Theseus (Greek mythology)—Juvenile fiction. [1. Theseus
(Greek mythology)—Fiction. 2. Greece—Fiction] I. Vasils,
Theodora. II. Title.
PZ7.K2155At 1987   [Fic]   87-24762
ISBN 0-8214-0879-8
ISBN 0-8214-0880-1 (pbk.)

This translation is dedicated to our mother,
Julia Fitsorou Vasils

Translator's Note

At the Palaces of Knossos was one of two serialized novels written by Nikos Kazantzakis for an Athenian youth periodical. The first of these, *Alexander the Great* (published in English translation by Ohio University Press, 1982), ran as a serial in the periodical *He Neolaia* until its interruption by the war in 1941. It was republished in a complete Greek volume in 1979. The companion novel, *At the Palaces of Knossos,* was never published serially but eventually came out in an unabridged volume in 1981 (Eleni N. Kazantzakis, Athens).

The English version of this work is taken from the author's typewritten manuscript which appears to be an early, if not first, stretched-out draft intended for serial publication. In preparing this edition for the English-speaking reader, the translator has deleted certain repetitious passages and has abridged and edited the work to adapt it to its present book format. The story line has been retained essentially intact, and the English translation in general remains faithful to the original.

A brief history accompanying the text has been added by the translator to aid the reader in placing the work in chronological perspective.

AT THE PALACES OF KNOSSOS

At the Palaces of Knossos

Noon, in the heart of summer. The sun cresting over Knossos is beating down on the world-renowned Palace, and the bronze double axes, the vast gardens, the multicolored rooftops, are shimmering under its acmic rays.

Oleanders are in bloom along the riverbanks. The river is rolling peacefully. To left and right, people have come to sit and eat beneath the cypress, fig, and olive trees that shade its banks.

Beyond, the plain is steaming. The harvesting is finally finished, and the threshing floors are piled high with corn and golden wheat, that divine crop that nourishes the people. Stretched out beneath the olive trees, the peasants silently chew their olives and their crust of bread and gaze wearily at the mounds of wheat that still await their winnowing.

A din, like the drone of a giant beehive, is rumbling from the Palace where slaves, emerging from the cellars, are buzzing through the corridors. Like industrious working bees, they beat a hasty path down the long narrow halls, climb the marble stairs, and bring food to the masters.

The bronze door facing the great courtyard opens and a man steps out. Slight, gray-haired, holding a small drum, he walks with purposeful stride to the center of the courtyard where he halts. There, with ceremonious pomp, he raises his arm, beats a sharp drumroll, *rat-a-tat-tat*, with the drumstick, and calls out in a high, shrill voice: "Silence, all! The Princesses are resting!" He takes two more measured steps, halts, beats another drumroll with the stick, and once again calls shrilly: "Silence, all! The masters are resting!"

At once the din ceases. The doors close. The slaves hush, and the Palace plunges into silence.

In the royal sleeping chambers the maidservants come and go on tiptoe, noiselessly preparing the bedding beneath the windows where the two Princesses will sleep.

Phaidra, the eldest of the two, is tall and dark, with luxuriant curly hair and a rich deep voice.

Ariadne, the younger, is slender, golden-haired, and very fair of skin. Her lips and pale cheeks are brightened with rouge, lest people think her ill. She is sitting at her window, fanning herself and looking out at the courtyard. Her gaze travels past the courtyard, past the yellowed plain beyond, and comes to rest on Juktas, the sacred mountain that resembles some gigantic head reclining face up against the sky.

"Aren't you coming to bed?" Phaidra had already come to stretch out on the all-white sheets and was calling.

"I'm not sleepy,"murmured Ariadne. "I'll just sit here and look out the window for a while."

Phaidra laughed.

Ariadne turned and looked at her sister sharply.

"It's nothing," said Phaidra. "Just something I thought of," but her voice was mocking.

Ariadne fluttered her fan. She bit her lip and kept silent, and soon her sister closed her eyes and drifted off to sleep. *Good*, the younger Princess murmured to herself, *now I can be alone*, and breathing with relief, she turned to the window again.

Out in the courtyard, a tiny creature had come to scamper up a column and was perched atop a glittering double ax, busily peeling a piece of fruit. At sight of it, the Princess's eyes lit up. It was her little pet, the baby monkey they had brought to her from Egypt. She laughed softly, reaching out across the window ledge to grasp it. "Kitz! . . . Kitz! . . . ," she called to it coaxingly. The monkey let out a playful screech and buried its snout in the banana.

"Come . . . come . . . ," cooed Ariadne, waving her fan enticingly, but the coy little creature wouldn't budge. For an instant it looked back at her mischievously and, lifting its little tail, fanned it at her slyly, mimicking the fluttering of her fan. The Princess laughed delightedly and reached across the ledge, beckoning it to come, but the pampered pet kept biting into the yellow fruit and wouldn't be enticed.

Ariadne was leaning across her window, following the monkey's playful antics, when suddenly she sat up sharply. A man had appeared in the deserted courtyard below, a slender youth, about twenty, with chesnut hair. He was tightly girded with a red waist-band from which hung a short, wide, gold-hilted dagger, and about his head was tied a thin gold ribbon.

"There he is again," she murmured under her breath and quickly turned to dart a look behind her, to make certain that her sister Phaidra was still asleep.

The youth was approaching quietly through the sun-splashed courtyard, looking intently about him. His eyes were taking in the narrow passageways, the staircase, the Palace. He was staring with consuming interest at each tier of the three-storied Palace, as though committing everything to memory—the windows, the balconies, the terraces. . . .

Ariadne watched with curious excitement. For three days now this stranger in foreign dress had been scouting the Palace, taking everything in. *Who could he be? He came and went all day and never spoke to anyone. All he did was look. And always, not far behind him, was that savage Malis, spying on him. . . .*

And indeed, someone was moving furtively behind a column, stalking the foreign youth. From her window, Ariadne could see the King's Chief Officer clearly. His upper body was naked, and an iron sword hung from his waist. The features on his fiendishly cunning face stood out sharply—the pointed chin, the shaved mustache. His beady black eyes were nailed on the stranger, and they held such savage hatred that Ariadne trembled for the youth. *Oh Mother Goddess, protect him!* she murmured silently, *don't let Malis kill him!*

The young stranger had crossed the courtyard now and was de-scending the theater steps, heading for the broad stone path that led to the exit of the Palace compound. Malis, his head thrust forward between hunched shoulders, was following stealthily be-hind, like a wildcat stalking his prey.

Where was he going? The Princess's heart beat loudly. He was making for the harbor! "He's leaving!" she cried softly in dismay and for an instant was tempted to call out to Malis, *stop him! don't let him leave!*, but quickly she restrained herself. She was a Princess, and it would be unseemly to expose her emotions.

She fluttered her fan. The sun was scorching. Out at the thresh-ing floors where the peasants had returned to their winnowing, a gentle wind was blowing. She settled back against her window and watched the rhythmic movement of their wooden pitchforks.

3

As they raised them high, the wind would toss aside the chaff, and the wheat would fall in piles at their feet. *Poor peasants . . . how they worked all year, ploughing the fields, sowing, harvesting, winnowing . . . and then along came the Palace guards and took away their labor, leaving them nothing but the chaff. . . .*

She was pondering thus, watching the peasants out in the plain when the doors of the vast storage house began to open, and out came the Palace slaves with their large empty sacks. "There they come, to take away the wheat," she murmured, and her heart went out to the winnowers.

The young foreigner, too, as he was striding away down the broad stone road, heard the sound and turned with curiosity to see. Some ten Palace slaves were emerging from the storage house. Beardless and naked, except for a piece of coarse sailcloth about their waists, they fell in step and began marching toward the threshing floors out on the plain.

Malis hid behind an olive tree. Dropping cross-legged to the ground, he waited, his eyes nailed on the foreign youth. For three days now, he had been stalking him, wondering who he was, what he wanted. "Whoever you are," he growled under his breath, "you won't get away!"

Suddenly the sound of angry voices erupted from the plain. Shouts, curses, threats. Malis leaped to his feet behind the tree. A fight was in the making at one of the threshing floors! He cocked his ear. The peasants were resisting, refusing to give up the wheat. They had raised their wooden pitchforks and were threatening the Palace slaves. Women's shrill voices were joining the fray. *They had done the planting!* they were shouting, . . . *they would do the eating!* They were coming to blows, and now guards from the Palace were rushing toward the threshing floor, their lances ready.

The foreigner, watching from the road nearby, was following the spectacle intently. "The moment has come!" he murmured, his eyes blazing, and he made to approach the threshers. But as he was striding toward the threshing floor, he felt a powerful grip on his shoulder and, swinging around, turned to confront the savage countenance of Malis.

The Chief Palace Officer was eyeing him menacingly. "Where do you think you're going?" he challenged.

The youth shrugged off his grasp. "I don't account to anyone," he said. "I'm a free man."

"No one is free here!" snarled the Palace Guard. "Everyone's a slave to the King!"

"I'm not from here," said the foreigner. "And I'm not a slave!"

"Where are you from?" demanded Malis. "Why are you here?"

"I'm here to see the King," replied the youth.

"*I* am the King's eyes and ears," declared Malis. "*I* give his orders when he's away!"

The youth looked at the Officer contemptuously. "I don't report to slaves," he said.

Malis glared. Grasping a whistle that hung from his neck, he blew it shrilly and at once six guards sprang forward from the Palace doors and rushed to his side with their lances at the ready.

"Seize him!" he commanded.

But as the guards prepared to seize him, the youth pulled out his dagger and sprinted backward, bracing himself against the great outer door. He was balancing lightly against the Palace door, his dagger raised high, when two of the guards approached and as they reached to grab him, he brought his dagger down and the two rolled in the dust.

Malis cursed. "Use your lances!" he shouted. "Kill him!"

But the youth leaped backward again, backstepping through the great entrance into the Palace grounds. He kept sprinting backward, propelling himself toward the main courtyard where he had seen the altar with the giant horns. *If he could reach it and grab the horns, no one could touch him, he'd be under the God's protection.*

The guards were stalking him cautiously, none daring approach too close. Seeing them hesitate, Malis cursed them and lunged for the foreigner himself. The youth had reached the main courtyard now and was racing toward the sacred bull-horns. He was running hard, streaking toward the altar, reaching up with outstretched arms to grasp the horns that were glinting in the sun when Malis, close on his heels, pounced and grabbed him, raising his dagger high.

"Malis!" a woman's voice pierced the air. The Chief Officer shuddered, his arm with the dagger freezing in midair.

"Malis!" the voice resounded again, this time followed by an angry rapping against an upper window of the Palace.

5

Malis raised his eyes. He knew very well to whom the voice belonged. The Princess Ariadne was standing at her window, waving to him threateningly with her fan. Her golden hair had fallen loose about her shoulders, and her eyes blazed with anger.

Malis lowered his head, muttering something inaudible, and turned away. The guards, too, backed away in fear and quickly scattered, guards and Chief Officer disappearing inside the shadowy passages of the Palace.

The youth lifted his eyes toward the window. But the window had closed, and a deathly stillness resettled over the Palace. "The Goddess Athena is with me," he murmured, wiping the sweat from his forehead. He put the dagger back in its sheath and sat down in the shade of the altar. *It was safe here. He could rest for the present.* Exhausted, he leaned back. The mission upon which he had embarked was awesome, fraught with danger. He closed his eyes. He sat contemplating his position when soon, in the stillness of the sanctuary, a gentle sleep overtook him and he was back in his country far beyond the waves, on the coastal beaches of his homeland, where weeping youths and maidens were kissing his hands, seeing him off on his ship. *Safe journey!* they were calling to him. *Save us!* Then they disappeared in the dream and only the sea remained stretching before him, with fourteen dolphins gamboling in its calm waters. . . .

"Hey, there! Wake up!" A voice nearby was chasing the dream away, and the youth opened his eyes to see a boy standing before him. The boy was wearing a yellow embroidered waistband, and a brass ring on his right ankle. "Get up!" he was urging with a friendly smile, reaching down to take his hand. "Come with me."

But the youth looked at him with curiosity and refused to move. "Who are you?" he said. "What do you want?"

"Don't ask questions," said the boy. "You're to come with me."

The young foreigner wouldn't budge.

"It's in your interest," urged the boy. "Come!"

Still the youth hesitated.

"Afraid?" the boy laughed.

The youth reddened and sprang to his feet. "Let's go!" he said.

The boy turned and led the way, and soon the two were striding across the huge inner door of the Palace and entering the corridors within. It was dark and cool and the air was filled with curious aromas. They walked through a first corridor, climbed a broad wooden staircase, and reached the next floor. Here light, coming from a high skylight, revealed mural-covered walls to the left and right of them. In the soft glow, the foreigner could make out colorful paintings of seas and swimming dolphins and fish leaping from wave to wave. They came to a small grated window behind which was a workshop. Here the boy stopped for a moment and peered inside between the thick bronze bars. The foreigner, too, came close and looked inside. In the dim light he could make out a small cell where an old man was sitting hunched over, appearing deep in thought. "A prisoner?" he whispered.

"It's Daidalos," said the boy. "He has a son, Ikaros, who's a friend of mine. The King won't let him out so that he doesn't give away the secret. He's the one who built the Labyrinth."

"The Labyrinth?" The foreigner concealed a shudder.

The boy looked up at him in surprise. "You haven't heard of the Labyrinth?"

"No. I'm from a distant city," said the youth. "How could I?"

"It's where they keep the Minotaur," the young boy whispered, uttering the word with dread.

The foreigner held his breath and kept silent. *Careful . . . he must not arouse suspicion . . . a slip, and he'd be lost.*

"The Minotaur," whispered the boy again, "the dreadful monster that eats the seven boys and seven girls that they bring to it from Athens every year."

"I've heard something . . . ," murmured the youth, trying hard to sound casual. But the turmoil in his breast was strangling him.

"You've heard something!" sputtered the boy. "Why the whole world is buzzing. . . ." He hesitated, darting a furtive look around him, and lowered his voice. "The whole world is buzzing with the injustice!"

The youth stood still. *"Injustice?"* he whispered softly. He put his hand on the boy's shoulder. "You, a Cretan, call it an *injustice?*"

The boy was silent. "I'm not a Cretan," he said at length. "I'm an Athenian!" and he uttered the words proudly.

The youth's hand trembled on the young boy's shoulder. "I've heard so much about Athens," he said, controlling the tremor in his voice. "Forgive my astonishment, but I've never been to

Athens, and I'm seeing an Athenian for the first time." He paused. Then presently, pretending a casual curiosity: "How does it happen that you're in Crete?"

"My father came from Athens," said the boy. "He used to work with Daidalos. He's a coppersmith. He was married here and I was born here . . . but my blood is Athenian."

"Why don't you go back to Athens?" asked the foreigner. "Don't you want to?"

"I do," said the boy, "but I can't. The King won't let my father leave."

"Why?"

"Because he's working on something secret . . . down in the dungeons."

"What secret?" casually asked the youth.

"Iron."

"What's your name?" asked the foreigner presently.

"Haris," said the boy.

"Where are you taking me?"

"To the Princess Ariadne."

"Why? What does she want of me?"

"I don't know," whispered the boy. "She told my sister Krino to bring you to her, and my sister deliverd her orders to me. My sister is her maid."

The Goddess Athena is with me, smiled the youth to himself again, and quickened his step.

They had climbed the stairs to the second floor now and at their approach black guards with gold rings in their ears leaped to attention. They glowered fiercely, the whites of their eyes flashing in the dimly lit hall, but when they recognized Haris, they moved aside and let them pass.

The air smelled more pungent here. Behind the closed doors they could hear the sound of high-pitched voices and laughter and the jangling of bracelets. Here, too, the walls were covered with exquisite drawings—dancing women with flowing hair; a boy dressed in blue gathering white crocuses in a garden of flowers; white doves, green parrots. . . .

They came to a low door with tall white lilies painted on it.

"We're here," whispered Haris. "I'll stand guard while you go inside. Good luck!"

The young man knocked on the door softly and at once it

opened. Standing behind it was a young girl, smiling brightly and nodding in silent greeting. She was wearing a yellow dress embroidered with three blue lilies.

Krino, guessed the youth without speaking. He stepped inside. At first he could barely make anything out. The room was in semi-darkness, half-lit from a window that was closed and covered with a pink translucent animal skin. There was a heavy scent of lilies in the air. He took another step inside and looked around. No one. The maid who had let him in vanished. He waited. "Was anyone here?" His voice resounded with impatience.

Light girlish laughter answered from the corner near the window. There, beneath the light, he could see the figure of a girl curled up on a low divan. She was pale and blonde, watching him with enormous black eyes that glowed in the semidarkness.

"Who are you?" he said, approaching the girl. He could see the glitter of a huge gold ring on her finger.

"It's not your place to question Princesses," the girl replied, a trace of laughter still in her voice. "Who are YOU?"

"Why have you brought me here?" demanded the youth. "Are you Ariadne, the daughter of the Cretan King?"

"I told you," said the girl, pretending annoyance. "Princesses are not to be questioned. Now answer my question. Who are you?"

The youth hesitated. "I'm a merchant," he said, "from renowned Cyprus."

"And what merchandise have you come to sell us?" smiled the girl mockingly.

"Copper."

"Copper!" Ariadne laughed. "We don't need your copper. We have a god more powerful now. Haven't you heard?"

"What god?"

"Iron!"

The youth tensed. He had heard a great deal about this new metal, this hard, all-powerful metal that made formidable new weapons. The blonde barbarians were bringing it from the north, but no one knew how to work it. The barbarians kept their secret well.

"And who among you is able to work it?" he said.

"I'm telling you for the third and last time, stranger," warned the girl. "You are not to question a Princess. Now, sit here, across

9

from me; you look tired, and I have much to ask you." Having said this, she clapped her hands and at once the young girl Krino appeared. "Krino, bring a goblet of old wine for our guest," she bade the girl, "and some of the fruit that arrived from Arabia." Then, turning to the young man, "sit," she repeated in a gentler voice. "I have much to ask you."

The young man sat down on a low, ivory-decorated stool.

"Where are you from?" began the Princess.

"I told you."

"You didn't tell me the truth. You're not from Cyprus . . . and you're not a merchant. Merchants don't walk with head held high the way you do, and they don't have your air of pride about them. They speak fawningly, not with your lordly manner. Where are you from?"

"I see I cannot deceive you, great daughter of Minos," said the youth. "No, I am not a merchant. I am the son of a nobleman."

"From where?"

For an instant the young man faltered. "From Sicily," he said.

"From Sicily?" Ariadne raised an eyebrow mockingly. "They say an ancestor of mine, the great Minos, was killed there . . . drowned in his bath." She smiled, her almond eyes sparkling. "You are ancient enemies of ours; what do you want here?"

"I'm traveling around the world to see new lands and meet new people," said the youth.

"Why?"

"Because I'm young. Sicily is too small to hold me!"

Ariadne sighed. *She, too, was young . . . and Crete was too small to hold her! But she was a woman . . . where could she go?* She stood up and opened the window, letting in the sun. Three strands of pearls around her neck glimmered and her hair, too, shimmered in a golden glow. She turned to the youth. Her lips were painted a bright crimson.

"Your ship," she said. "Is it anchored in our harbor?"

"Yes."

"You must leave tonight. At once."

"Why do you tell me this?"

"Because I have taken pity on you. That's why I've brought you here. To tell you to leave."

"I can't," declared the youth. "I'm waiting for your father."

"You must leave before he comes back. He has gone to a distant grotto to talk with the Great Goddess and receive her blessing. He'll be like a savage, full of power, when he returns. Heaven help you!"

"I'm not afraid," answered the youth. "What's there to fear?"

Ariadne looked at him closely. "Malis, the officer who tried to kill you, is going to make accusations against you."

"Against me?"

"Yes. You're a spy. You've been stalking our Palace, taking note of everything. Who knows what you have in mind. If you value your life, you'll leave."

The youth shook his head. "I'm not leaving yet," he said.

"Don't you love your life?"

"Yes. But I love something else even more."

"What?"

The youth was silent.

Ariadne clapped her hands and at once Krino appeared. "Bring your santouri," she commanded the girl. "I want you to sing for us." She turned to the young man again. "Tonight we have a full moon," she said. "We'll be celebrating the great purification ceremony in the central courtyard. This is the night my father will be entering the grotto of the Goddess. Stay for the ceremony if you like, so that you can boast in your lifetime that you saw the Cretans in their worship and dance rites. Afterwards, I'm warning you again, you must leave. You're young. Don't die before you've accomplished great things. Do you understand what I'm saying?"

"I understand," said the youth. "That's why I'm staying."

Krino returned with the santouri and settled cross-legged at her mistress's feet. "What do you command me to sing?" she asked softly.

"The song of the Minotaur," said Ariadne, looking at the young man evenly. "Sing of how he devours the fourteen bodies that come to us from Athens every year."

The youth lowered his eyes under her gaze and looked away to hide the angry glint that flashed through them.

My guess was right, the Princess smiled, . . . *he's the one.*

Krino began to play. A plaintive sound reverberated from the santouri, a profoundly mournful sound, like a dirge, like the sound of fourteen bodies weeping. She threw her head back, exposing her white throat, and began to sing. The song was a dialogue between seven youths and seven maidens. The seven youths were weeping, bidding the earth farewell; and the seven maidens were responding, comforting them with words of encouragement. Under her skillful fingers, the santouri, accompanying the threnodial verses, was the roaring, laughing monster that had the body of a man and the head of a bull.

She was still singing when the youth sprang to his feet. A tear had escaped down his cheek. "Enough!" he said hoarsely.

The Princess rose, too, a look of satisfaction on her face. She turned to Krino. "Thank you," she said to the girl. "You have never sung better. Leave us now."

The girl bowed low to her mistress and disappeared behind the heavy curtains.

When they were alone, the Princess turned her gaze on the young man. "I found out what I wanted to learn," she said.

"And what did you learn?"

"That you're not a merchant from Cyprus. And you're not a nobleman's son from Sicily."

"What am I, then?" laughed the youth.

"Careful!" warned Ariadne, "Walls have ears in this Palace."

"I have nothing to hide," said the youth.

"You have everything to hide," retorted Ariadne, "or you're lost!" She walked to the window again and looked out. The sun had begun to drop toward the west, and Juktas had taken on a rosy hue. The plain was filling with shadows. Out among the threshing floors the Palace slaves, their sacks slung over their shoulders, were still transporting the harvested wheat. From a distance, they looked like ants following one behind the other as they hauled their loads back to the Palace. Across the courtyard, two white doves were soaring over the altar and came to settle atop the giant sacred bull-horns. Ariadne stood silent at the window, watching the day end. *It would soon be time to dress . . . time to prepare the sacred serpents . . . and get ready for the ritual dance with Phaidra before the moon came out.* She stood a long while looking out at the gathering twilight, a melancholy sadness in her eyes.

The foreigner was watching her uneasily. *Could she possibly have guessed who he was? Would she betray him? His life, and the fate of his country were in her hands.* For a minute he thought of falling at her feet and entreating her but instantly rejected the idea. *Whatever was meant to be would be . . . he would not demean himself!*

Ariadne turned from the window and rested her gaze on the youth. She looked at him long and hard, until her eyes grew misty. "Will you leave?" she asked again, and this time her voice was all entreaty.

"No," the young man answered quietly.

"*THESEUS!!*" she said, punctuating each syllable sharply. "You're playing with your life!"

The youth paled. He stared at her, astonished.

The girl smiled. "You see? I guessed who you are. You're the Prince of Athens. You came to spy on our Palace and to learn our secrets so that when you come back in the spring with the others you'll know how to kill the Minotaur. Am I right? Speak!"

"You're right," confessed the youth.

"Well? Do you have anything to ask me? Since you, too, are a Prince, I permit you."

"What do you intend to do? . . . now that you know who I am."

Ariadne didn't answer. She stood up and began to pace the floor. She stopped at the window and looked out again. The slaves had begun to decorate the courtyard, preparing it with myrtle and laurel, draping broad red ribbons about the double axes. Malis was standing in the center, barking orders in a savage voice. Now and then he would steal a glance at the Princess's window. One would think he suspected the hated foreigner was up there.

"What do you intend to do?" Theseus's voice broke in again, quietly urgent.

"I haven't decided yet," said the Princess. "Don't be hasty." Her voice sounded hollow and strained. She bent over an azure vase and sniffed the lilies, then went to where a little ivory goddess was hidden in a recess of the wall. The goddess was clad in a curious flounced skirt; her upper body was bare, and entwined about her arms were two black snakes. Ariadne stood before the statue and looked at it in silence.

Theseus followed her closely. She appeared to be praying. "Whatever she decides," he thought resignedly, "I'm ready."

At last the young woman turned from the statue and approached the foreign youth. "Take this ring," she said, slipping off the huge gold ring from her middle finger, "and look at it."

Theseus took the ring that she extended and went to the window where he held it up to the light. Carved in its center was a bare-breasted goddess holding a taut bow. To her right and left were two lions standing erect with upraised tails; and along the edge was a man, raising his arms in terror, as though he were worshiping.

"I've looked," said Theseus, handing back the ring.

"Keep it," said the Princess. "I'm giving it to you. If you are ever in need of help, press the seal in wax and send it to me. Whatever danger you find yourself in, I will help you."

Theseus opened his mouth to speak, but before he could utter a word the door was flung open and young Haris burst into the room. "Malis is coming!" he warned in a whisper, motioning down the hall.

"You must leave!" said the Princess.

Theseus made a bound for the door.

"No! not there!" cried Ariadne, grasping his arm. "Krino!" The young girl had already entered on the instant. "Take him through the secret passage," she whispered, pointing to Theseus, and the two disappeared behind the curtain.

Malis was emerging on the threshold now. He glanced quickly about the room and bit his lip. *He got away from me*, he thought to himself, bowing low before the Princess.

"What is it, dear Malis?" asked Ariadne sweetly.

"It is time for you to prepare, my Princess," answered the Commander of the Palace Guard. "The moon will soon be up."

"I have said my prayers to the Great Goddess," said the Princess, pointing to the ivory statuette in the corner. "I am ready."

2

Out in the great courtyard, where slaves were busy adorning the tall columns with myrtle and laurel, worshipers were already streaming in for the evening's ritual. The harbor of Knossos was filled with the long swift ships of the Cretans who were arriving since morning from all over Crete to worship at the renowned capital of King Minos. Most, in observance of their vows, were making the one-hour trek from the beach on foot, some carrying lambs and kids on their shoulders; others, pigeons and partridges;

the poorer, flowers and fruits. All were bringing their promised offerings to the Great Goddess whom the Cretans had worshiped since ancient times. She was the goddess of the people, and of plants, and animals, and they called her Mother.

Young Haris, too, was out in the courtyard carrying armloads of green branches to help decorate the columns. With him was his friend Ikaros, a boy slightly older than himself, a thin, restless youth with chestnut hair and blue eyes. The youth was seemingly bent on mischief this evening, following after Haris and heckling him as he worked, pulling apart the branches that the boy entwined about the columns. Haris, scrambling up and down the columns, was trying to quiet him, but the youth kept cavorting underfoot and generally making a nuisance of himself among the peasants who were arriving with their offerings, until finally our young friend exploded in exasperation.

"Hey, Ikaros," he shouted, "get to work! Can't you see, the moon's almost up and we're a long way from finished!"

"I'm not a slave!" scoffed Ikaros, his eyes flashing. "I'm not a slave to be carrying branches and decorating courtyards for the ladies to dance in!"

"No? What are you then?" asked Haris jeeringly.

"I'm a free man!"

"Then leave the Palace if you dare!" answered Haris. "Since you say you're free, go ahead, try to leave!"

Ikaros reddened. "I will!" he flared. "You'll see! One day, together with my father, I'll leave!"

"How?" laughed Haris. "You'll have to turn into birds!"

"We'll turn into birds!" declared Ikaros hotly. "You'll se . . . ," but before he could finish, a powerful hand had grasped him by the neck and was swinging him around. The youth looked up startled. It was Malis, the fierce Palace Chief.

"Quiet!" he bellowed, giving Ikaros a cuff that almost knocked him off his feet. Then glaring up at Haris perched atop the column, he shook his lance menacingly. "YOU!" he commanded angrily. "Get down here!"

Haris scrambled down the column and Malis grabbed him by the arm. "Come here!" he snarled, "and tell me, where did you take the foreigner this afternoon when you went inside the Palace?"

Haris was silent.

15

"Speak!" shouted the Officer. "Where did you take him?"
Silence.

"Speak, or I'll beat you!"

"Beat me," murmured the boy, and would say no more.

Malis lifted his lance. His face was purple with rage. He prepared to strike, his lance poised in the air, when suddenly Ikaros, leaping up behind him, snatched the weapon from his hand, leaving him disarmed. Livid, Malis swung around and lunged for the audacious youth, but as he reached for Ikaros, he let go of Haris, and Haris, seizing his opportunity, turned on his heel and bolted. At the sight of him fleeing, the frenzied Officer let go of Ikaros to chase after Haris and now Ikaros, too, took off on the run.

A snicker sounded nearby. *Try chasing rabbits by the pair . . . and end up with empty air. . . .*

"What's that, old man?" Malis whirled around, ready to vent his spleen on an old peasant who had been watching the scenario and chuckling to himself.

"Nothing, my Captain . . . nothing . . . ," declared the peasant, cowering. Then taking courage, "I was just thinking of my two rabbits," he added, all innocence, "I brought them for the Great Goddess and they got away."

Glowering, Malis turned on his heel and strode hurriedly toward the Palace.

The ladies of the Court were emerging on the grand staircase now, clad in long festive gowns. They were descending the steps like peacocks, the hems of their bell-shaped skirts shimmering under the lavish embroidery of flowers, grapes, and seashells that adorned them. A soft night breeze was gently ruffling their hair that fell in crisp waves about their shoulders. Their lips were full and painted scarlet and necklaces of multicolored precious stones gleamed at their throats. Children, walking before them, were carrying small bronze censors, perfuming the air with precious scents.

Young men to the right and left of them were leading the way, carrying cone-shaped sacred vessels filled with milk and honey for the Great Goddess. The youths were dressed in shiny loincloths, tightly girded at the waist with silver belts. All were wearing dangling earrings, and about each youth's right arm was entwined a colored bracelet.

16

Above them in the eastern sky, a full red moon was slowly rising from behind the mountain. And now a joyous murmur went up among the crowds. The Princesses were emerging from the Palace door! They were crossing the great threshold, dazzling in the full splendor of their ceremonial dress—Phaidra, tall and vibrant; Ariadne, fragile and pensive—each with two huge snakes coiled about her naked arms.

The crowds pressed forward, staring open-mouthed in eager expectation. Some had climbed the trees to get a better look. Theseus, too, had come, and was leaning against a pillar, following the brilliant spectacle with curious excitement. He watched in wondrous fascination. Never had he seen such royalty. Such opulence, such grandeur! Riches like these were unknown in his father's kingdom. Athens was simple and poor, a mere collection of villages that only recently had banded together to form a kingdom. But they had begun to build ships now that would take them beyond their Greek waters, into the Black Sea up north, and as far as Egypt in the south. In time they, too, would have wealth. He was staring at the magnificence, marveling, when he felt a small hand tugging at his arm.

It was young Haris. The boy had slipped through the crowds and had come to stand beside his anonymous new friend. "What do you think of all this?" he beamed at Theseus, pointing to the brilliant pageantry with pride.

Theseus patted the boy's head and didn't answer.

"Do you have anything as great in your country?" persisted the lad.

Theseus looked down at the young face beaming up at him. A look of sadness clouded his eyes. He bent close. "Don't forget you're an Athenian," he whispered softly.

Haris blushed.

Theseus patted him on the head, ruffling his hair playfully. "Don't ever forget it," he said smiling, but his voice was somber.

The Palace ladies had reached the center of the courtyard now and were forming a circle. Linking hands, they began a slow, swaying dance, chanting the Goddess's sacred hymns.

The Princesses, too, had come to enter the circle. Standing in the center, one facing the other, the two sisters were waiting motionless as the crowd hushed in expectation. Suddenly, with a sharp thrust of their arms that wakened the snakes, the Princesses let out a piercing cry and the snakes lifted their heads and began hissing.

The throngs gasped and fell back. Theseus, too, involuntarily drew back in a spine-tingling reflex.

Haris laughed. "Did they scare you?"

Theseus kept his eyes on the spectacle. The Princesses were beginning to dance, a slow, calm dance, their bare white feet gleaming on the moon-splashed tiles. They were moving serenely, in subdued rhythm, gradually accelerating their tempo, picking up momentum, hands and feet moving ever more swiftly as they danced. The snakes were leaping up now from the girls' bare arms and coiling about the Princesses' necks. For an instant, they hid beneath the sisters' thick curly hair, then all at once their heads appeared above the dancers' foreheads, swaying back and forth in rhythm with the dance.

"How beautiful! How frightening!" murmured Theseus, unable to take his eyes from the serpent-haired dancers. What kind of people were these Cretans? How civilized, and yet how barbaric!

Phaidra was turning toward the east now, raising her arms to the moon, calling to the Great Goddess. "Oh Mother, hear our prayer!" she intoned in her deep voice. "Tonight the King will ask for your blessing. Give him strength, so that we, too, may be enriched. Glorify him, so that we, too, may be glorified! Oh Mother, heed us!" She spoke, and gently caressed the snakes that had come to coil around her arms again.

And now Ariadne stepped forth and raised her arms to the moon. The crowd hushed to hear. "Oh Mother of men, plants, and animals," she began in a high, endearing voice. "I, Crete, am calling you! Extend your hand and bless my fields; multiply my sheep; bring the sun and rain; clothe the earth with vegetation; give fruit to the trees; blow wind in my ships' sails! I, Crete, am your beloved daughter, Oh Mother. Heed me!"

A din, like a storm at sea, rumbled through the courtyard then as the crowds lifted their arms heavenward and began calling to the moon. The handsome youths who were carrying the cone-shaped sacred vessels knelt at the altar beneath the huge horns and began pouring their libations of honey and milk over the earth. When they had finished, a tumult broke loose among the throngs.

18

"We're all going to join in the dancing now," explained Haris, taking Theseus's arm. "Here . . . give me your hand. . . ."

"I don't dance!" said Theseus brusquely, and stood back against the column where he had been leaning.

The crowds began forming a circle. Linking hands, they formed a ring around the Palace ladies. In the center, the two Princesses had already begun to dance. Hair flying, each holding a hand over her bare breast, they were dancing a lively dance, their eyes to the ground. The Palace ladies, too, had formed a second circle and were dancing around the Princesses at a slower pace. The third and largest circle was made up of the populace, chanting sacred hymns and swaying in slow, dragging step around the Palace ladies, they, too, with their eyes riveted to the ground.

Throughout the vast throngs, girls clad in bright red dresses were strolling about, sprinkling the people with rose water from colorful aspergilla that they carried in their hands. The air was heavy with the scent of roses.

One beaming young lass with black laughing eyes strolled up to Theseus and, whispering something, splashed him with her perfumed water. Theseus bent down to make out her features in the moonlit night. He smiled, recognizing Krino.

"Safe journey!" whispered the girl returning his smile gaily.

Theseus bent closer to catch her words.

"Safe journey!" she repeated softly.

"I don't understand . . . ," said Theseus puzzled.

"I don't either," answered the girl. "I'm only repeating what my mistress told me to say to you."

Theseus threw a quick look across the courtyard where the dancing had stopped now. The two Princesses were leaving the circle, preparing to return to the Palace. In a bound, Theseus made after them.

"A foreigner!" a voice rang out as he approached. "Don't let him near the Princesses!"

Ariadne turned her head to look and saw him tall and fair among the crowd, thrusting out his arm, opening a path to reach her. She looked at him unmoved, her eyes hard and cold, as though she had never seen him before. Theseus stopped short. *What kind of people were these? One minute tender friends, the next. . . .* He felt for the gold ring that she had given him. *It was real; and yet.* . . . The Princess kept her gaze on him, stony and unyielding, and Theseus lowered his eyes, unable to hold out beneath the harsh, implacable stare. *I've been beaten*, he thought, shamed.

Ariadne turned away then and continued with her sister up the staircase, the Court ladies following like peacocks behind them, until they disappeared inside the Palace.

3

Theseus, too hurried from the courtyard now. Instinctively he headed toward the sea. He needed to be alone, to breathe fresh sea air, to clear his head. *Before he could reach a decision, he'd need time and solitude . . . he'd need to think over carefully all that he had seen and heard that day.* . . .

As he was turning north to take the broad main road that would bring him to the harbor, he heard a shout behind him. Someone was hurrying after him, calling to him to wait.

"I'm Haris's father!" the man was calling as he approached. "Your young friend's father."

Theseus looked annoyed. He was anxious to get to the sea, to sort out his thoughts in solitude. "If you'll forgive me," he said impatiently, "I want to be alone."

The man, about fortyish, held out his hand. "My name is Aristidis," he said. "I'd like to walk with you, if I may." He spoke in a deep, firm voice.

Theseus softened. He still wanted very much to be alone. "Your name," he said, "that's not a Cretan name."

"I'm not a Cretan," answered the man. "I'm from Athens."

"Ah, yes," remembered Theseus. "I had forgotten. Your son told me." He held out his hand. "Come," he said, "let's walk."

They walked in silence for a while, two shadows on a Cretan moonlit road. *Two Athenians*, smiled Theseus, observing the shadows they were casting on the ground, . . . *two compatriots trodding the land that had enslaved his country.* His face suddenly clouded. *For how long? . . . for how long would this glorified kingdom continue to rule his country?*

"Your lordship is a foreigner, too," observed Aristidis, breaking the silence. "My son has told me a great deal about you. All he talks about is you. You're like a Prince, he says. . . ."

Theseus smiled.

"Are you a Prince?" the man asked boldly. His voice was shaking with intensity.

Theseus didn't answer. A thousand thoughts were troubling him. What if the man were a spy? What if he had come to trap him? These people were cunning. They were worldly, powerful merchants, wise in the ways of deception. He would have to keep his wits about him. "What are you talking about?" he said casually, "I'm a man, just like you."

"A slave," murmured Aristidis bitterly.

"No! A free man!" declared the youth proudly.

"Then why do you say you're like me?"

Theseus was silent.

They walked on without speaking.

"We're all slaves here," murmured Aristidis, breaking the silence again.

"Why don't you leave?" said Theseus.

"They won't let me. I've learned the art of working iron and making new weapons. They're afraid if they let me leave I might go to some other country and teach the people this dangerous new skill."

Theseus threw him a covert look but didn't answer. He was struggling with the thoughts that were leaping in his mind. *Should he take this man with him? Should he bring him to Athens to teach his people how to work this iron . . . so that they, too, could make formidable new weapons and wage war on Crete to free themselves? . . . .*

"Why are you looking at me?" said the man.

"This is not the place to talk," answered Theseus. "Let's get to the harbor."

They lengthened their strides. The night air smelled strongly of harvested crops. Out in the vineyards, vines were still spiring tall with clusters of unripened grapes, and somewhere an owl, flitting up an olive tree, was rustling the branches under its weight. In the distance the sea, calm as milk, was shimmering into view. They could see the glow of the harbor lamps and feel the sea breezes moving inland, filling their nostrils with the briny smell of the water.

"A beautiful night," observed Theseus, breathing deeply of the fragrant air.

21

"A beautiful sea," murmured Aristidis. "A beautiful sea for a journey."

"If you were to find a ship in the harbor that would take you away, would you go?" asked Theseus.

The man sighed. "No one would dare take me," he said sadly. "They're all afraid of the King."

They were approaching the harbor now. In the half light of the moon, the myriad ships, their prows erect, were gleaming boldly. Guards on night watch were marching up and down the pier, lances glinting on their shoulders. Some sailors, drinking at a tavern that was still open, were singing softly.

"Let's stop and have some wine," offered Aristidis.

"I don't like taverns," said Theseus. "Let's find a place where no one can hear us."

They moved on until they came to a rock at the edge of the wharf and sat.

"Now," said Theseus to Aristidis. "Tell me about this iron of yours. I've heard a lot, but never 'til now have I met a craftsman who knew how to work it. Can you make iron knives?"

"I can," said the other. "And swords. And spear tips. And arrows for bows. Any army that is equipped with my weapons is invincible."

Theseus bowed his head. He pondered, struggling hard with his thoughts. Should he speak? Should he remain silent? What if the man were a spy?

He raised his head and looked at his companion long and hard. He could see the man's face clearly in the moonlight. An honest face, sincere, with eyes that harbored a profound and indescribable sadness.

"Would you leave with me?" he said at length, and his voice was barely audible.

"I would!!"

"Not so loud!" Theseus looked about him sharply.

"I would!" whispered Aristidis fervently, grasping the young man's hand. "Take me with you! I'll leave at once!"

"Your children," said Theseus. "Haris and Krino. You have no fears for them?"

"No," said Aristidis. "They're under the protection of the Princess Ariadne. No one would dare harm them. They're both in her service."

"Do you have a wife?"

"No, she died. I'm free."

"Do you know where I'm going?"

"Far from Crete. That's enough for me," said the man, his voice shaking with emotion.

Two night guards strolled by. They looked at the pair sitting on the rock and halted.

Aristidis had raised his voice. "Our beloved King will be returning from the cave of the Great Goddess tomorrow . . . ," he said to his companion.

The guards continued on their way.

"You're a crafty one," murmured Theseus.

"Necessity . . . ," laughed Aristidis. "When one is a slave. . . ."

The moon had risen to the center of the sky.

Theseus got up. "Let's go," he said.

They climbed down the rock and walked along the water, hugging the shoreline beach after beach, until they came to a large cove beneath some cliffs along the seashore. A small caïque, unlike any Cretan ship that Aristidis had seen, was rocking quietly in the water. A simple craft, with a tall mast and four oars. It was stark white and had two huge eyes painted on its prow.

Theseus whistled softly in the dark, and at once two men sprang from the small ship's hold and stood at attention.

"We're leaving!" the youth said to them, keeping his voice low.

"We're ready!" answered the men.

Theseus raised his eyes to the sky that had suddenly gone dark. A cloud was passing, covering the face of the moon. "Athena is with me!" he murmured, "this is the moment!" and he leaped into the caïque.

Aristidis, not waiting to be asked, leaped in, too.

"Who's this?!" The two sailors grabbed the blacksmith, glaring fiercely.

"Let him go," said Theseus. "He's coming with us."

"As you command, Prince," they mumbled and released their hold.

Prince?! Aristidis' head spun round. "You're a Prince?" he whispered.

"Don't talk, grab an oar!" said Theseus sharply.

Aristidis grasped an oar, his heart racing. The two sailors

grabbed up the other oars, and Theseus sat at the helm. "In the name of Athena! Forward!" he commanded.

The three began rowing silently, gliding the ship cautiously away from the shore. The moon was still behind the cloud and the harbor was plunged in darkness.

"Careful! Don't make a sound with the oars!" Theseus cautioned softly. They were nearing the harbor entrance, rowing carefully, when a voice rang out from the lighthouse above.

"Who's there?"

Theseus crouched low. "Hold the oars!" he whispered.

The caïque stopped. They waited. One minute. Two minutes.

"Who's there?" the voice called out again. They could see a lantern swaying up in the lighthouse from where the voice was coming.

"There's no one out there!" shouted a second voice from the opposite tower. "Stop yelling!"

"I thought . . . ," echoed the first, trailing off.

"You're drunk!" laughed the other. "Quiet down!"

Theseus waited. A cloud moved across the sky and covered the moon again.

"Now!" he commanded softly.

The caïque shot forward. It cut through the water, lightly disappearing in the darkness, and in minutes they were shearing through the open sea.

"Hoist the sails!" the Prince's voice boomed now. "We're free!"

Aristidis mopped the sweat from his face. "Thank God!" he murmured. "We made it!" He turned to Theseus. There were tears in his eyes. He grasped the Prince's hand and bent down to kiss it. "Where are we headed, my Prince?" he asked, his voice choked with emotion.

Theseus pressed his hand. "Haven't you guessed yet?" he laughed.

"No," murmured the man. "Where are we going?"

A smile of triumph played on Theseus's lips. "To Athens, my friend!"

4

24

Early the next morning, Haris hurried in tears to the Palace to find his sister and his friend Ikaros.

"Father's gone!" he sobbed as the two listened in alarm. "I waited for him all night and he didn't come home!"

"Didn't he tell you anything before he left?" his sister cried with disbelief.

"No, nothing. I was with him at the festival, but then I lost him. He always talked about going away . . . and now he's gone!"

"He must be with the foreigner," said Ikaros. "I saw him after the festival was over. He was with your friend the foreigner, walking toward the harbor."

"That must be it!" said Krino in a stricken voice. "He went away with the foreigner! It's all very clear to me now . . . last night, just before the Princess went out to take part in the dance, she called me to her and told me to find the foreigner in the crowd, and to say *safe journey!* to him. It's all very clear now," she murmured, ". . . he went away and took father with him!"

Haris burst into fresh tears.

"Wish them good sailing!" said Ikaros, putting his arm around the boy. "Our turn will come next!" He looked down the corridors that were filling now with slaves coming from the threshing floors. "Let's get out of here," he whispered. "I have something to tell you."

The youngsters wiped their eyes and followed him with heavy hearts out the crowded corridor into the courtyard. Throngs of men and women were already milling about, waiting to see the King return.

Ikaros led the way hurriedly down the staircase and headed for the great southern portico that housed the spring where the new arrivals stopped to refresh themselves and bathe their feet before entering the Palace. Here, too, the vast portico, with its tall columns and bright muralled walls, was buzzing with people streaming in from the neighboring cities to pay homage to the King.

The three made their way past the crowds until they finally came to a quiet ravine at the bank of the river where the murmur of the water and the chirping of a tiny bird in a myrtle bush were the only sounds to disturb the solitude.

"This is fine," said Ikaros. "We'll stop here."

They settled beneath a blooming oleander and looked at one another solemnly. "You know I have no other friends than you," began the older boy, his voice deep with emotion. "Whatever good comes to me in my life, I have sworn to share with you."

25

The brother and sister looked at him soberly. Never had they seen their friend so serious.

"Now listen carefully," he said drawing closer. "My father, as you know, is a great craftsman. There's no one in the world who could compare to him. . . ."

"We know," murmured the two. Everyone knew of Ikaros's father, Daidalos. He was the one who had built the new twisted labyrinth where the Minotaur was kept.

"My father was the first to give life to statues," continued Ikaros. "Until now, all statues had their arms and feet stuck to their bodies. Like mummies. But my father freed their arms and feet and gave sight to their eyes."

"We know," said Krino. "That's why all your father's statues are tied down with ropes, so they won't get away."

"All that's nothing," said Ikaros with a shrug. "What I'm going to tell you now is the real miracle!" He lowered his voice. "Before I tell you," he whispered bending close to the pair, "you must swear that you won't give away the secret to anyone."

"We swear!" murmured the children.

"Even if you're tortured . . . or killed!"

"We'll never tell!" declared the two.

"Then hear the secret: For three years now, my father has been working to make wings—designing a pair that he could attach to his shoulders, and one that he could attach to mine, so that we could escape from the Palace, and fly away where we can be free."

Brother and sister gaped in disbelief.

"Wings?" exclaimed Krino, looking at him with dread and incredulity. "Wings? Have you lost your mind, Ikaros? Or has . . . ," the girl faltered.

". . . Or has my father lost his?" finished Ikaros.

Krino reddened.

"No, Krino," he said quietly. "I assure you there isn't a brain in the world that works like my father's. The first two wings are finished already; my father has made a trial run with them."

The pair stared in awe, not daring to question their friend's word.

"Starting tomorrow," he continued, "he'll begin working on the other pair for me. . . ."

"And you'll be leaving?" Haris cried in dismay.

"*We'll* be leaving," said Ikaros. "All of us! I begged my father to make a pair of wings for each of you. I told him I wouldn't leave without my friends." He stood up. ". . . But we must keep all this to ourselves," he warned. "Not a word to anyone! We'll bide our time. When the blessed day arrives, I'll let you know. And then . . . *whrrr!* . . . we'll soar away like birds!"

The children were on their feet. They fell on Ikaros, embracing him with tears of hope. "We'll fly to Athens!" shouted Haris. "We'll fly to Athens where my father was born!"

"Where mine, too, was born," said Ikaros. "We'll all go to Athens, where we'll live in freedom!"

A rumble could be heard now, as from an approaching multitude. The three conspirators hastened out of the ravine. They could hear the rumbling clearly, a chanting din from afar, accompanied by the clanging of metallic timbrels. It couldn't be the royal entourage returning already; the Goddess's grotto was up in the Diktys Mountain, some seven or eight hours away, and the King was not expected to return until late that afternoon.

They scrambled up a nearby hill. In the distance they could make out a throng of people coming, moving briskly, almost running. A priest was in the lead, dressed in hairy sheepskin and carrying a metal triangle which he kept striking in rhythmical beats with a metal rod.

It was the paean procession, a ritual observance of the harvesting that had just been completed. The priest, running ahead of the others, was chanting in a booming voice the thanksgiving hymn to the Great Goddess who had provided wheat to mankind. And the reapers, their wooden pitchforks slung over their shoulders, were following behind in a cloud of dust that was rising from beneath their running feet. The procession approached, sped past the hill where the three youngsters stood watching, and disappeared at a turn in the road toward the Palace.

"Poor peasants," said Ikaros. "If only they had wings to free themselves."

"The wings your father makes are not enough," the thoughtful Krino murmured quietly. "Here different wings are needed . . . wings of the spirit."

"Let's go," said Ikaros. "And let's not mention wings again. If anyone hears us, we're lost!" He headed down the hill and soon the three young friends were hurrying through the streets of Knossos, in the humble peasant quarter where the city's poor lived. People everywhere were preparing to welcome the King. House-

27

wives were tidying their houses, scrubbing their thresholds, hanging colored blankets from the windows. Young girls were watering the plants on their doorsteps, feeding the poultry, tying gay red ribbons on the household cats. Today all plants, animals, and humans were expected to be joyous.

The workshops and stores along the cobblestone streets were buzzing. Throngs of people, streaming in from the countryside, were jamming the narrow alleys—dark, long-haired, hook-nosed people, with eyes full of passion and fire.

Ikaros steered his friends through the crowds, acting as guide for the benefit of Krino who seldom set foot outside the Palace. The girl, looking about her wide-eyed, was astonished at the crush. "They're here for the bazaar today," Ikaros explained, leading expertly past the throngs.

They turned into a narrow street lined on either side with workshops—the famous workshops of Knossos. Krino sniffed. "How lovely!" A sweet aroma of cypress shavings filled the air. They had come to the Street of Carpenters, to the workshops that produced the famous cedar chests of Knossos. In shop after shop, artisans, stooped over their workbenches, were engrossed in their wood, carving it into the exquisite chests and furniture that Crete exported to distant lands.

The three continued on, toward the din of heavy hammers striking against anvils. "Cover your ears!" laughed Ikaros. "We're coming to the coppersmiths."

Ahead of them an enclave of small, blackened workshops—the copperworks of Knossos—were looming darkly to the right and left of the narrow street. A glow from a fire was coming from each of the tiny foundries. Inside, black slaves were working the bellows, blowing the flames to keep them constant, while in the center the coal-blackened mastersmith, clad in a leather apron, his powerful arms bare, was hammering away at the copper.

"What do they make here?" asked Krino in wonder.

"What don't they make!" said the older youth importantly. "Hoes, shovels, plowshares, axes, knives, lances, shields. . . ." He walked to one of the foundries where the walls were covered with weapons—swords, short double-edged knives, curious shiny shields. It was the foundry of his father's friend, Master Thurses, the famous sword craftsman. Every sword that came from this forge was prized, stamped with the outline of a hand holding a flame—the seal of the master. It was Ikaros's ambition to some day own one.

"Let's hurry," urged Krino, hoping to get a glimpse of the bazaar before heading back to the Palace. "I have to get back before the Princess wakes up."

Ikaros tore himself away from the coveted display and hurried the pair through the streets, past the workshops, past the potters and painters and sandalmakers, until they came to a broad prosperous looking avenue where the famous textiles of Crete were sold. "Look at their coat-of-arms," he said, ". . . a spider, weaving her web."

"How clever!" cried Krino stopping to admire the exquisite cloths. An accomplished weaver herself, she eyed the finely woven fabrics appreciatively.

"If you had a coat-of-arms," said Haris to Ikaros, "what would you choose? I'd choose an olive tree."

"I'd choose two giant wings," said Ikaros. "How about you, Krino?"

"I'd choose two bull's horns," answered Krino blushing.

"You love the sport that much?" said Haris looking at his sister uneasily.

"Yes," said the girl. She remembered how she had wanted to compete in the games at the great festival last year, and how he, fearing for her safety, had stopped her. She loved playing and wrestling with the giant bulls and trained diligently. For her there was no greater thrill than pitting her fragile body against the monstrous beast with the terrible horns and subduing the raw omnipotent power with her wits.

Ikaros hurried them on until at last they came to the edge of the city. Stretching before them was a circular elevated plane, bordered all around by trees—the great plaza where the bazaar was set up. In the center spired the altar with the giant horns of the Bull, and next to it, the bronze statue of the Great Goddess. Voices and clamor. People were everywhere, spreading their wares on the ground and setting up shop with whatever they had brought to sell.

The three plunged into the bustling square, past rows of vendors squatting beside their myriad goods—piles of wheat, sesame, barley, lentils, chick-peas, beans. . . . They passed a stall where some peasants were selling a kind of barley beer, sealed in jars that were ornamented with a barley motif. Alongside the beer were cheeses and honey. Another group were selling herbs: sage, thyme, savory, mint, and the coveted dittany. Krino stopped to sniff the sweet-smelling herb. There was no more prized herb for fragrance or healing in all of Crete.

Ikaros led on. He had spotted the fishermen who had set up shop under the Great Goddess's statue, fierce-looking, sun-baked men, hawking their catch in raucous voices. All the sea's treasures were spread out in broad, shallow baskets at the Great Goddess's feet—crabs, oysters, cuttlefish, octopuses, sea urchins—filling the air with the smell of the sea. Ikaros drew near. He sniffed the briny air and breathed in deeply. How he loved the sea! The burly fishermen were standing over their catch, bellowing out the praises of their fish in voices hoarse from straining. One old seafarer, towering above the others, was standing over a basket filled with sponges and conches. Gleaming like a pearl among the sponges lay an enormous twisted conch. Ikaros moved closer, his eyes on the magnificent conch. "If only I had money . . ." he sighed, gazing at it longingly.

The old seafarer smiled. "What's your name, my boy?"

"I'm the son of Daidalos," answered Ikaros.

The seaman looked at him in surprise. "The great artisan?"

"Yes," answered Ikaros. "Do you know him?"

"Do I know him!" The old salt's eyes lit up. "One day he came out here to the harbor. I was sitting in my boat, sorting out my catch. It was a day when I had happened to hit on a hugh starfish, the size of my two hands. I was sitting there, looking at it and admiring it, when I heard this voice: *Hey, there, Palikar.* . . .

"I looked up and saw a man dressed in foreign clothes. 'What do you want, effendi,' I said to him.

"How much do you want for the starfish? he said.

" 'It's not for sale,' I said. 'I like it, and I'm keeping it for myself. I'm going to nail it here on the prow of my ship, where I can look at it.

"Sell it to me, he said, *and I'll carve one on your prow even more beautiful; one that will never spoil.*

" 'And who is your lordship,' said I, 'that boasts he can carve a starfish more beautiful than this one?'

"I'm Daidalos, he said, *the King's masterbuilder.*

"I stood up then, out of respect. You see, I had heard of him.

'Here,' I said, 'you're a great artisan, you deserve to have this,' and I gave him the starfish.

"*Wait*, said your father, then. *I'm coming aboard your ship*, and he made a leap and came aboard. He took out two small tools from under his belt and knelt at the prow. He put down the starfish beside him and started to carve. He'd look at the starfish, then at the wood, and carve. And in a little while, what should I see? A huge starfish with five tentacles wrapped around the prow, as though it were alive.

" 'Only a god could perform such miracles,' I said to him, and took his hand and kissed it."

The old seafarer paused. "If you ever go out to the harbor," he smiled down at the three companions, "ask for old Olynthos's boat and you'll see the carving." He reached into the basket of sponges then and picked up the sea conch. "It's yours," he said, giving it to Ikaros. "I don't want money. Just take it, and tell your father 'greetings from old Olynthos the sponge diver.' "

Ikaros grasped the sea conch. "I'll remember you every time I blow it!" he declared warmly.

The two young companions stood watching silently, impatient to be off.

"Hurry, Ikaros!" they clamored when he had thanked the seaman and turned to them again. "We're late!"

"I should be at the Palace!" said Krino.

"And I should be at the harbor looking for my father!" said Haris.

"And I should be at my father's workshop, helping him," said Ikaros. Now that his father was working on the wings, he would allow no one to help him but his son.

The three broke into a run, Haris racing toward the harbor, and Ikaros and Krino heading for the Palace. Krino ran without stopping. All thoughts were on her mistress now. "Surely she would be awake by now, waiting to be dressed!"

"Don't worry!" Ikaros called to her as they sped through the narrow city streets. "You'll make it! See . . . we're flying like birds!"

The sun was high in the sky, and slaves were hurrying through the courtyards when the pair arrived at the Palace. At the watchtowers the guards with their bronze-glinting armor were standing erect at their posts, looking over the plains and the sea. The youth and maiden hurried through the southern gate, passed the guest portico with the refreshing spring, and disappeared in the cool winding corridors of the Palace. "We'll say good-bye here," whispered Ikaros. "I'll see you tonight," and he quickly left her to hasten toward his father's workshop.

For a moment Krino stopped to watch the handsome youth hurry away down the corridor. A tender warmth was in her eyes as they followed his strong, lithe form. Then turning away, she raced up the steps, two at a time, and ran without stopping down the long corridor of the women's quarter until she came to her mistress's apartment.

The rose-colored window in the Princess's bed chamber was closed. Light was filtering weakly into the luxurious room, softly illuminating the lilies that gleamed whitely in their azure vase. The Princess was lying in bed, her blonde hair covering the soft white pillow upon which she rested. Her eyes were open.

"Come in," she called sweetly to Krino. "You're late."

Krino reddened. "I thought you were asleep, my Lady," she stammered.

"I couldn't sleep," sighed the Princess. She looked at Krino anxiously. "Did you deliver the message?"

For an instant the girl stared at her mistress in confusion. "Of course, my Lady," she recovered, quickly remembering the message. "I sprinkled rose water on him and whispered 'safe journey!'"

"And what did he say?"

"He said 'I don't understand.'"

The Princess sat up angrily. "He didn't understand? Is that what he told you?"

"Yes, my Lady. But I think he understood all too well," said Krino smiling.

"Why do you say that?"

"I don't know if you'll be happy, or sad, my Lady," said Krino hesitantly. "But I must tell you. . . ."

"Tell me what? Speak up!"

"He's gone," the girl said softly.

A crimson flush spread across the Princess's pale countenance. For a moment she was silent, trying to compose herself. "How do you know?" she managed at length, when she could sound casual.

Krino told her everything she knew. When she had finished, Ariadne rose from her bed. "Come, dress me," she said.

Was she pleased? Was she saddened? Krino watched her silently as she helped her dress. Ariadne had picked up a small gold mirror and was studying her face. "Put some rouge on me," she said.

Krino laid down the comb with which she had been arranging her mistress's hair and brought out a small ivory box from which she began to rouge the young woman's cheeks and lips. She opened another box containing a blond dye made from saffron and applied it to her lashes and brows. All this she did with expert skill.

Ariadne watched her absentmindedly. "So he left with your father," she murmured when Krino finished.

"That's what I think, my Lady," answered the girl. "Haris has gone down to the harbor to see what he can find out."

Ariadne lifted her eyes to the window. "Open it," she said to the maid. "Look and see if he's out there."

"Who? . . . of course, my Lady," said Krino, instantly realizing *who*. She hurried to the window and opened it. The sun streamed in, and fresh air filled the room. The din of the crowds that had gathered below could be heard. Krino leaned out and surveyed the courtyard, her alert eyes sweeping in everything—the altar, the stairs, the doors, the column where he usually came to lean. No one.

"No one's there," she said.

Ariadne didn't answer. *He must be gone,* she thought. *It's for the best.* For a while she remained silent.

"Krino," she said finally, calling the maid to her. She took the young girl's hand. "My little Krino," she whispered gently. "Do you love me?"

Krino flushed. "I would give my life for you, my Lady," she said, choking with emotion.

"I don't want so great a gift," said the Princess. "All I want from you is this: if you are questioned about the stranger, say you know nothing. Do you know who he is? Were you eavesdropping when I was talking with him?"

"No, my Lady," said the girl. "I wasn't eavesdropping. But for a minute you raised your voice, and I heard. I know who he is."

"You must not tell anyone. Do you hear?"

"I hear, my Lady."

"And your brother Haris, too. Tell him he is not to say a word to anyone. He's a brave boy, and I know he won't be afraid."

"No, he won't be afraid," Krino assured her proudly.

"Has my sister wakened yet?"

"I don't know, my Lady. Shall I go and see?"

"No. You are not to tell her, either. No one must know. No one. Understand?"

"I understand."

"Now bring me the chest, where I keep my bracelets."

Krino went to a low table and picked up a large cypress chest that was decorated with birds made of mother-of-pearl. She brought it to Ariadne and placed it on her knees. The Princess opened the chest and took out a gold bracelet. On it was etched a scene depicting a youth and a maiden frolicking in a garden filled with flowers. "Give me your hand," she said to the girl.

Krino extended her hand. Her heart was racing.

The Princess slipped the precious bracelet around the young girl's arm. "It's yours," she said.

"Mine!" cried Krino. "Why?"

"To remember me by." She looked away, out the open window toward the sea. "I may be going away," she said softly. "I may be leaving. . . ."

5

The air was hot and scorching, stinging Haris's face as he sped along the main royal road to the sea. It was thick with dust raised by the caravan of men and beasts that were hauling loads to and from the harbor. Myriad carts, yoked to oxen or horses, jammed the road in both directions, carrying Crete's bountiful goods to the ships for export beyond the seas, or bringing back treasures to the Palace from around the world.

Haris pushed doggedly past the slow-moving caravan, impatient to get to the harbor where he was certain he would find some clue to his father's disappearance. He could see the tall masts of the ships as he approached. Two-masted, three-masted ships; mooring ships; embarking, horn-blasting ships; approaching, open-sailed ships. Everywhere ships! And everywhere a deafening roar!

He approached the wharf and stared in awe. The waters were filled with ships. Would Athens ever equal this? He stared and his heart felt suddenly heavy. Who could defeat such power? The King had no need of armies or walls to defend his land. With these floating fortresses, as he called his ships, he could fight his enemies before they dared approach his shores. Crete could rule and tyrannize the world forever.

He looked about him, dispirited. The harbor was glutted with people and cargo. Horns were blasting, dockhands shouting, orders reverberating from the watchtowers, voices shrieking to be heard. Everywhere din and clamor. And everywhere ships. He began to pick his way uncertainly along the pier, past the towering mounds of freight, past the giant jars and barrels destined for foreign ports. Whom could he ask? Where could he begin? Strangers, all. Dazed, he stopped at a protruding rock near the edge of the pier and sat down to collect his bearings. He sat amid the staggering confusion and stared at the mooring ships. Cypriot vessels not far from where he sat were unloading copper—big round chunks, like giant loaves of bread. Some Egyptian ships, anchored alongside, were bringing in bananas, dates, and ivory. One of them had begun unloading a herd of tiny monkeys and some black-skinned slaves. Farther down the wharf, a ship from some unknown distant land was unloading yellow-haired slaves. And another, tin and amber. . . .

For a brief spell Haris forgot himself, caught up in the extravagant display of wealth before his eyes. How big the earth was! How rich, how beautiful, how full of variety! His friend Ikaros was right. How much better to spread sail and roam the world, than to sit rooted like a tree.

He was staring hard, lost in wonder at the revelation before him when, above the din, it seemed he heard the sound of a familiar voice. He listened. Someone was calling him. *Hey, there, young Haris!* . . . It was his uncle Kaphisos, his mother's brother, coming toward him! He must have just anchored! Kaphisos was captain of a ship from Rhodes and had, indeed, just anchored, and spotting his young nephew sitting forlorn at the edge of the pier, he called to him and was hurrying toward him in surprise.

"Uncle!" With a sob at the sight of one of his own, Haris was on his feet, racing to his kin, and before the startled man could open his mouth to speak, the boy had flung himself into his arms and was blurting out the story about his father. He sobbed with relief, unburdening himself in his uncle's strong embrace, and when he had finished his incoherent tale, the captain shook his head in disbelief.

"Impossible!" he said. "Who would dare take the blacksmith aboard his ship? The King would have his head! It must be something else."

"But what?" sobbed the boy.

"Come with me," said Kaphisos. "It's too noisy here. Let's go to my ship where we can talk," and taking his nephew, he led him a short distance down the wharf to a ship where a wooden plank extending from the stern served as a bridge and, walking the plank, they went aboard and settled in the ship's prow.

"Now," said the captain, "start from the beginning. Tell me everything, step by step, so that I can understand."

Haris began with the foreigner—how he had been stalking the Palace every day, and how Ikaros had seen him and Haris's father walking together at the harbor. He told his uncle all he knew, and as he talked, he felt his heart lighten.

When he had finished, Kaphisos sat for a long while with his chin in his hand. "You're right," he said at last. "I'm convinced. Your father has gone away with the foreigner. It must have been something very urgent that took him away; he's not a man to act without thinking. Trust him."

"I trust him," said Haris. "But if only we knew where he went . . . what he's doing . . . when he'll be back."

"Don't worry," said Kaphisos. "He'll write to you when he can. Now go back to the Palace. In the meantime, I'll scout around and see what I can find out. I have friends here." He patted his nephew's head. "Courage!" he said to the boy. "You're twelve years old; you're no longer a child. This ordeal is the hardest you've had to face 'til now. Confront it like a man. Have faith in your father. But more important, have faith in yourself. Remember, it's in the thick of the storm that the good skipper shows what he's made of."

When Haris left his uncle Kaphisos and returned to the Palace, he found Ikaros waiting for him. The youth had come to sit beneath an olive tree outside the Palace gate, to eat his simple noon-day meal and watch the dusty road where Haris would be returning from the harbor. All morning he had been thinking about his friend with growing trepidation. If, indeed, his father had gone off with the stranger, it would turn out bad for him and Krino. The King would be in a rage and would certainly take it out on them.

It was past noon when he finally spotted Haris hurrying back on the long dusty road.

"Well?" he called out to him as he approached. "Did you find out anything?"

Haris looked pale, and his jaw was set. He sat down beneath the shade tree to catch his breath and looked at his friend soberly. "My father's gone," he said. "He's gone off with the stranger. I'm convinced of it now."

Ikaros received the news in silence. The foreboding in his breast was mounting. He listened solemnly as Haris described what he had seen and heard, and when the boy was finished, he sat in gloomy thought.

"Why so quiet?" Haris asked uneasily.

Ikaros didn't answer. He was pondering the dilemma, uncertain whether to voice his fears to his young friend.

"You know something that you're not telling me!" said Haris. "Speak! I can take it!"

Ikaros reflected for a while, weighing his thoughts carefully. He knew the other didn't lack courage.

"All right," he said at last, "I'll tell you what's on my mind. That brute Malis is sure to go straight to the King tonight and tell him everything about the stranger—how he was here spying on the Palace for the past three days, and how he disappeared. . . ."

"I'm sure you're right," said Haris.

". . . But that's not the worst of it. What's worse is that he disappeared taking your father with him. Do you realize what that means?"

"Yes. It's scary!"

"It's high treason!"

"High treason! Why?"

"Because your father knows a State secret. He knows the secret of working iron. And now that he's gone, the King will suspect that he's going to teach it to other countries—countries that until now only had copper weapons. If others learn to. . . ."

"I understand," said Haris.

". . . The King will be in a rage. He'll send ships out every-where to track down your father. And maybe. . . ."

Haris looked at him apprehensively.

". . . He'll want to get revenge and take it out on you and Krino."

It was true. The King would be furious at his father and would want to take revenge on them. Haris sat pondering the awful truth in silence.

"You did well to tell me," he said quietly.

"Yes. It's best to know the danger—and meet it head on."

The two sat huddled together, reflecting on the terrifying consequences.

At last Ikaros stood up. "I should be getting back to my father's workshop," he said. "Maybe our solution will come from there."

"You think so?" Haris didn't much believe in Ikaros's dream.

"I know so! One day, Haris, you and I are going to put on wings and fly away from this Palace that has us enslaved!"

One day . . . but right now we'd better brace ourselves to get through this ordeal! thought Haris. "I hope you're right," he murmured gloomily and, rising, followed Ikaros back to the Palace.

6

When the two friends met again late that afternoon, the trumpets were blaring the King's arrival. The royal entourage had been sighted, and great throngs were spilling into the streets to welcome him, waving laurel and palm branches.

Ikaros and Haris had come to wait outside the Palace entrance where they could watch the King's party as it approached along the royal road. They had climbed an olive tree, and from their vantage point above the crowds that lined the broad main road, they could make out the procession clearly. In the lead came the royal guards, bare-legged and bare-chested, their leather aprons tightly girded at the waist, earrings at their ears, and a giant plume atop each head. All were carrying red spears and small bronze shields that were embellished with a curious design resembling the figure *8*.

Behind them came the Palace nobles, borne on litters by black African slaves. They, too, were adorned with colorful plumes and earrings and golden bracelets. Ikaros and Haris knew them all by name—Nimrod, the King's chief hunter, a fierce-looking wiry officer sporting a scar on one cheek; and Oneirokritos, the dream interpreter, a corpulent, beardless old man with a heavy necklace of blue stones around his neck. All were wearing necklaces of precious stones—a strand, or two, or three—each according to his rank, and as they passed, they raised an indolent hand and waved indifferently to the cheering crowds.

Behind the nobles, drawn by four white bulls, came a great gold-embellished chariot, draped in costly purple. Inside, in a pearly iridescence of bejeweled plumes, sat a shriveled old man upon a golden throne. His bald, toothless head was crowned with a glittering gold tiara that was adorned with seven white ostrich plumes, and in his hand he held a silver staff embossed with three gold lilies at its tip.

The crowds set up a chant: "Long live the King! Long may he live!" and as the chariot passed before them, they reached toward it, tossing handfuls of new wheat upon it. But the old King inside stared stonily ahead, never budging, never throwing them a glance.

At the entrance to the Palace the procession halted. The slaves set down the litters and lifted the nobles out. As soon as the nobles were on their feet, they converged on the royal chariot to lift the King out. They spread costly rugs on the ground and, lifting the royal personage carefully in their arms, they set him down. And now, all stood motionless, turning their eyes to the Palace where the daughters of the King had appeared on the marble staircase and were slowly descending, a step at a time.

The Princesses, clad in ceremonial dress, their hair falling loose about their shoulders, were descending like goddesses, dark-haired Phaidra, goddess of the Night, fair Ariadne, goddess of the Day. They descended slowly, in measured step, and when they reached the bottom they approached their father and bowed. First the eldest bowed and kissed his hand, then the youngest, Ariadne.

A hush fell over the crowd. The trumpets had ceased, and nothing could be heard but the rustle of the Princesses' skirts and the gay jangling of the nobles' bracelets and earrings.

The King put out his bony, withered hands and placed them on his daughters' heads and blessed them. Then raising his royal staff, he gave the signal to proceed into the Palace. At once two nobles ran to him supporting him on either side, and as Malis, in full uniform, went before them opening the way with his double ax, they lifted him up the great staircase, barely allowing his feet to touch the marble steps.

When they reached the grand central courtyard, they halted. Here the King stood before the altar with the sacred bull-horns and held out his arms. His lips appeared to be moving, as though in prayer, but no words were audible. When he finished this mute prayer, he bent over the sanctuary where a bronze bowl filled with new wheat had been placed, and grasping a handful of the wheat, raised it high. The crowds surged forward. "Back! Back!" shouted the guards, and the crowds fell back.

The King raised his fistful of wheat and turned to the north, flinging the wheat in the air. He filled his fist three times more and flung the wheat to the east, to the south, and to the west, and each time, the crowds surged forward, grabbing up the kernels that scattered on the broad courtyard slabs. This wheat was considered sacred, and everyone took great care to save it throughout the year. They put it in tiny sacks and hung it about their necks to ward off the evil eye.

Haris had gathered up a few kernels, too. "For my sister," he said to Ikaros who was laughing at him. "I'm giving them to Krino, to make a good-luck charm for her hair. . . ."

"Aren't you embarrassed, believing such fairy tales?" needled Ikaros.

"It's the custom," mumbled Haris, redfaced.

The King by now was entering the great portal of the Palace. For a shimmering moment as he stepped across the threshold, the glitter of gold filled the doorway, then disappeared with him inside the dark halls.

The sun had gone down, and an evening breeze was bringing in the scents of thyme and oleander from the riverbank and the mountain opposite.

"Let's walk," said Ikaros, breathing deeply the cool night air.

The two strolled leisurely along the teeming Palace grounds, stopping now and then beneath the low-built balconies to eavesdrop on the nobles who were holding court there. The gardens and balconies were buzzing with animated talk as those of the nobles who had been left behind went seeking out the lucky ones who had accompanied the King, curious to hear the stories the returning nobles were relating with great relish and embellishment.

At a tiny garden in the east wing, Malis had taken aside his friend Nimrod, the King's chief hunter, and was firing questions at him. A small crowd had gathered.

"Only three nobles were allowed to go into the cave," Nimrod was boasting, and he, the chief hunter, was one of them. . . .

"But did you actually go inside?" Malis was asking.

"Of course, my dear commander. The minute we saw the full moon come up over the mountain, we lifted the King in our arms and went into the cave. It's pitch dark inside . . . you walk and walk, through pits and ravines, until you think there's no end . . . and suddenly you hear a terrible roar and the whole cave shakes . . . and you know it's the god Tauros. . . ."

"Like hearing a fairy tale," snickered Ikaros.

"Shh!" murmured Haris. "Let's listen!"

"Come on," laughed Ikaros, moving on, "my grandmother used to tell me stories like that."

"I know," whispered Haris, "but I want to hear the ending."

"Is that all that's bothering you?" laughed Ikaros. "Come, *I'll* tell you the ending. Once upon a time. . . ."

"I'm serious," said Haris, following peevishly after Ikaros. "I wanted to hear what it's like in the cave."

"That's what I'm going to tell you," said Ikaros. "I found out from my father. He was there and he knows. He was there with the King once, back in the days when the King still liked him." He looked at Haris mockingly. "Hear, then, the tale, according to my father:

". . . This bull that roars— and that the King's hunter says is the god Tauros—is no god at all, but a genuine bull. He's tied to a crag inside the cave, in front of a huge pit. They've gilded his horns, and they've tied a double ax between them. And in the pit, under the crag, sits the old priestess. You know her. . . ."

"The one with the white hair that we see at the festivals? . . . the one that foams at the mouth?"

"That's the one. She's dressed like the Great Goddess, in a long skirt with flounces, and her hair is braided with two snakes, and she sits there with poppies in her hands and some ears of corn. The King goes up to her and says: 'Great Goddess, Mother of men and animals and plants, give me your blessing. Give me strength to continue to govern Crete.' And the old woman opens her fists and the King fills them with gold. And he says to her: 'Do you want more?' And she says: 'I want more.' And the King fills her fists again and says to her: 'Are you satisfied?' And she says: 'I'm satisfied.' And he says, 'Then give me your blessing.' And the old woman puts her hands on the King's head and says: 'The blessing of the Great Goddess be upon you! Receive new strength and govern Crete!'

"And the King, they say, takes the new strength, gets back in his chariot with the four white bulls, and comes back to the Palace. There. That's all there's to it."

Haris was listening soberly. "Did you notice how he doesn't say a word when he comes back?" he murmured, ". . . as if he's afraid of losing his strength?"

"That's because he's not allowed to speak all day," said Ikaros. "But starting tomorrow. . . ."

"God help us!"

7

Night was settling in earnest over the Palace now. Inside, servants were scurrying through the long corridors, igniting wicks and filling the great stone lamps with oil. Their glow could be seen through the tall Palace windows. Out in the courtyards the cry of the sentries echoed familiarly from the watchtowers. *Guards, be vigilant! Be vigilant, guards!*

Voices and laughter were echoing everywhere. It was the time of night when the Palace was filled with the sounds and clamor of slaves emerging from the cellars, toting their massive trays, and hurrying with the evening meal to their masters' quarters.

In the royal wing, brilliant with luminous lamps, the King was waiting for Malis whom he had summoned to appear before him. He was impatient to hear all that had transpired in the three days of his absence and, just as Ikaros had fearfully predicted, the King had lost no time in sending for his trusted chief.

The fierce commander could be seen hurrying through the corridors toward the royal wing, moving in long, rapid strides, his sandals scraping loudly against the tile slabs. One could sense his agitation. Beads of perspiration were trickling down his forehead as he approached the royal chamber. For a moment he stood outside the King's closed door and hesitated, wiping away the sweat. He coughed a nervous cough and, taking a deep breath, put out his hand to open the door but, as though thinking better of it, pulled it back and adjusted the two red feathers on his head, instead. He straightened the two red feathers, tightened his belt, took one more deep breath and reached for the door again, this time pushing it open and cautiously stepping inside.

The vast, gold-embellished chamber of the King was aglow with the light of myriad lamps scattered all about, and a fragrant scent filled the air. The King was seated on an elevated throne at the far end of the room, near two giant bronze censers that were burning perfumed incense at his feet. His eyes were closed and he looked tired. His thoughts, if one could read them, were on this very matter of his weariness: *He was tired of playing these games . . . tired of dragging himself through mountains and caves to talk to a sly old woman who was never satisifed, no matter how much gold he gave her. All this trekking back and forth was exhausting him . . . but what could he do? He had to go through the pretense. He had to keep them believing that he talked with the gods . . . How else would he keep them submissive. . . .*

Malis approached and the old King opened his eyes. "I hear you," he said, acknowledging the Palace commander.

"Oh long-abiding King . . . Oh sovereign of the sea . . . ," began Malis drawing close.

"Skip the formalities," said Minos wearily. "Get to the report."

Malis cleared his throat and nervously began with his report. He started with the harvesting, describing how the threshing and winnowing had been completed and how the threshing floors had overflowed with wheat and barley. Next he described how he had supervised the filling of the Palace storage jars and how he, personally, had sealed the jars with the royal seal.

"Everything occurred in perfect order then?" observed the King when Malis paused. "You have nothing special to report?"

43

"Just a slight disturbance, my King . . . ," answered Malis cautiously. "The people rebelled at giving up all the wheat, but I sent in soldiers and got them back in line."

"You should have killed a few, as an example!" said the King. *The crops were his . . . the land was his . . . the people were his . . . they worked, and he, the King, gave what he pleased. That was the law. That was how he found it from his ancestors, and that was how he would keep it. . . .* "Anything else?"

Malis swallowed nervously. This was the moment he was dreading. How was he going to explain what happened with the stranger without bringing the King's wrath down on his head? "The day you left, my King . . . ," he stammered, his voice choking in his throat.

The King looked at him sharply. "Speak up!" he glowered. "What dreadful thing are you holding back?"

Malis drew in his breath and plunged into his story. He explained how a stranger, a youth, had come to the Palace and had asked to see the King. He explained how the stranger insisted on waiting for the King and would talk with no one else. He described the youth's appearance, the birthmark on the cheek, the noble bearing that betrayed a noble ancestry, and how the youth had roamed the Palace grounds, inspecting everything minutely—the towers, the doors, the workshops—and how he had stared at the workshops and finally gone into Master Thurses's forge and ordered a gold studded sword. He explained how he, Malis, had suspected the stranger of some treachery and challenged him, and how the stranger had fled through the courtyard with Malis in pursuit, and how he had cornered him before the altar and was about to kill the youth with his knife when the Princess Ariadne, watching from her window, called to him to let the stranger go.

The King was listening, interrogating tersely, biting his lip.

"I kept watching him in secret," continued Malis, "and after a while a boy came out to the altar where the stranger had gone to sit and took him into the Palace, toward the women's quarters."

By now the King was on his feet. He came up close to Malis, withering him with a look. "And then? . . ."

"And then I lost him," said Malis trembling. "I thought they had taken the stairs behind the courtyard, and I ran there, but they were gone. I searched everywhere, I combed the halls, the storage rooms, the workshops; they had disappeared. Then a terrible thought came to me, and I ran to the room of the Princess Ariadne. . . ."

The King groaned.

". . . But the Princess was alone. She was preparing for the evening's ceremony."

"Who was the boy?" The King demanded.

"The son of the blacksmith," answered Malis. "His name is Haris, and he has a sister who's the Princess Ariadne's favorite slave."

"Bring him to me!" commanded the King. "But wait!" He suddenly held up his hand as Malis turned to go. "Bring me the stranger first!"

Malis froze. Cold sweat broke over him.

"At once!" shouted the King angrily. "I want him here at once!"

"It can't be done, my King," said Malis weakly. "He's gone."

"Gone!"

"He disappeared, my King. He was at the consecration, where I was keeping my eye on him, but suddenly he disappeared . . . in the night. I sent guards everywhere, to the cities, to the villages, to the harbor. But he's disappeared."

"Fool!" bellowed the King lifting his hand. "Idiot! Get out of my sight!"

"My King," mumbled Malis, going down on his knees. "There's something more. . . ."

"More!" roared the King. "I've been gone three days and already you have the Palace in shambles! What more is there? Speak!"

"The blacksmith . . . ," stammered Malis.

The King started. He reached for Malis and grasped him by the shoulder. "Get up!" he shouted. "Look me in the eye . . . and measure your words carefully. The blacksmith . . . what. . . ."

"The blacksmith has disappeared, too," murmured Malis.

"With the stranger?"

"I don't know. . . ."

The King looked about the room. His eyes searched wildly for something to grasp—a lance, a sword, anything with which to strike this idiot chief. A cluster of bronze oil lamps were hanging from the chandelier beside his throne. He grabbed one and threw it, ignited as it was, at Malis's face—oil and all.

Malis dared not move. He didn't so much as lower his head or raise a hand to shield himself. The lamp struck him squarely in the face, splattering oil down his neck, his chest, his feet. He stood there mute, blood spurting from his forehead.

"Fool!" raged the King. "Imbecile! You let them escape right out of your hands! Now what?"

"Command what you will, my King," murmured Malis wiping the oil from his face.

"Go!" groaned the King. "And put a ring of guards around the Palace! Make sure no one leaves. They might still be hiding in some cellar. You hear?"

"I hear you, my King."

"Now get out of my sight. I'll deal with you tomorrow!"

"I kiss your feet, O long-abiding King," murmured Malis, falling trembling at the old man's feet again.

"Go!" bellowed the King, lifting his foot and giving him a savage kick to the head. "I'll settle the score with you tomorrow!"

Dripping with oil, wounded and humiliated, the fierce commander crept backward on all fours to the door. He opened it, looked furtively to the left and right down the long empty corridor, saw no one was there, and quickly stepped outside, keeping to the shadows along the walls. In the dark, his eyes were shooting sparks.

There was no sleeping for the King that night. He lay on his bed staring with wide-open eyes at the murals on the canopy above his bed. A thousand suspicious thoughts were racing through his mind. The stranger could be a prince from Asia . . . or from Cyprus, or Syria, or even Egypt. Or possibly, the son of some barbarian noble from the North—from Macedonia or Thrace, or beyond from the Hellespont. All those kings were jealous of his wealth and glory.

Suddenly a thought struck him. Could the stranger be an envoy from Athens . . . sent by old Aigeus? He had been hearing rumblings of rebellion from there lately. Athens was rearing her head.

She had been annexing her neighbors and was getting ideas about becoming a mighty kingdom. His spies brought him rumors that she was entertaining the notion of overthrowing the Cretan yoke, what nerve!, and of refusing to pay the blood tax—the tribute of the seven youths and seven maidens that he forced her to send to feed his Minotaur every year. "That must be it!"

He rose in agitation from his bed. Dawn was finally breaking. Through the open window he could make out Juktas still plunged in blue darkness. The morning star was twinkling brightly. In the distance, the peaks of Ida were taking on the first soft blush of dawn. He leaned against the window. The smells of newly harvested soil were rising from the earth. "I've grown old," he murmured, taking in a deep breath. "How much longer do I have to enjoy the beauties of this world?" He looked out at the profound stillness, his gaze drifting northward toward the sea. For a long while he stood at his window, pondering, his eyes fixed reflectively on the sea.

8

The sea was calm. Gentle waves were caressing the shores of Santorini . . . Melos . . . Naxos . . . Poros . . . all the captivating islands that were scattered on the azure waters north of Crete. And cutting quietly through the waves, speeding north toward Athens, was a tiny white caïque, with two huge eyes painted on its prow . . . and in it was Haris's father, sailing away, away, away, until he disappeared with the caïque into the horizon where the sea merged with the sky. . . .

As dawn was breaking young Haris, asleep on his spartan mattress, was dreaming of the vast blue sea. In the morning when he wakened, he didn't remember the dream, but his heart felt heavy. He wakened with his father on his mind. He lay in bed thinking gloomy thoughts when a sound at the door broke into his brooding. It was Krino. Her face was ashen as she slipped into the room and quickly closed the door behind her.

"Haris," she whispered urgently, tiptoeing across the tiny room to his bed. "The King knows everything! Last night Malis. . . ."

"Yes, I know," said Haris sitting up, "last night Malis went to the King."

"Now he'll be looking for you!" trembled Krino, pale with alarm.

Haris took his sister's hand and held it. "There's nothing to worry about," he said, sounding reassuring. "It has nothing to do with me."

"It does," persisted Krino. "He thinks you know who the foreigner is. . . ."

"But I don't!"

"Malis told him you took him to the Princess's room . . . and he thinks you know who he is, and where he went!"

"How do you know this?"

"I heard the King telling the Princess. He came to her room at dawn this morning and woke her up. He was furious. I could hear them arguing. He was threatening her and she was screaming back *I don't know! I don't know!* When he finally left she called me in and told me that he'd be sending for you and to tell you not to betray her."

"I won't!" declared Haris. "I swear, I won't betray her!"

Hardly had the boy uttered the words when the door burst open with a violent kick from the outside and a fierce-looking guard stormed into the room. In a stride, he was across the tiny cell, grabbing Haris by the neck and dragging him out. "Get going!" he barked at the boy's startled query. "The King wants you!" He was raising his arm to strike Haris a blow when Krino let out a scream.

"Don't touch him!" she cried, running to her brother. "He's in the Princess Ariadne's service, and you'll have *her* to answer to!"

The guard shuddered and let his arm drop.

For a desperate instant Krino clung to her brother. "Be brave," she whispered, holding him to her.

"I will," the boy mumbled, struggling to keep his voice steady.

Krino let him go and hurried back to find the Princess, to tell her they had taken Haris.

The guard, meanwhile, was setting Haris a rapid pace, marching him quickly through the winding corridors toward the King's room. As they were passing the workshops where the artisans were quartered, Haris stopped for an instant to peer through the bars of the little window over Daidalos's shop. He could see Ikaros inside.

"Ikaros!" he shouted, but the guard shoved him on.

"Keep moving!" he warned, and Haris hurried on.

Inside the little shop, Ikaros heard and jumped from his bench to come to the door. He looked down the corridor and saw Haris hurrying alongside the Palace guard and understood. "Courage, Haris!" he called after his friend.

The guard turned and raised his spear menacingly, then pushing Haris forward, disappeared with him around the bend.

The King was sitting on his throne. The throne, shaped to hold a single body, was made of costly alabaster and carved with great craftsmanship. It was placed between two muralled walls that were lavishly painted with clouds and lilies. One of the walls had a curious-looking animal painted on it, about the size of a lion, with a mane of peacock feathers and a curled tail. The strange-looking beast was stretched out among the lilies, its pointed head raised upright, looking toward the royal throne. Three thick squatty columns made of cypress wood supported the room's ceiling. They were painted black, with bright red crowns.

The King, sitting on his sumptuous throne, was tapping his foot agitatedly. His eyes were looking past the room, out the open door. The mountain across the plain was by now bathed in morning light and the trees were glistening in the olive groves, their silvery leaves rustling with the swallows that were pecking at the air. The King was gazing out the open door but seeing none of this.

Somewhere in the women's quarters a parrot in a cage began to screech raucously. "Good Morning! Good Morning!"

The King started from his throne. He went to stand against a column. *They'll never escape me!* he muttered, clenching his fist. *I'll track them down . . . and I'll skin them alive! . . .* He turned at a sound at the door. A guard had appeared, holding Haris fast by the arm.

"Come in!" he commanded, pointing impatiently to Haris. "You," he said to the guard. "Leave us!"

The guard left, and Haris came down the four steps alone.

The King checked his fury as he watched the boy approach. "Are you the son of the blacksmith?" he asked when Haris had drawn near.

"Yes, King," said the boy, raising his head.

"Where is your father?"

"I don't know."

"Who was the foreigner that you were talking with?"

"I don't know," murmured Haris again.

"What happened to him? Did he leave?"

"I don't know."

I don't know! . . . I don't know! . . . That was all he had been hearing all morning from his daughter Ariadne. The King glowered. *He couldn't have a Princess whipped by slaves . . . but this one . . . this one and his sister were a different matter! . . .* He grasped Haris by the shoulder and slammed him against the wall. "Are you going to tell me the truth?" he growled, "or shall I have you beaten until you're bloody?"

"I'm telling the truth, my King."

The King released his grip. "Guards!" he thundered, clapping his hands sharply.

Two guards appeared holding red spears.

"Bring Krino, the Princess Ariadne's slave, to me at once!"

The two guards bowed and turned to go.

"Wait!" he called them back again. "Take this wretched boy away and give him a hundred lashes!" He looked hard at Haris, "Are you going to tell the truth now?"

"I told it," said the boy.

"They're going to break every bone in your body! Didn't you hear what I ordered?"

"I told the truth," murmured Haris.

"Take him away!" commanded the King. "And when he's ready to talk, bring him back!"

When the guards had taken Haris away, the King began pacing the floor again. A fearful suspicion was taking hold in his head. So this was the blessing the Goddess had given him! He laughed a sardonic laugh. While she was placing her hand on his head, a stranger was stalking his grounds, stealing his Palace secrets, making off with his blacksmith. "It's all Malis's fault!" he growled. He stopped pacing the floor in the low-ceilinged room and went to the door.

"Find Malis!" he commanded a guard. "Tell him to report to me immediately!"

The guard went off on the instant.

The King leaned against the door and wiped the sweat that was running down his bald head. "It's all his fault!" he raged. "He should have seized the stranger at once and thrown him in the dungeon."

A minute went by. Two. He leaned against the doorjamb, waiting. Three minutes went by. He counted impatiently.

Malis appeared.

At sight of the chief, the King exploded. "As of today," he bellowed, "I am stripping you of your office!"

"My King . . . ," murmured Malis, turning green.

"Silence! You should have seized him and thrown him in the pit! Now go!"

"My King . . . ," tried Malis again.

"GO!"

Malis bowed low, almost snapping in two, and retreated staggering out the door.

"I am King!" ranted Minos, banging his fist against the pillar. "My Palace is on firm ground. It will not fall!"

Light footsteps sounded at the four stairs. The King turned. A young girl was entering the room, a maiden gently sweet and charming.

Minos watched her approach. "Krino?"

"Yes, my King."

"Tell me," he said, looking at her sternly. "Who was that stranger who came to the Palace and talked with your mistress?"

Krino remained silent.

"Who was he?"

Still silence.

"Speak!" shouted the King, grasping the girl by both shoulders and banging her against the wall. "Speak! Or I'll kill you!"

"Kill me, my King," was all Krino would murmur.

"Guards!!" Minos was livid.

Two new guards appeared.

"Take her and throw her in the dungeon! In the deepest pit!"

The guards reached for Krino.

"Don't touch me!" said the girl softly, drawing herself up. "I can walk by myself."

The King slumped in his throne. He watched the proud maiden walk from the room, a guard on either side, and fell wearily back in his seat. "I'm tired," he murmured, ". . . so tired." It was almost noon and the cicadas outside were chattering in fever heat.

He could hear the roaring of the bulls being led to water down at the river. He closed his eyes. *He was feeling faint . . . so very faint. . . .* He rested his head against the alabaster back and before he knew it, old and weary as he was, he dozed off on his throne.

9

Night. All were asleep in the Palace. The wind was howling through the trees, thrashing about the branches. In the distance, a dog was barking. An owl hooted, *whoooo-whooo-whoo!* Flitting from tree to tree, it was adding its mournful cry to the night.

Out among the dried-up wells at the far end of the Palace compound, a solitary figure was crouching in the darkness over an open pit. All around were deep holes—dried-up old wells that made up the Palace prison cells. The figure, a youth, was leaning over the rim of the pit, calling urgently to someone deep inside.

No one was answering. The youth thrust his head deeper into the black hole. It was dark, the narrow shaft went down at least seven fathoms, and the youth could see nothing.

"Krino!" he called anxiously. "Can you hear me?"

A muffled sound came from its depths.

The youth strained closer. "Krino!" he called again. "It's me! Ikaros!"

A faint cry, *Ikaros*, could be heard. Then, barely audible, the voice rose plaintively. "How is Haris?"

Ikaros bent lower into the well. "He's in bed," he called down into the blackness. "I left him sleeping."

The fragile voice trailed upward again, full of anguish. "Is he in pain?"

"A little," the youth called back.

"Is he wounded badly?" from the depths of the pit.

The youth hesitated. "He's a little black and blue," he lied.

In truth, Haris's body was covered with welts and bloody wounds. The guards had beaten him brutally. They kept beating him, demanding that he confess. "I told the truth!" the wretched boy would cry and clench his teeth as the lashes rained on him, cutting through his flesh. They kept it up for a hundred lashes until they left him raw and bleeding on the ground and Ikaros gathered him up, unconscious, and carried him to his bed. Ikaros had sat up with him through the night, putting oil on his wounds and comforting him. Mercifully, Haris finally fell asleep, and the youth was able to leave him for a while and come to Krino with some food.

"Have you eaten anything?" he called down to her.

"No," faintly.

"Are you hungry?"

Again, a hollow "no."

"I'm sending something down to you," he said, lowering a small packet attached to a string. In it he had put some bread and some olives and figs, and a small pitcher of water. "Hold out your hand."

Krino felt for the package with her hand. "I have it," she called up to him. "Now go! Don't let them see you here!"

"I'm going," said the youth. "I'm going back to Haris. Goodnight for now. . . ."

"Ikaros!"

"I'm here, Krino."

"Is the Princess well? Have you seen her?"

"She's well. I saw her going to her father's this afternoon."

"Go, now," urged the voice from the black hole again. "Go, before they catch you here."

"I'll be back tomorrow, Krino," Ikaros called down gently. "Goodnight for now."

"Goodnight, dear friend. Goodnight!"

Silence filled the pit again.

Back in the Palace, Ikaros stole down the stairs and headed for the humble basement cell where Haris lay. A small earthen lantern was flickering feebly in the room as he entered. The youth tiptoed quietly so as not to waken his friend, but Haris's eyes were open.

"Where were you?" the boy whispered weakly from his bed.

"I went to see Krino," said Ikaros coming to sit by the cot.

"What did she tell you? Is she afraid down there in the pit?"

"She asked about you," said Ikaros. "I told her you were fine." He looked down at his friend anxiously. "Are you hurting, Haris?"

53

"A little," murmured the boy. "But I'll be all right. You should go now and get some sleep."

"I'm sleeping here tonight," said Ikaros. "I'll keep you company."

Haris reached out feebly and pressed Ikaros's hand.

"Go to sleep," said Ikaros softly.

Haris closed his eyes. Ikaros, too, curled up in the corner and closed his eyes. The two boys lay still in the silence.

"Ikaros. . . ."

"I'm here."

"You're a true friend. . . ."

"Go to sleep."

Haris closed his eyes again. He lay very still. Every move was agony. He hurt terribly, but along with the tormenting pain, he was experiencing a profound consolation. He was remembering his father's words—*a man's worth shows up in the difficult moments of his life*—and he was pleased with himself. Try as the guards would to break him, he had held fast. . . .

Ikaros lay awake, curled up in his corner. At last he heard Haris's easy breathing and he, too, drifted wearily into sleep.

10

Captain Kaphisos was sitting before a small table at a waterfront tavern, opposite his old friend Captain Tsekouras.

"Bon voyage, Captain!" he was calling heartily, raising his cup high. Inside he was seething. The brutal flogging of his nephew Haris, and the plight of his niece Krino down in that vile pit, made his heart chafe for the day when the King would pay dearly for the injustice against these two orphaned children.

Outwardly, he was genial. He had learned that his friend, the old sea captain, was preparing to sail the next morning, and so he had invited him to dine with him at the tavern on this eve of the other's departure. In truth, he had reason to suspect that his friend was on a mission for the King, and the dinner invitation was a pretext for Kaphisos to fill him with wine and loosen his tongue. Something the old captain had let drop—something about tracking down a man who had mysteriously disappeared from the Palace—gave Kaphisos the idea that Tsekouras might be sailing off to find Haris's father.

"Bon voyage, Captain Tsekouras!" he beamed across the table

at his friend. He knew the old man's weakness for wine and filled his cup again. "I trust we'll meet again soon. Surely you can't be going far in that little boat of yours. . . ."

The barb hit on target. Tsekouras straightened up as though his spine had been jabbed with a needle. "You're mistaken, my friend!" he declared. "Captain Tsekouras is not afraid of the sea!"

Kaphisos smiled to himself, pleased. "I didn't mean to offend you, my worthy Captain," he replied. "Who among us doesn't know of Tsekouras's bravery? I'm only referring to your little boat. . . ."

"I assure you, Captain," bristled Tsekouras, "my ship is not as insignificant as you make it out to be!"

"Surely it can't hold up on a long voyage," persisted Kaphisos. "The most it could manage, I'd wager, would be making it to Melos. Beyond that, I doubt. . . ."

"Melos!" sputtered Tsekouras. "Melos!" He pounded his hand on the table. "Why, do you know where I'm going?"

"No, my friend," answered Kaphisos, drawing his chair closer.

Tsekouras picked up his cup and drained it. "You should only know!"he snorted.

"You don't mean to tell me that you're on some important mission!" needled Kaphisos, laughing.

Tsekouras's red face flushed deeper. "I see you don't think much of me, Captain," he declared, drawing himself up. "Listen, then, and learn what it means to be Captain Tsekouras!" He threw a cautious glance around him.

Kaphisos drew closer. "I suppose," he goaded, "you're going to tell me that the King himself is sending you. . . ."

It was more than poor old Tsekouras could bear. "That's right!" he shrilled, "the King himself is sending me!"

Kaphisos let his jaw drop. "The King! The King himself is sending you?" he allowed, pretending to look amazed.

Tsekouras was lording it now. "Do I have your word you won't tell?" he said, patting the other condescendingly on the shoulder.

"Is your secret so astonishing, then?" whispered Kaphisos, without giving him his word.

"Of course!" crowed Tsekouras. "I'm not sailing out to sea just to haul back cargo from Rhodes and Cyprus, like you. I'm out to haul in big fish. Hear this, my friend. . . . I'm sailing out to hunt down an important personage—a Prince!"

"You don't say, Captain!" declared Kaphisos. "A Prince! Does the King have that much faith in you?"

Tsekouras flushed with pride. "I'm going to comb the seas from Egypt to Thrace," he gloated. "I'm going to find this Prince and drag him back by the hair to the Palace."

Kaphisos filled their cups again. "To your health, Captain!" he said. "I see that you're a very important man. . . ." He paused. "But I knew all this," he said slyly.

"You knew!" exclaimed Tsekouras leaping to his feet.

"Sit down!" laughed Kaphisos. "I knew all along . . . I've known for days."

Tsekouras stared. "But it's a State secret. . . ."

"So what?" The thrice-cunning Kaphisos shrugged. "I know even more," he smiled, "something that your lordship, of course, doesn't know."

Captain Tsekouras's eyes bulged from his head.

"That's right," repeated Kaphisos. "I know something more. But it looks as though the King hasn't taken you into his confidence. . . ."

"Me?" shrieked Tsekouras beside himself. "He hasn't taken ME into his confidence?! And just who, may I ask, do you take me for?"

"What can I say, my friend?" drawled Kaphisos. "I esteem you very much . . . but it seems the King . . . well, since he didn't reveal the entire secret to you. . . ."

"He did!" exploded Tsekouras. "He told me everything! But I swore I'd never tell!"

Kaphisos laughed snidely. "That's easy to say," he goaded. "You pretend you've taken an oath not to tell, and that way you get yourself off the hook. What do you take me for?"

"What do you take *me* for?" sputtered Tsekouras. "I'll prove to you that I know everything! Since you already know the secret, it doesn't matter that I took an oath." He looked about him, then leaned close to Kaphisos's ear. "I'm sailing off to track down the blacksmith," he whispered. "He's disappeared . . . he's gone off with that Prince that I was telling you about. The King doesn't want the people getting wind of it. There. That's the secret."

Kaphisos put out his arm and clasped the hand of his simple friend. "Bravo, Captain!" he said. "I see now that the King does, indeed, esteem you, and takes you into his confidence! Let's drink the last cup to your health." He filled the cups and raised his own ceremoniously to his lips. "I drink to your health, Captain Tsekouras!" he declared. "I see with joy that the King—long may he live—recognizes your worth and entrusts you with the State's secrets. May you carry out your mssion and return victorious!"

"Thank you, good friend," murmured Tsekouras, and his breast heaved with pride. "Till we meet again. . . ."

"I wish you luck," smiled Kaphisos, rising from the table now. Having nothing more to learn, he was anxious to leave. "May the Great Goddess who watches over Crete be with you night and day."And having said this, he strode away, leaving Tsekouras.

Offshore, the islet of Dia was glistening in a rosy glow. The sun had begun to set, and the peaceful waters of the sea were taking on their winelike hue.

Kaphisos walked along the pier, smiling to himself. Simpleminded Tsekouras fell right into his trap. In his vanity to show that he was in the King's good graces, he had betrayed the secret. Dark red clouds were gathering out on the sea. "We'll have high winds tomorrow," he murmured, "high winds for Tsekouras's sails." He sat for a while on a rock at the far end of the pier. *So the King was sending out ships to capture Aristidis . . . God help him! He was capable of chopping the poor blacksmith to bits! If only he knew where Aristidis had gone, he'd have steered that simpleminded Tsekouras in the opposite direction.*

11

Early the next morning, Captain Tsekouras opened sail and thrust out to sea. A strong wind was blowing and the keel creaked loudly as the ship floundered in the waves.

Cretans were dauntless sailors and no tempest could frighten them. They took to the waters from early childhood. The sea was their playground, where they learned to swim and cavort and scramble up and down the ropes and masts of the myriad ships. As young boys they learned to handle the vessels with ease, plying the oars, taking in the sails, letting them out—all with never a fear of the storms. They had taken the sea's measure and were the finest seamen in the world.

Kaphisos, standing on the wharf, was watching his friend's ship being buffeted about by the angry waves. He had no wish to see Tsekouras's ship sink; no, he didn't want anything like that to happen to poor Captain Tsekouras. But what he did want was for him to come back empty-handed, not to find anyone, neither the foreign nobleman, nor his dear friend Aristidis the blacksmith. He smiled to himself. How he'd laugh if the King were to summon *him*, too, and command him to sail out to find the two fugitives. He'd play him a good game. Oh, he'd punish that sly old fox all right!"

One would think he had read the King's mind, for an hour had not passed when who should appear at the wharf, just as Kaphisos and his sailors were settling down in the stern of their ship to mend their sails, but a guard from the Palace. He stood at the wharf opposite Kaphisos's ship and lifted his arm to the Captain.

"Are you Captain Kaphisos?" he called.

"Aye, that I am!" answered Kaphisos. "What orders do you bring?"

"The King wants you!" announced the guard.

"*Me?*" feigned Kaphisos. "What does he want with me?"

"I don't know. You're to come with me!"

Now the captain suspected all too well what the King wanted. He rose quickly to his feet. *So far so good,* he chortled to himself. *He's sending me on the chase! We'll have a good laugh!* He girded himself with his finest belt, put on his new sandals, slipped two large gold bracelets around his arm—the ones he always wore on holidays—and bounded ashore. "Let's go!" he said, his eyes beaming.

Before noon they were entering the great North Gate of the Palace. They cut through the broad paved street, passed the stone theater to their left with the tall royal box, crossed the great courtyard, entered the cool winding corridors of the Palace, and headed for the royal apartments.

The King was sitting on the terrace, beneath a huge velvet canopy that had been set up over his head to provide him with shade. At his side, on a low stool decorated with mother-of-pearl, was a large gold tray piled high with grapes and figs. The King looked pensive. He was gazing out at the sea toward the north. Until now, he had dispatched five ships to hunt down the fugitives. And now he was summoning the renowned Captain Kaphisos. He knew the Captain's sister had married that cursed blacksmith, and he knew of Kaphisos's high regard for his brother-in-law. He knew everything about Kaphisos. His secret police saw to that. They kept a record in the Palace of every man living in the Kingdom. The King could look up the record and know each man's virtues and failings, what he said, what he thought. He had looked up Kaphisos's record that very morning: *A good captain. Fearless. Made frequent trips to Rhodes, Cyprus, Egypt. Commanded a ship that could hold up to 150 jars. Clever. A man not easily fooled. Loved wine and gold but was honorable, could not be bribed.* The King smiled. "Very well," he muttered. "We shall see. He's clever. So am I. We'll tangle and see who wins!"

The guard appeared on the terrace. "My King," he announced, raising both arms, "Captain Kaphisos!"

The guard disappeared and Captain Kaphisos entered. His small black eyes were dancing. "I worship your Kingship!" he said. "I am at your command."

The King watched him carefully as he approached, taking in the sturdy body, the sly piercing eyes, the high forehead. *Terribly clever looking . . . caution would be needed here. . . .*

"Welcome, Captain Kaphisos!" he said in a honeyed voice. "I have summoned you to entrust you with an important mission. A mission that is of interest to you personally."

"I hear your orders, my King," answered Kaphisos, smothering his glee.

"A great misfortune has befallen my Palace," said the King. "A misfortune that concerns you, too, Captain."

"Any misfortune of yours is a misfortune of mine," declared Kaphisos. "Are we not all your servants?"

"I mean a misfortune that concerns your family," explained the old King.

"My King!" Kaphisos caught his breath. "You frighten me! A family misfortune of mine? I don't understand."

"You will," said the King. "My blacksmith, Aristidis—hadn't he taken your sister for his wife?"

"Yes . . . my God, has anything happened to Aristidis?"

"A savage pirate came ashore," explained the King, "and saw him walking on the wharf at night and seized him and threw him in his ship and carried him away."

"What? They've abducted Aristidis?" exclaimed Kaphisos, clasping his hands in mock dismay.

The King shook his head ruefully. "And all I can think of are

59

his poor children," he sighed. "Their tears and their grief break my heart."

"Revenge, my King!" shouted Kaphisos. "Revenge!"

The wily King eyed him closely. *Was he pretending? Was he really hearing this for the first time? Didn't his nephew tell him anything?* . . . "Captain Kaphisos," he said aloud. "I'm pleased to see that you love our blacksmith as much as I do. You can imagine what the unfortunate man must be suffering in the hands of the pirates, far from his children."

"Revenge! Revenge, my King!" roared Kaphisos again, letting two tears slip from his eyes.

"Yes, revenge!" said the King. "That's why I've summoned you. I'm entrusting you with a great mission—to sail off with your ship and find me the poor blacksmith, wherever he is, and bring him back to me."

"My King," shouted Kaphisos, dropping all pretense now. "I swear I'll cross every sea, I'll put in at every shore, I'll search everywhere, and I'll find him!"

"And you'll bring him back to me!" repeated the King, emphasizing every syllable. Then lowering his voice: "Come here," he commanded, "come closer, and listen well to what I tell you."

"I'm listening, my King."

"There are sorceresses abroad, who feed foreigners magical potions. They give them magical fruit that they call *lotus*, and when the poor captives eat this, they fall under a magic charm and don't want to leave and return to their country . . . they forget their homeland, their children, everything. Do you follow me? They might have put a spell on our poor blacksmith, and he might not want to return to Crete."

"I understand, my King."

"He might resist you. But you're not to be fooled. The magic potions will have crazed him, and he won't know what he's saying. You are to seize him by force, and bind him tightly, and throw him into your ship. You hear me?"

"I hear you, my King," answered Kaphisos. "I hear you and I will carry out your command."

"Get on with it, then! Speed has a charm of its own. Prepare to leave tomorrow. And take care! Keep the secret guarded. Don't tell a soul why you're leaving and where you're going!"

Kaphisos bowed and made to take his leave, retreating backwards from the royal presence. He was about to step across the threshold at the other end of the room when the King pointed his finger at him threateningly.

"Captain Kaphisos!" he called to him. "If you betray me, I'll have your head!"

Kaphisos retreated, taking the steps two at a time. Out in the great courtyard he thought for a second of going to find Haris, to tell him the good news, but instantly rejected the impulse. "Keep your head, Kaphisos," he muttered, thinking better of it. "The King suspects you . . . don't do anything foolish, or you're lost!" And hurriedly he took the road leading to the harbor.

12

Meanwhile, far from the Palace of Knossos, our two fugitives were cutting through the sea in their swift ship, their eyes fixed ahead on the land that was coming into view. They could see the mountains of Attica rising in charming symmetry ahead—Hymettos, Pentelikos, Parnes—and their hearts were racing.

"Hail, Attica!" shouted Theseus, lifting his arm in salute. "Hail, my beloved land!"

Aristidis, too, was gazing out at the land of his birth and his breast stirred. How long it had been since he had left it! How long he had yearned to escape that hated Palace at Knossos and return to his homeland, a free man! And now he was here! But his heart was heavy. He was thinking of his children, Krino and Haris, whom he had been compelled to leave behind without so much as a parting word, and with difficulty was holding back the tears.

"Patience, comrade," murmured Theseus. "Come spring, all our sufferings will be over. I give you my word."

Aristidis shook his head. "The Kingdom of Crete is too great," he said sadly. "Who could rise against it, with its thousands of ships, its endless wealth? It is omnipotent. There is nothing it doesn't have."

"Except one thing," said Theseus, "the most important."

"What thing?" said Aristidis dubiously.

"A soul."

The blacksmith was silent.

"The Kingdom of Crete," said Theseus, "was an omnipotent Kingdom once upon a time—when it had spirit. But now, it has ended up a gigantic body without a soul. It can barely balance itself on its wobbly feet. Let a strong spirit come along and blow on it, and it will topple."

"I hope you're right," murmured Aristidis.

"Don't doubt it for a minute, my friend," said Theseus. "I ask one thing only of you. I shall be sending out ships to bring back iron from the north, and I want you to begin at once to prepare weapons for me. I'll give you my best smiths, so that you can teach them to work the iron. Everything must be ready by spring. Everyone in my Kingdom will be put to work—young and old, men and women. With the coming of spring, we must liberate ourselves!"

The ship was fast approaching the Attic shores now, and the charming little houses on the slopes of Lykabettos could be clearly seen amid the stately pines. Alongside Lykabettos, a lower hill was coming into view. At its peak, encircled by a hedge of walls, a wooden temple could be discerned. "The Akropolis," smiled Theseus. The walls encircling the little temple were glistening rosily, laughing in the last bright rays of the setting sun. "Well met, oh Goddess," he called out and lifted his arm to the temple in a reverent salute.

The sun was sinking fast and all around the mountains were taking on a tender violet hue. Pentelikos with its glistening black olive groves, Hymettos with its lush green pines, were shimmering softly. The walls of the Akropolis were beaming rosy tints, and down below, reposing at its feet, lay Athens in a wash of muted light.

"What beauty!" whispered Aristidis, his heart swelling with pride. "What simplicity and grandeur!"

Theseus was quiet. His thoughts, as they approached, were on his father now; he knew with what concern the King would be awaiting him!

And indeed, for days now, old King Aigeus, with his retinue of advisers, had been climbing the Akropolis and standing before the crude statue of Athena, offering prayers to the Goddess for the safe return of his son. Every morning, since Theseus had left on his perilous mission to Crete, the King would climb the sacred hill to the wooden temple that overlooked the sea and, having first paid homage to the Goddess, protectress of his city, would take up watch at the entrance of her sanctuary and gaze far out on the waters to wait for Theseus's ship. As each day passed without a sign of the familiar sails, the King's apprehension would mount until by morning of the seventh day, he could barely endure the agony of his suspense. If any evil were to befall the Prince, his Kingdom would be lost. To whom would he leave his throne? He was old. He had no other son. Who, other than Theseus, would be capable of subduing the bandits and wild beasts that threatened Athens's borders? And who, among the Athenians, would be able to free them from the dreadful tribute they were forced to pay every year to the Minotaur?

These were the thoughts that were tormenting the aged King when, on the morning of the seventh day, as a brisk breeze began to blow inland, the familiar caique with the red, wind-filled sails was finally sighted on the horizon.

By sundown, the ship had entered the harbor. The city's populace were all turned out—the King, the Court, the people—all were at the waterfront cheering the ship as it approached. A god-like youth was standing at the prow, lifting his arms to them, and the throngs pressing against the shore cheered wildly. Indeed, as he drew near, his chestnut locks about his handsome face aglow beneath the sun's last golden rays, their Prince seemed like a god to them. And when, in a bound, he was leaping ashore, embracing his father, greeting his people, the cheers reverberated to the skies. All were crying openly as old Aigeus, the agony of waiting over, clasped Theseus to his bosom, unable to speak through the tears that choked him. "My son! My son!" was all that he could murmur.

13

While Athens was celebrating her great joy, down in Crete the Cretans were preparing for the autumn harvest. The vintagers were gathering in the vineyards, plucking ripened grapes, hauling them to the wine presses, stomping them, filling their mammoth decorated jars. All the Palace smelled of must.

The skies over Knossos were growing darker, the air colder, the days shorter. The leaves on the trees were turning yellow and beginning to fall.

One day, the sky thundered and turned black. The clouds descended over the earth and by evening the autumn rains broke loose. It rained all night, the waters spilling in giant sheets down the mountain, swelling the river and running roaring into the sea.

Haris lay awake in his cell. It was two months since his father had disappeared and his sister Krino had been imprisoned in the well. How was she going to survive the cold and the rain? He lay awake worrying, pondering what he could do. Tomorrow he would go to the Princess and fall at her feet. He would plead with her to intercede. It seemed she had forgotten Krino.

But the Princess had not forgotten her beloved little slave. At every opportunity she would implore her father to release her, but he, ever hostile, vowed to leave her in the pit until his ships brought back her father, bound hand and foot!

She lay awake in her room now, listening to the first rains. It was not yet dawn when she rose from her bed and summoned her slave. Taking the girl, and a large bundle, she stole from the Palace and hastened in the night toward the dark pits. At the well where Krino was imprisoned, the Princess crouched low over the rim and peered inside. "Courage, Krino!" she called softly into the black hole. "I've brought you food and warm woolen clothes."

In the depths of the pit Krino stirred. A grateful murmur trailed upward.

"Be brave, my little Krino," whispered the Princess. "I'm going to free you!"

The shivering girl reached up for the bundle and choked back her tears. How many times she had heard these words from her mistress.

"Courage!" called down the Princess again. "I'll be back tomorrow," and rising, hastened back to the Palace.

Autumn advanced. One by one, the chores in the field were completed, the jars in the Palace filled. The harvesting over, all thoughts were turned now to the great holidays that were approaching.

At the Palace, the halls were buzzing with preparations for the long-awaited festival. The grand Court Ladies had summoned their seamstresses to prepare new wardrobes for the gala ceremonies, and day and night nimble-fingered slaves could be seen toiling over costly fabrics, embroidering lilies and dolphins and corncobs in red linen thread.

All were murmuring impatiently for the bull sports to begin.

Out in the plain, where the powerful bulls were grazing, their glossy bodies gleaming in the sun, slaves were preparing the threshing floors where the proud beasts would pit themselves against the youths and maidens who were trained to vie with them. Every day now, the cowherds could be seen leading the huge animals down to the river to bathe them and polish their horns and paint their hooves with brilliant red dye.

Haris and Ikaros watched all these joyous proceedings with heavy hearts. As long as Krino was imprisoned in the pit, they could feel no joy.

Ariadne was watching the festive preparations and smiling. She had a plan.

The days passed and the ships that her father had sent out to find the blacksmith and the foreigner began returning. One by one, from Cyprus, Egypt, Sicily . . . the ships returned, and one by one their captains hastened from the harbor to the Palace to fall trembling at the King's feet. With each report they gave, the King would draw his brows and scowl. Eventually, old Captain Tsekouras, too, returned empty-handed from his mission and fell trembling at the King's feet. The terrified captain gave his report and barely escaped with his head.

But one day, the last of the ships pulled into the harbor. The captain leaped ashore and sped with great haste to the Palace to find the King. "I think I have discovered who the stranger is!" he announced triumphantly and proceeded to report all that he had seen in Athens. He described old King Aigeus, and the King's son Theseus, "a youth, handsome and strong with chestnut hair and a birthmark on his cheek. . . ."

The King struck his staff on the tiles. "He's the one!" he shouted. "That's how Malis described him to me . . . with chestnut hair and a birthmark on his cheek."

"That's how he described him to me, too," said the captain. "The minute I saw him, I knew; and when I made inquiries, I found out that he had been away on a sea voyage and had only just returned to Athens."

"He's the one!" declared the King again. "And the blacksmith? Did you inquire about the blacksmith?"

The captain trembled. "I did," he answered. "But I couldn't find out anything more."

"Enough! Come back tonight," said the King. "And have your ship ready. You'll be sailing out again when it gets dark." Having said, he turned and summoned a guard. "I want you to bring the blacksmith's son to me at once!" he commanded. "And tell the scribe to come here, too, with his writing tools."

The guard vanished, and the King rubbed his hands together. "I have them in my clutches!" he muttered gleefully. "They won't get away this time. . . ."

He was rubbing his hands when Haris appeared at the door. The King's lips curled malevolently. "Get ready!" he said, as the boy descended the four steps and entered the Throne Room. "You're going away!"

Haris looked at him startled.

"You're sailing tonight! Now go!"

The young boy paled. "Where are you sending me?" he murmured in terror.

"Wherever I please!" snapped the King. "Now GO!"

Haris hurried away, and the scribe entered. A short, slight man with long gray hair, and long fingers. He was carrying a tablet of soft wax and a wooden box filled with curious-looking symbols: lines and circles and tiny houses and heads of animals.

"Sit," said the King, "and write!"

The scribe sat at the foot of the cypress column where the King was pointing and opened his box. It was divided into small squares, and each square contained one of the mysterious-looking symbols.

TO THE KING OF ATHENS, AIGEUS, MY SLAVE . . . dictated the King. I, THE KING OF CRETE, MINOS THE 33rd, LORD OF LAND AND SEA! . . .

The scribe was taking the wooden symbols, one by one, and pressing them with amazing nimbleness into the soft wax, and the words were leaping easily and clearly, making a circle at the outer edge of the wax, then another inner smaller one. . . .

66   . . . I, KING OF KINGS, COMMAND YOU: IN THE SPRING, WHEN THE SEVEN YOUTHS AND SEVEN MAID-

ENS ARRIVE HERE TO BE EATEN BY THE MINOTAUR, I
DEMAND THAT AMONG THE YOUTHS SHOULD BE
YOUR SON THESEUS! I HAVE SPOKEN!

"Bring it here!" The King commanded when he had finished.

The scribe approached and held out the tablet for the King to
affix his royal seal. The King removed the ring from his middle
finger, pressed it deep into the center of the wax, and slowly lifted
it out. The royal seal appeared etched in clear relief: a wild bull
with huge twisted horns, and a double ax standing upright between them, and at the feet of the bull, a slain man.

14

"Ikaros! Ikaros!"

Old Daidalos was bent over his bench engrossed in his work,
deaf to the shouts that were coming from the small barred window
over the workbench.

"Ikaros!" Haris was raised on his toes at the window, franti-
cally calling his friend.

Daidalos lifted his head and saw Haris's frightened face pressed
against the window. "What is it, Haris?" The old artisan rose in
concern. His son's young friend sounded terrified. Had they hurt
the boy . . . had they tortured him again? He went to the window. "Ikaros isn't here," he said gently. "Why do you want him?"

"I must see him!" said Haris, tears streaming down his cheeks.
"Where is he?"

"Probably at the pigeon house; I sent him to bring me a
dove. . . ."

Haris let go of the bars at the window and flew off.

In the small courtyard he could see Ikaros emerging from the
pigeon house, clutching a dove that he had just snatched from its
nest.

At the sight of Haris coming toward him, Ikaros held up the
bird in triumph. "Caught!" he laughed, but instantly the laughter faded from his lips. "What's wrong?" he queried, noting
Haris's stricken face.

"I'm going away!" said Haris.

"Away! Where?" Ikaros's voice caught uneasily.

"I don't know."

"You're not making sense. . . ." declared Ikaros.

"The King just called me and told me to get ready, that he was sending me away on a ship. . . ." said the boy.

"On a ship! You're leaving on a ship?"

"It looks that way."

"And you're crying?" Ikaros looked at Haris enviously. "Isn't that what we've always dreamed of? To get away from Crete . . . to freedom?"

"Yes. . . ." A sob caught in Haris's throat. "But what about Krino? Where will I leave her?"

"I'll look after Krino," said Ikaros. "I'll stand by her! You go on your way and don't worry, I'll look after her like a brother. Besides, who knows, you might even. . . ."

"What?"

". . . You might even find your father out there somewhere."

"But what if the King is sending me away to kill me?"

"Don't be stupid. If he wanted to kill you he could do it right here. What's to stop him? You wouldn't be the first."

"You're right," murmured Haris, "Your mind's working better than mine."

"When did the King say you're sailing?" asked Ikaros.

"Tonight. Late. But I should be going now . . . I want to say good-bye to Krino."

"Wait, there's time yet," said Ikaros. "We'll go together when it gets dark. If the guard's still there, we'll tell him the Princess sent us. He'll back off. Come, stop worrying, everything will turn out fine. You'll see."

"Let's walk a while," said Haris, somewhat comforted. "I want to say good-bye. Who knows when I'll ever see this land again."

"First let me take this pigeon to my father," said Ikaros. "He wants to study it, to see what makes it fly." As they walked back he related how the idea of the wings had come to his father. He had been looking at the pigeons in the courtyard one day, he said, when the thought occurred to him that they, too, were heavier than air. Yet they could fly. What was the mechanism that lifted them? This was what he had set about to find out, and this was how the idea had come to him to make wings for people."

When they had delivered the pigeon, the two friends took leave of old Daidalos and, hand in hand, headed for the broad main staircase. They raced down the steps, hurried through the streets,

68

past the little houses of Knossos, and soon were in the grassy meadow where the bulls were grazing. Here they stopped for a while to admire the animals that would be taking part in the bull sports, then continued on until they came to the river's edge.

The sun had begun to incline toward its western groove, and the birds were returning in joyous profusion to their nests. Two peacocks, strutting about a harvested vineyard, paused for a moment, spread out their shimmering plumes, and admired their beauty.

"How beautiful this land is!" murmured Haris. "How can I leave it?"

"All lands are beautiful," said Ikaros. "There where you will be going, you'll find new beauties. If only I were free!" he sighed. "How I'd travel! How I'd roam the world from end to end and see everything there is to see!"

"I'd be satisfied with a little house in the middle of a garden," said Haris, "where I could live with my father and my sister. I'd be satisfied to work all day, learning my father's craft, and at night come home to my garden and hoe and water and prune my bit of land. That's what would make me happy."

"Not me!" declared Ikaros. "I want to travel, to see new places and new people, and not be tied down anywhere! That's what it means to be happy! A man's soul isn't a limpet, to cling to a rock. It's a bird! and it wants to fly!" He looked at Haris wistfully. "Promise me something," he said.

"Anything!" the boy declared.

"Promise me you'll write. Wherever you go, write to me, so I'll know where you are. Who knows . . . some day you might see the three of us—my father and Krino and me—dropping out of the sky like pigeons out there."

"If only I could see that day!" said Haris passionately through the tears, "I'd be willing to die that very hour!"

"We don't want you dead!" protested Ikaros. "What good can you do if you're dead? You must stay alive! All three of us must stay alive, so that we can all live together in freedom some day! We must work together, Haris. We must open a shop . . . and make wings . . . and share them with everyone!"

Haris smiled.

"Don't laugh," Ikaros said soberly. "The day will come, I promise you, when people will fly like birds. No more of this

69

dragging around on foot . . . traveling by donkey and ox cart to get anywhere. People will have wings. And they'll fly like eagles from mountain to mountain and soar over the seas!"

"Dreams."

"They may be dreams now," declared Ikaros, "but the day will come when the dreams will become real. You'll see."

The two walked on. A cool wind was rising, playfully ruffling the young boys' hair.

The sun went down, and still the two walked on, engrossed in sober talk—two friends, hand in hand along the river's edge, taking their farewells.

The first star came out.

"The Evening star," murmured Haris. "Time to head back."

"Yes," sighed Ikaros. Now that the hour of parting was upon them, his heart was aching terribly.

15

At the Palace, the captain was standing before the throne of King Minos, listening attentively.

"Take this tablet," the King was commanding. "It's a letter from me to the King of Athens. You will sail tonight. And when you reach Attica, you will go up to Athens. There you will go to the Palace where you will present yourself to my slave Aigeus and give him this letter. Do you understand?"

"I understand, my King."

"And you will take the son of the blacksmith with you. I suspect the blacksmith is in Athens, pirated there by that brazen Theseus. You must find him. I am giving you his son to use as a decoy. Understand?"

"No, my King."

"You're stupid! Now listen. You've seen how birds are caught, haven't you? The hunter places a decoy in a snare and it sings and sings until the other birds, hearing it come close and then *phrrupp!* the snare snaps shut. Understand?"

"I'm beginning to, my King."

"You're to remain in Athens and parade back and forth with the boy, and wherever he is, the blacksmith is bound to catch sight of his son one day and fall on him and snatch the boy away from you.

When that happens, you are to go back to King Aigeus and say to him, 'either you give me the blacksmith, or the Cretan ships will come and set fire to your crops and your orchards and your Palace.' Do you hear?"

"I hear you, my King. What you command will be done."

"Now go. Call the boy, and take him away. And if you don't succeed, I'll have your head!"

The captain knelt, kissed the feet of the King, and hurried off in terror. When he was gone the King clapped his hands. At once the guard on duty outside his door entered. He was clad in a bronze suit of armor and on his head he wore a large feather. He stood at attention before the King.

"Go up to the royal chambers," commanded Minos, "and inform the Princesses that the Great King invites his daughters to dine with him tonight. Tell them they are to dress in their finest, as though for a celebration. And summon the chief gardener to appear before me."

The guard saluted and hurried off.

Before long, the gardener arrived. A lean, sly old bird, with a green feather on his head.

"Old gardener," said the King, "gather the brightest flowers from the garden and decorate the table. I am dining with my daughters, the Princesses, tonight."

Next, he summoned the Officer of the Guard. "Tonight," he said, "I want the guards to be served a double ration of food and a double ration of wine. I am pleased, and I want everyone in my Palace to be pleased."

It was a mild autumn evening and a warm breeze was blowing. The jasmine and honeysuckle still blooming in the royal gardens were throwing off sweet scents, and the wispy sighs of nightbirds carried softly from the olive grove. From his window, the King could see the first of the stars in the sky. He glanced at the two tall windows that were glowing with light from within the Princesses' apartments. "Dinner will be late tonight," he thought. He knew his daughters' vanity . . . by the time they put on all their finery, he would do well to pass the time with a game of chess. He clapped his hands. The guard entered.

"Summon the dream interpreter!" he commanded.

The guard hastened away and Minos settled back on his throne

71

again and waited. Soon a corpulent old man entered the room, approached the throne, and silently took his place opposite the King.

The chessboard lay open on a small table between them, illuminated by three torches from an alabaster lamp that was hanging from the ceiling.

The two began positioning the chessmen in their places. The King's were made of ivory; the dream interpreter's of gilded cypresswood. The chess table was decorated all around with silver daisies. Inside, it was divided in sections by wide strips of ivory and crystal. It had twelve gold circles carved at one end, and at the other, there were four ivory towers.

"I'm in a frame of mind to beat you tonight," said the King arranging his chessmen.

"I dreamed we were playing chess and that I won," answered the old man shrewdly. "That means I'm going to lose."

"Then we're even," chuckled Minos. "You win in your sleep, and I win awake. We've divided the Kingdom between us."

"Yes," laughed the dream interpreter, "I take the shadow and you take the meat."

"Let's go!" commanded the king, making a move with his chessman to the tower on the right. "I begin the attack!"

Out in the courtyard, slaves were preparing the royal table. Servants were hurrying back and forth from kitchen to table, carrying trays of food and decorated pitchers of wine. Gardeners laden with flowers were adding colorful touches with freshly cut blooms to the festive board.

Night progressed. The stars filled the sky. The chessmen under Minos's hand advanced and were now surrounding the tower. Two, three more successful moves, and the King would capture it. He turned for an instant from his playing and called to a slave. "Go tell the Princesses not to hurry," he commanded. "Tell them to take their time."

In the royal bedchamber, the Princesses were finishing their toilette. Slave girls, kneeling at their feet, were adjusting the elaborate skirts, sewing tiny silver bells at the hems. Phaidra, in a playful mood, was chattering and teasing Ariadne. Ariadne, sober and preoccupied, was barely answering her sister. The two were standing before a pair of tall mirrors held up for them by slaves, waiting for Phaidra's maid Myrto to finish tying pretty bows of ribbon on her mistress's waistband. "Bring me my three coral necklaces," Phaidra bade the girl when she had finished. "They'll go well with my black dress."

"And bring out the sacred snakes!" Ariadne called after her. "Have them ready for me."

Phaidra turned to look at her. "You're going to dance tonight?"she exclaimed in surprise.

"Yes," said Ariadne.

"Why?"

"To please Father."

"You never wanted to before."

"Tonight I do."

"You must want some special favor," said Phaidra. "The old man goes crazy when you dance."

"Maybe."

"What do you intend to ask for?"

"You'll see."

Phaidra pursed her lips. "You've changed lately," she said. "What's come over you?"

"Nothing," answered Ariadne peevishly. "Don't ask questions."

Myrto brought out the three coral necklaces from the large cypress chest where they were kept locked and handed them to the Princess. Phaidra took them and held them up against her glowing throat. Her bosom was bare, covered only by a flimsy white tulle. Her lips were tinted a brilliant red, and her eyes, painted by her slaves with a filmy border of blue, looked enormous, almond-shaped and downy, like a doe's.

"You look beautiful," said Ariadne, regarding her sister admiringly.

Phaidra smiled, pleased. "You dance better than I do," she acknowledged in return.

A slave appeared at the door. "The King has finished his chess," he announced. "He invites you to come down."

At once the maids picked up the lamps and began filing out the room. The Princesses followed. Slowly they descended the stairs, the maids lighting the way before them. They walked leisurely, regally, glittering like peacocks with outspread plumes—Phaidra in her gown of black with its red embroidered birds and yellow ears of corn, and Ariadne in her gown of blue with its gold embroidered fishes.

The King was waiting out in the courtyard. He smiled to himself as he watched them approach. *They were beautiful. It was time he summoned the great princes from the lands and islands beyond the seas, to select bridegrooms for them.* "Welcome!" he beamed cordially as they drew near.

"You do us great honor, Father," said Phaidra.

Ariadne remained silent.

The three sat at the table, the King at the head on a high throne, Phaidra to his right, Ariadne to his left.

The slaves took their positions, sitting cross-legged at the garden entrance behind the cypress column, and began playing the flute; light, playful tunes, to enhance the masters' appetites.

Ariadne was silent, her eyes on her father. She was watching him uneasily. The slaves in attendance at the royal throne were filling and refilling his goblet with wine and he, in unusual high spirits, was draining it with the greatest of pleasure. *What,* she wondered, *was he so pleased about?*

Cup after cup, the King downed his wine, smiling to himself. He was reflecting on the ship that was sailing away and on the letter it was carrying to the King of Athens. In his imagination, he already had that insolent Theseus in his clutches and was throwing him in the Labyrinth. In his mind he was envisioning the hated youth being crushed in the Minotaur's ferocious grasp. *And the blacksmith, too,* he was chortling to himself, . . . *he had put a good bait on his hook . . . he'd snare that blacksmith, too. No one could escape him! No one!*

He rubbed his hands contentedly. The meal was over and two slave girls came forth and began sprinkling the air with rose water. Two others brought a gold basin and pitcher to the table for the King and Princesses to rinse their hands. And now, at a signal from the King who rose and bade the slaves leave, the servants disappeared, leaving the royal family to themselves in the starlit courtyard.

The King turned to his youngest daughter. "Ariadne," he said, "do you want to please me tonight?"

"I'm at your command, Father," answered the Princess. *Her little plan was working.*

74 "Dance for me," said the King.

Ariadne rose from the table. "What dance will please you, Father?" she asked sweetly.

"The one that you'll be dancing at the festival of the Bull," said the King, "the dance of Man and Bull. That's the one I like."

Ariadne smiled.

The lanterns were snuffed out and the stars shone forth in the sky. A gentle breeze was blowing. Two owls across the mountain were hooting a monotonous, melancholy cry; and from the watchtower, the call of the nightguard echoed its familiar intonations: *sentries be vigilant! . . . be vigilant sentries! . . .*

The Princess solemnly untied the ribbon in her hair and let the thick tresses spill loose in waves about her shoulders. She looked across the courtyard toward the column where her slave had come to stand, and clapped her hands sharply. "Bring out the snakes!" she called aloud.

At once, the slave girl hidden behind the pillar, came forward with the snakes. The Princess took them from her and began caressing them. She gently stroked the snakes until their little tongues, darting in and out, began to hiss contentedly. She grasped them firmly by the middle then and almost imperceptibly began to move, arching a bare foot on the flat courtyard tiles, feeling the ground cautiously, as though it were a precipice and she were testing to find solid ground. Slowly, she lowered her head, in the manner of a bull preparing to gore his prey, and with a sudden swift thrust, she began to dance.

She danced possessed, whirling and leaping across the tiles, hair flying, body spinning and swaying. Now she would quicken the tempo; now she would come to a sudden stop, her body taut and motionless, stretching from her toes like an arrow on the verge of being sprung. Whirling, stopping, charging, she spun and swayed to the fierce rhythm of the dance.

The King was straining in his throne, watching with bulging eyes, his bald pate gleaming ivorylike beneath the star-illuminated sky. What he was seeing in the nimbus out there in the courtyard was no longer his daughter, but a glistening bull, wrestling and playing with a human. Now the bull would charge with lowered head and upraised horns; now the man would materialize, motionless and slender as an arrow. He was watching enthralled, his dry ashen lips trembling with passion.

"Ariadne!" he shouted at last in a hoarse, strained voice. "Enough!"

The Princess smiled to herself and stopped. Her body was

steaming lightly, glistening with a filmy mist. She returned to the table and sat down. The slave girl behind the column hurried to her again and covered her with a robe. She sprinkled rose water on her perspiring neck and temples and took away the snakes that she uncoiled from her arms.

"You've never danced so beautifully!" whispered Phaidra, embracing her. "Now you can do whatever you want with the King."

The old King, too, reached down and kissed his daughter. "Ariadne," he said deeply moved, "you have given me great joy tonight. Ask me for anything you want."

Ariadne, breathing deeply, didn't answer.

"Come," said the King. "Isn't there some favor you want from me?"

"There is," the Princess answered softly.

"Speak, then. Ask for anything you want."

The Princess hesitated. "Will you swear you'll grant me what I ask for?" she said, looking at her father coyly.

"I swear by the Great Mother Goddess!" declared the King.

Then, most endearingly, Ariadne put her arms around her father and bent close to his ear. "Free Krino," she whispered softly.

The King looked across the courtyard toward the steps where two bodyguards were standing like statues. "Guards!" he called to them.

At once the two leaped to attention.

"Go immediately," he commanded, "and remove Krino from the pit and bring her here!"

The guards bounded down the steps and disappeared.

"Thank you, Father," whispered Ariadne, and she embraced the King again with fervent gratitude.

Almost at once the guards returned and Krino, pale and emaciated, was standing before them on trembling, wobbly limbs.

"Kneel, and kiss your mistress," commanded the King. "She has freed you!"

Krino knelt, and clasping the Princess's bare feet, broke into violent sobs.

16

Ikaros was restive. With the great festival just a day away, his father's workshop couldn't hold him, and he had come outdoors to roam the Palace grounds and look for his friend Menas.

The Palace of Knossos was no ordinary Palace, confined to a single structure. It was, in reality, a small city, with streets and squares, temples and a theater. It had parks with myriad exotic flowers and trees—palm, quince, plum, peach—with monkeys and canaries and partridges.

The Palace also had workshops, where all manner of craftsmen labored: artists, sculptors, engravers, carpenters. . . . Its pottery workshops were renowned throughout the world. The magnificent vases they produced, with their splendidly rendered flowers and fish, and exquisitely sculpted bulls and acrobats, were marketed as far as the outer reaches of the Mediterranean.

The Palace also had its weaving industry, and its wine and oil presses, its dye-works, goldsmiths' shops, coppersmiths' shops—all with their own coat of arms—the weaving workshops a spider, the oil presses an olive leaf. . . .

Ikaros roamed the Palace grounds stopping now and then at this or that workshop to watch a potter at his wheel or an artisan painting a flower on a vase. He was roaming aimlessly, wandering off northeast of the Palace, when he found himself before the old school of his childhood. The Palace also had its school—a single great room with stone benches all around and an elevated chair where the teacher sat.

He paused before the door of the little school to look inside. There was the familiar elevated chair where the teacher sat, and all around the stone benches where the pupils sat. A teacher was sitting in the elevated chair, holding a small pupil by the hand. In front of the teacher's platform there was a lower one where the pupils came to stand and learn to carve the strange markings of the Cretan language in soft clay. They would carve out the markings, and if they made a mistake they would erase it by kneading out the clay and starting over again. Ikaros smiled at the familiar scene. How many lickings with the rod it had taken for him to learn to read and write! Even then, his mind was always wandering, his eyes always gazing out the schoolroom window at the flitting sparrows and the green fields beyond. He could still hear himself protesting to his father. *I don't want to learn reading and writing! I'm going to be an architect . . . I'm going to build bridges and ships . . . what do I need with learning!* He laughed now at the recollection. How his father had tried to drum sense into his head! "An illiterate man is a blockhead!" he would harp at him. One day he showed him a block of wood. "Look," he said to him, "do you like this stump?" Ikaros had looked at it and turned up his nose. "Wait a bit," his father said, "you'll see," and he picked up his tools—the adz, the saw, the plane and chisel— and began to clean and carve the wood, and before long the stump was unrecognizable, changed from a raw mass to a beautiful little statue of a youth with girded waist and curly hair, holding a lily in his hand. "You see?" his father said, "this is what the soul of man is like . . . when left uncultivated, it's a stump of wood, a block-head. But look what happens when you work it!"

Ikaros smiled. The lesson had hit home. He had been attending school regularly after that, and "the wood," as his father said, had started to become a man.

He was still reflecting on the little incident, when he turned at the sound of a familiar voice. It was Krino.

"Krino!" he shouted. "It's you!" and he grasped the girl's hand. "Are you happy now?" he beamed, regarding her joyfully.

And indeed, in the sunlight again, after her long ordeal in the black pit, Krino had cause to be happy, but her heart was still heavy.

"I'd be happy, if only . . . ," she said, and her voice broke.

"I know . . . I know . . ." whispered Ikaros pressing her hand. "But you mustn't worry about Haris. He'll be all right. He's out at sea and most likely he'll find your father. It's all going to work out fine.

The girl shook her head.

"You'll see," said Ikaros, "he'll be all right. I had a dream; a good dream. I dreamed we were dolphins—you, Haris, and I— and we were happy. We were cutting through the sea and laughing. That means the three of us are going to escape."

"I shall not rest," said Krino, "until I hear from him and he tells me where he is and what he's doing."

"Where are you headed?" asked Ikaros.

"To the goldsmith's" answered Krino. "I must hurry. My Lady has sent me to have her bracelet repaired; it's the one she must wear tomorrow when she dances at the festival."

"I'll walk with you," said Ikaros, and together the pair set out in the direction of the goldsmith's. They hastened through the streets and alleys until they came to the little street of artisans where they found the goldsmith's shop.

The goldsmith's shop was a narrow little room with a tiny window overhead protected by thick bronze bars. A fire was burning in the corner beneath the window where the artisan was seated. He was pounding with a small hammer on a great fine sheet of gold. For a moment Ikaros stood at the door to watch. The sheet of gold under the blacksmith's hammer was taking on the shape of a human face. With each blow it was growing more lifelike . . . the nose, the mouth, the eyes. . . . Krino, too, stood watching in awe. The goldsmith hammered the gold a little more, corrected the mouth, looked at it carefully, then took a thick needle and etched the lids on the eyes. Satisfied, he held it up for the boy and girl to see.

"It's a death mask," he smiled. "For a nobleman from across the sea. A King, they say, died in Mycenae and they want to cover his face with this gold. Such a custom they have."

Ikaros left Krino with the goldsmith and, cutting across the narrow alley of shops, hurried off to find his friend Menas. The air in the streets was charged with expectation and he could barely contain his excitement. For days now envoys from the vassal states of Crete had been pouring into Knossos to attend the sacred rites honoring the Bull-god. Bearing gifts for the sovereign King, they had come from every realm of his dominion to see the celebrated games where the select trained bulls would vie with the famous bull leapers of Crete.

He made his way through the crowds, striding rapidly toward the Palace storehouses where he was to meet his friend. The youth was already waiting at the entrance, looking about him with incredulous eyes. He was a plump, tawny-skinned boy of about thirteen, with long curly hair and a large aquiline nose, a country boy from inner Crete, come with his father to Knossos from the distant city of Lato to see the great festival and visit with his friend Ikaros at whose house he was staying. He had been wandering all morning, his eyes bulging with astonishment at the immensity of the Palace with all its brilliance, its statues, its murals, its thousands of slaves scurrying about like ants since dawn.

"You haven't seen anything yet," laughed Ikaros coming up on him from behind.

The boy turned. "I'm in a daze!" he exclaimed, greeting his friend joyfully. He was standing in awe before the storehouse entrance, watching the Palace slaves hauling in the magnificent

79

gifts that the visiting envoys were bringing. A scribe, sitting close by, just outside the entrance to the vast storehouse, was recording the fabulous gifts in his tablet of clay: so many sheep and cows, so much wheat and oil, so many gold goblets, so many knives and swords, so many slaves. . . .

He was sitting cross-legged on the flagstones, carving the figures into the soft clay with great care. Single units were indicated by a small vertical line (|), tens by a short horizontal line (—), hundreds by a circle (O), and thousands by a circle surrounded with four tiny lines $\oplus$. As he recorded each gift on his tablet, Palace slaves would haul the offering into the storehouse with the other reserves. The wheat they poured into the mammoth jars that lined the storeroom floors; the sheep and goats they herded into stables. . . .

"Let's go inside," said Ikaros. "They're opening the secret chests." He loved to watch the guards unlock the chests that were buried beneath the floors and admire the stupendous wealth that was concealed in them.

Inside the storeroom, Palace officers, holding great mysterious keys, were on their knees before the giant jars unlocking the stone chests that were hidden in the ground. The chests, all in a row, were fitted at the bottom with a huge stone slab which, when lifted, revealed yet another stone chest, all lined inside with lead to protect the contents from the dampness. These were the secret coffers that contained the Palace treasures that were not in daily use.

The two boys crept up close behind the officers and craned to see. The open chests glittered inside with awesome treasures. There were huge crystal vases bedecked with precious stones, priceless embroidered fabrics, thick gold goblets, bracelets, rings, necklaces, earrings. There were great gleaming chunks of ivory, enormous inert slabs of pure gold. . . .

Such wealth! Menas let out a stunned gasp.

Ikaros looked at the guards nervously and nudged Menas, signaling him to be quiet. But an officer had already heard and whirled around to glare at the pair that had dared to come so close. "Off with you!" he ordered menacingly.

The guileless boy looked up in surprise and went to open his mouth again, but Ikaros tugged at his arm. "Don't!" he warned in a whisper. "Let's go!" and holding fast to the boy's arm, he backed off and the two hurriedly scampered away.

Out in the courtyard, they stopped. It was a beautiful day. The autumn sun glowed warmly, and the sea beyond was shimmering with a silvery cast. A steady stream of pilgrims were climbing the grand staircase. Voices in dialects from every part of Crete filled the air—dialects from Lato, from Praisos, from Tylissos, from Gortyn. . . . Pilgrims from all over Crete were streaming in, even from distant Kydonia on the western coast, and from as far away as Palaiokastro and Zakro on the eastern coast.

"All Crete is here," marveled Menas, staring at the myriad assortment of native dress.

"Not only Crete," boasted Ikaros, proud to be showing off the opulence of his city, "this is nothing! I'm going to show you people from even more distant lands. Come," and taking his friend, he led him through a vast corridor. The walls of the corridor were covered with brilliant murals—five hundred, at least—depicting all manner of Cretan life: handsome youths bearing sacrifices to the Great Goddess, cone-shaped vases filled with honey and milk, bulls with golden horns, beautiful ladies carrying gifts to the Great Goddess, doves and snakes and peacock feathers and enormous exotic flowers. Two murals, at either end of the long corridor, were painted by Ikaros's father. Menas came up close to look. Daidalos had painted a boundless sea on the first mural, where fish with wings were flitting from wave to wave. "Like swallows," murmured the boy, staring at the winged fish in wonder. "Are there really such fish?"

"Of course," said Ikaros, lording it slightly over the boy from the provinces. "They're called flying fish. But being from an inland town, you wouldn't know."

"And they really fly?"

"They really fly."

Ikaros moved on to his father's other mural. This painting, too, was filled with wings—with great numbers of exotic blue birds. A falcon, swooping down on them, was scattering the terrified birds, and they had spread their wings and were flying off toward the edge of the mural where the dark blue sea could be discerned.

"See," said Ikaros, "how good it is to have wings? All you have to do is spread them and fly away . . . away from the falcon." He was thinking of Haris, and his heart ached.

"Come," he said abruptly. "We've almost forgotten where we're going."

They hurried through the remaining corridor and reached a stairwell.

"Where to now?" queried the young friend.

"Up these stairs and to the Guest House."

The pair took the steps two at a time and came to a long corridor where a series of low doors lined the walls to the left and right. All were made of cypress wood, painted in different colors—yellow, red, blue—and over each door was hung a tablet with letters. Ikaros walked up to the doors and peered at the tablets.

"What do they say?" asked Menas.

Ikaros turned to the boy in surprise. "Don't you read?" he exclaimed.

"Of course I read!" said the boy, "but not your Palace writing. This is more complicated than ours."

Ikaros went to a yellow door and bent over the tablet. "Here's where the envoys from Cyprus live," he said. "They arrived yesterday, with gifts for the King—they brought huge bronze cauldrons and trays, and sacks and sacks of *porphyra*."

"*Porphyra?*"

"They're tiny seashells," explained Ikaros. "You boil them and pierce them and get a beautiful purple dye from them." He walked to another door. This one was painted green. "Envoys from Egypt," he read aloud from the tablet. "They've brought gifts of ivory and some enormous elephants' teeth and huge baskets filled with bananas and dates."

"Bananas and dates are things you eat," he explained again, laughing at the baffled look on the face of the country boy.

"And here," he said, walking up to the adjacent black door and peering at the tablet, "here live. . . ."

But just then the black door opened and two black giants emerged on the threshold, black as pitch. They had bronze rings in their noses and ears and wore little bells at their feet. The boys started; they made to retreat, but one of the giants put out his hand and patted Menas's head. Poor Menas shrank back and threw Ikaros a frightened look. The two giants laughed.

"What are they saying?" whispered Menas in alarm. The

towering blacks were talking in a strange tongue and gesturing in sign language.

"I don't know," said Ikaros, "but I think they want us to wait here." The two giants had suddenly turned and disappeared inside the room, and no sooner had Ikaros surmised their meaning when they were back on the threshold again, their hands filled with dates, motioning to the boys to open their palms.

"Take them," whispered Ikaros. "These are the dates I was telling you about."

Menas took the dates. He bit into one and let out an appreciative murmur and the two men laughed, pleased. Nodding and laughing at the young pair, the black giants closed their door and strode off down the hall, turning to look back, still laughing amusedly, until they disappeared down the stairs.

"They're like honey," murmured Menas, biting into another date. "I'll save the rest for my father. He's probably never eaten any."

"Here, take mine, too," said Ikaros.

"What about you?"

"Oh, I've eaten them before," bragged Ikaros. "Here in the capital we've had our fill of things like this."

Menas was growing tired.

"Come, we'll go out and sit by the spring," said Ikaros.

Out in the sunlight they headed for the south entrance, toward the spring. It would be shady there, and they could wait out the day watching the pilgrims coming in from the harbor. Scores of worshipers were still streaming in at the south entrance, pausing at the spring to refresh themselves. After their long trek from the harbor, they would stop at the spring to wash the dust from their feet and proceed up the great marble stairway to the Palace. There they would rest on the stone benches that were provided for them and admire the brilliant murals of red-footed peacocks that graced the walls.

17

The great day dawned. Sentries atop the towers trumpeted their conches, heralding the arrival of the momentous hour when man would pit himself against the bull.

At the Palace, royal baths and bedchambers came alive. Slaves hastened to their masters; slavegirls to their mistresses. The halls reverberated with the sounds of lords and ladies bathing, dressing, grooming—all adorning themselves in their best finery and jewels for the great occasion.

In his father's workshop beneath the Palace, Ikaros had wakened long before the conches blazoned forth the dawn. At the sound of their first blast, he leaped from his cot and shook his friend Menas who was sleeping on the mat beside him.

Daidalos, too, lay awake on his bed across the room. He could hear the two boys stirring, moving about quietly so as not to waken him. He lay with his eyes closed, listening to their sounds as they washed and dressed and finally tiptoed out the door. He was deep in thought, his mind on his work. A most difficult work, almost superhuman, this goal of his, trying to construct wings that would attach to men's shoulders so they could fly. Night and day his mind was on his work, searching, probing, trying to figure out a way. That there was a way he had no doubt. After all, man's mind was a spark from God. He, too, had a God inside him . . . with love and perseverance, he would find a way.

He opened his eyes. Light was beginning to filter through the window, illuminating the wall across the room where his tools were hanging. In a corner, the rays fell on some half-carved blocks of wood and, moving upward along the wall, sought out a small statue of a slender youth holding a lily that was nailed over Ikaros's pillow. The old artisan smiled. *With this little statue he had managed to teach Ikaros to read and write. Now . . . if only he could manage to complete these wings before he died—to free his son and not leave him behind still a slave.* He sighed. *It was too late for HIM . . . he was old . . . he had lived his life; but at least his son. . . .*

He sat up sharply. *No! His heart was still warm . . . his mind was strong and active . . . his hand sure and steady!* "On with it!" he muttered and sprang from his bed.

Quickly he washed and dressed, took down his tools from the wall, and fell to work. The world outside his window hurried past. He worked, oblivious. Once a shadow darkened his pane. He looked up.

"Still working, old Master?" A crony had stopped to beckon.

He peered at the withered old face pressed against the window and mumbled a kindly greeting. *No time for holidays, old friend,* and he bent over his workbench again.

The crony withdrew from the little barred window and shuffled away. *He shouldn't have bothered him . . . who knew what that brilliant old brain was working on this time!*

The din outside the craftsman's door grew louder. Shouts, laughter, squabbling voices, rang urgently through the halls as servants raced pell-mell up and down stairs, opening doors, shutting them, answering to orders that officers were shouting in confusion. In the kitchens, they were lighting fires, readying the Palace ovens. A din of lowing animals carried from the riverbank where lambs and cows were being slaughtered.

Out in the meadows the freshly washed bulls stood ready, sleek and shiny in the sun. For days now, the cowherds and goldsmiths had been at work on them, washing them, gilding their horns, painting their hooves with brilliant red dye.

The people were gathered at the hill, sitting on the stone tiers carved along its slopes. Opposite them was the small stone amphitheater where the King and the lords and ladies of the Court would come to sit with the foreign dignitaries. In the center stood the large threshing floor where the trained acrobats would be vying with the bulls. The threshing floor was surrounded by a tall fence, and in its center spired a slender column at the top of which was nailed a bronze double ax.

Ikaros and Menas, at the hillside since dawn, were sitting at the bottom tier of steps, to be closest to the action.

"The bulls will be practically on top of us," laughed Ikaros. "Don't get scared."

"What's there to be scared of?" said Menas nervously.

"They can get awfully close," laughed Ikaros, but just then a stir began to rumble through the crowd, cries went up, and people began scrambling to their feet, craning to see.

"Over there!" said Ikaros, pointing to the Palace doors that were opening now and letting out the first of the sentries. "Take a good look. You're never going to see anything like it again."

And indeed, the spectacle unfolding was exquisite. The tall palatial doors had opened wide, and sentries with red lances and curious bronze shields were emerging into the sunlight, aligning themselves to the right and left of the doors and forming a double-lined path clear down to the stone amphitheater where the nobles would come to sit.

And now the Court was emerging—generals, captains, priests, officers—all adorned with bracelets and earrings and precious jewels.

Behind them, glittering like peacocks in their plumes, came the Court ladies clad in gold-embroidered gowns, sprinkling the morning air with the tintinnabulation of their bracelets and earrings.

At a signal from the conches blasting loudly, the lords and ladies halted. The crowds surged to their feet, all eyes riveted on the great palatial door where the King had now emerged in a dazzle of gold. He was standing at the threshold motionless, crowned with a golden diadem, his bald head covered with seven enormous plumes that swayed over him in a rainbow of varied hues. At his waist a belt was glittering with precious stones, and on his feet were crimson sandals. On either side of him his daughters came to stand—Phaidra to his right, and Ariadne to his left, both dressed as priestesses in long multicolored skirts and tightly fitted bodices. On their heads they wore cone-shaped hats adorned with golden sequins. Their feet gleamed bare, their breasts, too, were bare, and snakes entwined their naked arms.

The old King raised his hands as though to bless his people, then putting one foot forward in its lily-embroidered sandal, he stepped across the threshold and at once the glittering procession resumed the march.

They reached the amphitheater, the King took his seat upon his throne, his daughters to the right and left of him took theirs on lower thrones; and after they were seated, the lords and ladies took their seats, too.

The conches ceased. The sun, clear over the mountain now, was shooting down its rays, illuminating the beaming faces, playing on the gold adornments of the brilliant gathering below. In the sudden hush, a gentle rustling could be heard, carrying faintly from the ladies still settling their sumptuous gowns in the royal seats.

86   And now two priests emerged and strode across the threshing floor toward the spiring column with the double ax. They halted before the small altar at the column's base and, intoning a few

words as though in prayer, tossed two handfuls of incense into a flame that was burning there between two stone bull-horns. Instantly a puff of smoke exploded, filling the air with its aromatic scent.

At a signal from the King, then, the two Princesses rose from their seats and descended the stairs. Solemnly, with downcast eyes and regal measured steps, they walked to the center of the threshing floor and halted.

"They're going to dance now," whispered Ikaros.

The King up in his throne leaned a taut neck forward.

The sisters stood motionless, Phaidra tall and regal, Ariadne pale in the morning sunlight. Phaidra was the first to stir. With a quick, sure movement, she began the dance. Striking her foot against the ground, she flung the snakes above her head and approached Ariadne, nudging her lightly, as though to challenge her. Then just as quickly, she retreated, twirling lightly in the air.

Ariadne, looking solemn and serene, stood motionless. Phaidra rushed at her again, beating at the ground with one bare foot in that repeated pawing motion. She nudged Ariadne again, this time with a vigorous lightning jab and, letting out a powerful cry, stopped short.

The long blonde braids shook slightly on Ariadne's shoulders, and the snakes uncoiling on her arms raised up their heads and hissed. Stealthily, like something stalking, Ariadne began to stir. Suddenly, without warning, she sprang at Phaidra. Phaidra took three rhythmic steps backward and began, with long swift strides, to dance a circle around her sister. Ariadne, too, was racing alongside her now, dancing a narrower inner circle of her own.

The crowd held in its breath. Nothing could be heard but the snakes that were sitting erect on the Princesses' bare arms, moving their small flat heads and hissing.

Menas watched transfixed, murmuring in fascination.

"Can you guess what they're doing?" whispered Ikaros.

The two sisters were coming together now. They had joined hands and were dancing as one, their heads tossing gaily with joyous abandon.

"Phaidra's portraying the bull, and Ariadne the human," explained Ikaros. "They were enemies when they started, and now they've made up and are dancing like friends. . . ."

The sound of conches blared and the two sisters stopped. They

87

turned toward the King, bowed low in respect, and now their slave girls hurried out to them to sprinkle rose water on their perspiring bodies and escort them back to their thrones.

Menas, following them with awestruck eyes, shook his head. Never in his life had he seen such a dance! He was about to speak when two black trumpeters suddenly emerged at the top of the amphitheater. They put two enormous conches to their lips and the entire hillside echoed with a resounding blast. At once, a thunderous stampeding of feet was heard, as though myriads of snorting animals were on the run.

"The bulls are coming!" laughed Ikaros reassuringly, and barely had he got the words out when the gates to the threshing floor burst open and seven bulls bounded in. Three were black and three a russet color. One, the largest, was stark white. They charged through the gate and began running abreast in a circle around the arena, all seven with their gilded horns and crimson hooves gleaming in the sunlight. Round and round they ran, as though looking for the humans they were to vie with until, shiny with perspiration, the white bull came to a halt. He stood snorting in the center of the arena, alongside the tall column, and extending his neck, let out a roar.

At once, seven athletes leaped atop the stone enclosure of the threshing floor. Four were men and three were women, all wearing identical dress, a form-fitting garment with a narrow leather belt that tightly clasped their waists.

The King, high on his throne, clapped his hands and instantly, as though anticipating the signal, the seven athletes leaped into the arena.

Menas gasped.

"Wait," laughed Ikaros. "You'll see now." His eyes were on a lissome young girl striding lightly across the threshing floor. She was slender and fair, about sixteen, and walked with a firm quick step. He leaned forward. Suddenly his face turned ashen. *Krino!* His eyes, fastened on the girl, filled with dread. *She had said nothing to him about this.*

Krino's passion since childhood had been to compete in the bull sports one day. She was an excellent athlete, and she had trained long and hard. Last year when she was ready, Ikaros had convinced her brother Haris not to allow her to compete. Now, with Haris away, she was free and had entered herself in the games. Her mistress encouraged her in the sport, and Krino had entered with Ariadne's blessing. Early that morning, the Princess had taken her aside and counseled her. "Take care," she cautioned, "make sure you choose the white bull. He's mine, and I have faith in him."

She was striding buoyantly across the arena now, arms outstretched, heading straight for her mistress's trusted bull. The animal, watching her approach, was pawing furiously at the earth and roaring. As she drew near and reached to grasp his horns, the beast thrust low his head and lunged to gore her.

Ikaros held his breath. *This was the most difficult part of the sport . . . she had but a second to grab the horns and hang on . . . It was Krino's first time in the public arena . . . would she keep her calm? . . .* In the fleeting instant that the thought flashed through his mind, Krino was grasping the animal's horns and clinging with a sure grip, balancing herself lightly on her toes. The angered bull flung back his head to shake her off and, taking impetus from the animal's upward thrust, Krino vaulted light as a feather over his head and landed on his back. Steadying herself on her hands for an instant, she clicked her heels twice in the air, then with another sudden burst of energy, turned a somersault over the animal's back and propelled herself into the arms of a man waiting behind the bull to catch her.

Ikaros let out his breath. *Splendid, Krino . . . Bravo!*

Up in the amphitheater Ariadne rose from her throne and waved her ostrich feathered fan at her beloved slave.

The other athletes, too, were hard at play with the bulls, grasping the animals' horns, swinging themselves over their heads, leaping off the animals' backs, and beginning all over again. The crowd was applauding, shouting its approval, and the ladies in the amphitheater were fluttering their fans and waving them enthusiastically at the athletes who were performing with the greatest grace. The sport continued thus until the sweat was pouring from the bulls and the athletes were panting for breath.

It was almost noon when the King finally lifted his arm, signaling the trumpeters. The conches blared, the seven athletes stopped, the gates of the arena opened, and the cowherds filed in and cautiously approached the inflamed beasts. Stroking them gently about their necks, they led them out, to drink and graze and rest.

The crowds, too, scattered now toward the fields, to stretch out on the grounds and picnic on the bread and food and wine that Palace slaves were passing all around. This was the day the King fed his people.

At the amphitheater where the nobles sat, slaves were bringing out huge trays from the Palace kitchens, piled high with food and fruit and drink to refresh the lords and ladies.

The King, dining with his two daughters, turned to Ariadne. He was curious about the young girl who had wrestled her white bull.

"That was Krino," smiled Ariadne, her face aglow with pride. "My little slave Krino—the one you freed from prison."

The King's beardless jaw hardened. The girl's father loomed darkly in his mind again. He still had no word from the ship that he had sent to Athens to find the blacksmith and that hated foreigner who had escaped with him.

"So that was Krino?"

"Yes, Father. She wrestled the bull well, don't you think?"

"Yes, very well." But in his mind the King was thinking of how to punish her. Innocent though she might be, he would punish her to hurt that faithless blacksmith. He turned to a slave standing behind the royal throne holding ready a crock of wine. "Fill my cup," he commanded.

The slave filled the gold cup and placed it in the King's hand. Minos took the cup and held it high. "I drink to your health, Ariadne," he said. "I drink to your health, Phaidra," *and may the Great Goddess help me fulfill what I have in mind!* He looked around and summoned one of the two Negroes who were standing ready to sound the trumpets. "Come close," he commanded, and when the Negro bent close, he furtively whispererd something in his ear, and the Negro made obeisance and sped away in haste.

The sun was on the decline now and the second phase of the games was about to resume. In this second phase the King was to choose one of the seven athletes, the one who had excelled in the morning games, and charge him with the honor of wrestling with the fiercest bull, alone.

The seven athletes appeared and aligned themselves before the King. They stood with bowed heads and waited for him to select the best among them, to bestow the victory crown upon him, and enjoin him to wrestle the bull.

The King looked them over carefully, scanning them one by one with his small cunning eyes. Suddenly he lifted his hand and pointed to Krino. "You!" he decreed.

The maiden knelt, kissed his feet, and he placed the victory wreath upon her hair. "Go now," he enjoined her mockingly, "wrestle the white bull!"

Krino rose, flushed with joy, and raced on wings down the amphitheater steps. Shouts and hurrahs filled the air around her. "Bravo, Krino! Bravo!" Court ladies cheered and waved their fans. The King looked after her and glowered. *You'll pay, daughter of the accursed blacksmith!*

The gate to the arena swung open and the lone white bull charged out. It streaked across the arena to the spiring column in the center and there stopped short, letting out an eerie, savage groan.

Ikaros sat up. Something was wrong! The animal, its eyes a bloody red, its tail taut and sticking upright in the air, was banging its horns frenziedly against the column, threatening to knock it down.

And now Krino was entering the arena, striding lightly toward the bull, her arms outstretched. She drew near, reached cautiously toward the animal, and just as she was thrusting forward to grasp its horns the rabid beast charged, and quickly she skipped backward. The bull let out a roar and, lowering his powerful head, lunged at her again, but sprinting to the right, Krino barely cleared the treacherous horns, and the heaving animal, hitting nothing but empty air, crashed to the ground.

The crowd cried out in horror. Ikaros was on his feet. Menas grasped his arm in dread. The King, stroking his beardless chin, was murmuring in satisfaction. *The Negro had done his job well with the intoxicating wine . . . there was no escape for her now.*

The bull, covered all over with dust, picked himself up and looked about the arena. Spotting the foe, he pawed furiously at the earth and came charging at Krino again with murderous rage. Krino, too, was sprinting toward him, reaching desperately for his horns. She leaped, grasped them, and clinging tightly with all her might, braced herself for the moment when the bull would toss back his head and she could take power from his rhythm to vault over his back. But this time the bull didn't throw his head upward. Instead, he let out a groan and, flinging his head from left to right, began shaking her like a rag in a side to side motion as she dangled from his horns.

Ariadne turned aghast to the King. "Father!" she cried, "the bull is drunk! Command them to stop the game!"

But the King kept his gaze on the arena. "Quiet!" he said. "Don't spoil the holiday."

Ariadne looked at her father sharply. A terrible suspicion was taking hold in her mind. "Father! . . . ," she said again.

"Quiet!" commanded the King, cutting her off angrily.

The bull, meanwhile, was racing round and round the arena, flinging Krino from side to side with jolting ferocity. The crowd, on its feet, was following the spectacle in horror.

Ariadne rose from her throne and without looking at her father for permission, signaled to the Negro to sound the trumpet. But the Negro glanced at the King and remained motionless.

Krino was barely hanging on now. Exhausted from the relentless shaking, she was hanging by her fingertips. Ikaros watched in dread. Two . . . three minutes at the most . . . and she'd fall off and the bull would make a thousand pieces of her. He looked about him desperately. Tiers of horrified people, and no one who could do anything to save her! Row by row, he scanned the faces and for an instant his glance settled on a man in the row behind him. The man had on a red apron. A thought flashed through his mind. "Your apron!" he shouted. The man looked at him in surprise. "Your apron! Your apron!" shrieked Ikaros above the din, and pouncing on the startled neighbor, began pulling at his apron. The bewildered man undid his belt and before he could hand the apron over to the crazy youth, Ikaros had snatched it and went vaulting like a bolt of lightning over the fence and into the arena.

The crowd gasped. No one breathed. All eyes were on the youth streaking across the arena toward the bull.

Ikaros, racing headlong at the animal, was waving the red apron in front of him. At first the rabid beast, in all his thrashing frenzy, seemed not to notice, but as the youth approached and the bull caught sight of something red coming at him, sparks flashed from his blood-gorged eyes and, dropping low his head, he let go of Krino and lunged with inflamed fury at the red cloth.

"Ikaros!" Menas screamed in terror from the ringside. Tears were streaming down his cheeks.

Ikaros sprinted aside. Waving the red apron in front of him, he sprinted agilely, racing to the left and right of the infuriated bull, and shouting to Krino.

Krino, who had fallen dazed to the ground, raised herself slightly.

"Run!" screamed Ikaros, not taking his eyes from the bull. "Jump over the fence!"

But the girl didn't stir. Her eyes were riveted on the crazed bull charging after Ikaros, and she trembled for the youth.

"Krino! Go!" shouted Ikaros again.

But Krino wouldn't budge. The faithful girl could not bring herself to flee while Ikaros was in danger.

"KRINO!!" shrieked the frantic youth for one last time. The bull had caught up with him now and he could feel the beast's hot breath on him. He was racing just steps ahead of it, swinging the red apron desperately from side to side. The bull was gaining. With a mighty lunge it pierced the flimsy cloth that Ikaros was swinging to the right now and, charging furiously into empty air, crashed headlong in the dust. And now Ikaros was streaking across the arena toward Krino. The crowd held its breath. The youth swooped the girl up in his arms, made a dash for the fence, leaped over the top, and deposited Krino, half-swooning, in the amphitheater on the other side.

The crowd roared.

The King rose angrily to his feet. He nodded brusquely to the two black trumpeters, and the pair put their conches to their lips and signaled the end of the games.

Ikaros, back in his seat now, wiped the sweat from his face. Menas was fanning him, hovering over him, bursting with admiration. "You were a real hero!" the boy fairly sputtered in awe.

Ikaros waved him off, laughing nervously. He was looking across at Krino in the amphitheater and couldn't contain his joy at having rescued her. He was still clutching the red apron and turned now to give it back to his neighbor.

"It's yours!" smiled the man. "Keep it to remember your heroic deed today."

Ariadne, in the little amphitheater, looked at her father. "Someone gave the bull wine to get him drunk," she said accusingly. "Who was it? He must be punished!"

The King glowered. "Don't meddle in things that don't concern

93

you!'' he said angrily.

Ariadne didn't answer. She rose from her throne. "I'm tired,'' she said. "I'm returning to the Palace,'' and calling Krino to her, she left. At the Palace entrance she turned to her beloved slave. "They want to kill you, my little Krino,'' she whispered, taking the young girl's hand. "They want to kill you! But I'm not going to let them!''

Across the amphitheater, Ikaros, too was on his feet. Gathering up the red apron, he signaled to his friend. "Let's go,'' he said to Menas. "The games are over.''

The King rose, too. There was the matter of the sacrifice to be attended to—the bull that he must offer to the Great Goddess— and then the crowds would scatter.

On the way back to the Palace, the King drew aside his general. "Who was that young man?'' he demanded.

"The son of old Daidalos, my King,'' the officer informed him.

The King said nothing more, but through clenched teeth, he vowed to punish him.

18

A week went by. Two. The rains had started in earnest. The skies were incessantly covered with clouds, and a cold wind was blowing.

Ariadne had lit a large bronze brazier in her room and was sitting on her couch, her braids loosened, gazing at the glowing red coals. Her mind was far away, beyond the sea.

Krino was sitting at her feet sewing. She was working on her mistress's spring wardrobe, embroidering delicate white lilies on a flimsy cloth of blue. Her mind, too, was far away, beyond the sea. Haris was late in writing, and she was worried. What could be happening to him?

The Princess turned from the fire and rested her gaze on her beloved slave. "What are you thinking?'' she asked softly.

"My brother,'' answered the girl, ". . . and my father. . . .''

"Don't worry,'' said the Princess soothingly. "They'll be all right . . . you'll get a letter soon.''

"It's been so long,'' murmured Krino and bent over her work again.

The sound of Phaidra's singing could be heard from the adjoin-

94

ing room. She was singing a lively tune, her deep voice filling the air with a melodious sweetness.

"My sister is fortunate," smiled Ariadne. "She doesn't worry about anything. She's beautiful and cheerful and sleeps easily at night, free of cares."

"And you, my Lady," said Krino looking up. "You should be fortunate, too. You're a Princess, you're beautiful, you're good . . . you lack nothing."

"Yes," murmured Ariadne and fell silent.

"I lack one thing," she said presently.

"What, my Lady?"

"Happiness."

Krino reached across the straw mat and embraced her mistress's feet. "Is there something that you want that you don't have?" she asked tenderly.

"I want to go away! I want to travel, to breathe freely! There . . . that's what I want!" declared the Princess, short of bursting into tears. "Living in this endless Palace suffocates me!"

She fell silent again. The aroma of sage and mint carried from the corridors where slaves were brewing herbal teas for their mistresses to keep them warm.

"Krino," she said after a while. "Bring me my writing things."

Krino rose and hurried to a drawer hidden in the wall where she took out an ivory writing tablet, a slender reed pen, and a bottle of red ink. "Here they are, my Lady," she said, placing them carefully beside her mistress.

Ariadne took the writing tools and settled on the couch. Krino went to sit at her feet again and resumed sewing. Now and then, she would lift a curious eye to look at her mistress. Something was troubling the Princess. She always asked for her writing things when she was troubled. She'd write and write as she was doing now, then erase what she had written, and begin over again. What could she be writing?

Ariadne, oblivious to her slave, was curled up on the divan, writing a song; a doleful song that spoke of oceans and voyages . . . and of ships' red sails . . . sails that unfurled and sailed away . . . sailed away and never returned. . . .

In the silence, nothing could be heard but the scratching of the pen on the ivory tablet and, from time to time, a sigh.

A profound stillness had settled over the room, mistress and maid working quietly, each absorbed in her own thoughts when a knock at the door shattered the thoughts and the quiet.

Krino rose and hurried across the room. "Who's there?" she asked, and waited.

"It's me!" a familiar voice answered.

"Ikaros!" she cried joyfully and opened the door.

It was indeed Ikaros, beaming broadly at the threshold.

Ariadne looked up. "Come in! Come in!" she called from her couch. "What brings you here?"

"A letter from Haris," announced Ikaros.

"From Haris! Is he well? What does he say?" Krino could barely contain herself for joy.

"He's fine . . . he's fine!" laughed Ikaros.

Ariadne put away her writing. She was certain in her mind that Haris's father had fled with the handsome Prince of Athens and was anxious for news to confirm her suspicions.

"Where's the letter?" she asked, all eagerness. "Where is it from?"

"From Athens," said Ikaros coming into the room.

A violent flush spread across Ariadne's face. "Give it to me," she said. "Let me read it!"

Krino ran to the window to open it wide for the Princess to read by. Her heart was pounding loudly.

Ikaros took a small papyrus roll from his bosom, unrolled it, and gave it to the Princess.

Haris, the son on the blacksmith Aristidis, greets Ikaros, the son of the great artisan Daidalos, and he greets his sister Krino, read the Princess aloud.

First, I inform you that I am well. And now, I will tell you in a few words my story: After we left Crete and had sailed out into the high sea, I went up to the captain and asked him where we were going. The captain is a good man and took a liking to me. To Athens, he said. And what will we be doing in Athens? I asked him. I can't tell you, he said. It's the King's secret. He could see that I was concerned so he said not to worry, that he didn't have orders to harm me. We're just going to roam around there for a few days, he said, and I stretched out on the prow and tried to sort things out.

It was a fine voyage, the sea was calm, we passed many is-

lands, stopped off at Melos, with a beautiful harbor and little white houses. There were many Cretans there and they treated us well, and then we embarked again and sailed north.

On the morning of the third day we sighted a long stretch of land. We stopped at a small harbor where some huts were scattered about. Here's where we're dropping anchor, the captain said. We went ashore, the captain and I, and the sailors stayed behind in the ship. The city is a bit far from here, the captain said to me, two hours by foot. He took with him a small box that he tied tightly around his belt. If I lose it, he said, I'm done for. I learned later what was in the box.

We walked fast; it was kind of cold. It had rained and the road was all muddy. We came across some vineyards and some olive groves and some fields where peasants were ploughing. I tried talking to them but they didn't understand our language.

We finally got to the city. How I had wanted to come to my native country, Athens! But now that I'm here, I don't feel joy. I don't know anyone here, and no one knows me. Besides, the city is poor. It really isn't a city—it's a lot of small villages joined together. And the Palace is like a great big peasant house.

We went to the house of a friend of the captain's. Here's where we'll stay, he told me. You're not to go out except with me. Never alone! That's an order! Do you give me your word? Yes, I told him. I didn't say anything, but my heart grew tight inside me. So I'm a slave here, too, I thought to myself. The captain took the small box and went out.

I stayed in the house with the owners—an old woman who kept mumbling, and an old man who just kept sitting in front of the fire, not paying any attention to her. Once he turned and told me that his grandson would be coming from the palace to keep me company. He's the chef there, he said.

I was tired and laid my head on my knees and soon fell asleep. I don't know how long I was sleeping when the old man's grandson woke me. He's about twenty years old, with big strong arms, and a black mustache and beard. His name is Demos. I stood up and greeted him politely and he laughed. Forget the manners, Cretan boy, he told me, sit down and eat, I've brought a pot of pork and vegetables from the palace that'll have you licking your fingers. I sat with them at the table, and while we were eating I found out that Demos knew the captain.

*He was taking the breakfast tray to the King's room, he told me,
when to his surprise, there was his old friend Captain Tyllisos.
He was opening a small box that he took from his belt and was
delivering a letter from the King of Crete. So that's what was in
the box, I thought to myself. A letter from the King of Crete to
the King of Athens. There must be something in it about me!
But what? If only I could find out.*

*I learned, too, that the King's son was away hunting bandits
that had come down from a place called Parnetha and were
raiding his borders.*

*After we ate, Demos had to go back to the Palace. Come with
me, he said, a ship's leaving tonight for Crete and you can send
back a message if you want. I can't, I said to him, and explained
about my orders. But you can do me a favor, I said. You can
deliver a letter for me to the ship's captain to take to my sister in
Crete. Fine, he said. Have it ready by midnight when I get back.
He left, and I was alone with the two old people, but they soon
fell asleep by the fire and I wrote this long letter. I still don't
know why I'm here and how long I'll be staying, but I'm writing to let you know that I am well, and not to worry. . . .*

When Ariadne had finished the letter and Ikaros had bowed and
left, the Princess turned to Krino. "Well?" she said to the girl. "Do
you understand now?"

"Understand what, my Lady?"

"Why the King sent Haris to Athens."

The girl looked puzzled. "No, my Lady, I don't understand."

"How innocent you are." Ariadne patted Krino's curly head.
"I'll tell you what the King is plotting," she smiled. "My father is
very clever. No doubt he has suspected that the foreigner who
came to the Palace must be some prince. His mind has somehow
leaped to Athens. He suspects it was the Prince of Athens who
came to spy on the Palace and talked the blacksmith into going
back with him to make new iron weapons for the Athenians. And
having come to this conclusion, he put his plan to work. Do you
see now what he's doing?"

Krino shook her head, still mystified.

"It's simple," said the Princess. "He sent Haris as a decoy. I'm
sure of it."

"A decoy??"

"Yes. Didn't you hear what Haris wrote? He has orders not to go out alone. Why? Because my father knows that Athens is a small city, and if he sends Haris and the captain to roam the streets out there together, they're bound to be seen some day by the Prince, and he'll walk up to Haris and talk to him. The captain will report this to my father and he'll be sure then that the foreigner who came here and became friends with Haris was the Prince of Athens."

"I see," murmured Krino, the light of understanding spreading slowly across her face. "And this way, too," she exclaimed excitedly as the further possibility began to dawn, "Haris might meet up with my father!"

"Yes, exactly. And my cunning father will catch your father, too. Two rabbits on a single bait, as the saying goes."

"I'm afraid," shuddered Krino.

"Don't be. I won't let them fall into the trap."

"What will you do?"

"I have my plans, too."

19

The next day Ikaros was sitting beneath his favorite olive tree outside the Palace gates, eating his midday meal. A gentle sweetness was in the air. After the heavy rains, it had turned mild, and a brilliant sun was shining again in a cloudless sky. The first winter flowers, the narcissus, with their heavy intoxicating scent, had burst into bloom. Whole quadrangles of the stark white flowers, with their charming yellow-yoked centers, were blooming in the royal gardens. Princess Phaidra adored them with a passion, and every day now she would come out to stroll through the gardens to look at them.

Ikaros had cut a few and was holding them to his nose, breathing their perfume with pleasurable sensation, remembering a story his grandmother once told him . . . *the narcissus had not always been a flower,* she told him, *but a handsome youth. He was very handsome and everyone loved him. But Narkissos was terribly vain, and thought of no one but himself—how he would bathe, how he would comb his hair, what perfumes he would put on, what clothes he would wear to make himself even handsomer. Every morning, as soon as he wakened, he would run to the spring*

99

and bend over the water to admire his face mirrored in the stream. One day, as he was bending over the water, admiring himself, he grew dizzy and fell in and drowned. They dragged him out and buried him, and over his grave sprang these flowers that we call narcissus. . . .

Ikaros was inhaling the sweet fragrance of the flowers and remembering the old myth when suddenly he sat up. Someone was coming down the road from the direction of the harbor. A man was approaching, escorted by two Palace guards. "It's him!" he cried, recognizing the captain that the King had sent away to track down Haris's father. "He's come back!" and springing to his feet, he raced out to the road to greet him.

Captain Kaphisos was approaching, dressed in his finest, and the expression on his face showed he was pleased. Ikaros, bounding toward him down the road, caught up with him and, arms uplifted eagerly in greeting, approached, but the captain, without a flicker of recognition in his eyes, looked at him coldly and strode past.

Ikaros stopped short. *He must not have recognized me,* he thought in bewilderment. But instantly he rejected the idea. Something was wrong. Surely, Captain Kaphisos had recognized him, he was certain of it. But for some reason he did not want to show it. *Why?*

The captain, of course, recognized Ikaros all too well. He knew the youth would be asking questions. What could he tell him? Something different than what he was going to tell the King? It was too risky. The lies he planned to tell were for his high and mightiness alone. Best not to speak . . . and he looked past the youth indifferently. It was a dangerous game he was playing. Would it work? He'd soon find out.

The King was still at table, dining, when the captain and the two guards arrived at the Palace and climbed the stairs to the royal chamber. Four slaves were in attendance at the meal, the first bringing the food up to the door of the King's chamber, the second taking it and placing it before the King, the third tasting it to make certain it wasn't poisoned, and the fourth filling the King's gold goblet with wine.

The two guards escorting Kaphisos opened wide the door to the royal chamber and heralded their arrival. "Oh long-lived King!"

they announced in booming voices, "Captain Kaphisos, bringing important news!"

At once the King broke off eating and signaled to a slave to bring the rinsing bowl. He hurriedly rinsed his hands and mouth, the food no longer interesting him now, and with a final splash of rose water on his palms for fragrance, he turned, impatient for the captain's news, and nodded to the guards at the door. "Let him enter!" he commanded. "And let all others leave the room!"

The slaves hurried out and Captain Kaphisos strode buoyantly into the room. "My King," he declared exuberantly, "I worship your grace!"

"Welcome!" responded the King. "If I can judge from the look on your face, you bring good news, Captain Kaphisos."

"As good as can be, my King!" answered the captain. "I think I have found the avenue through which we are going to recover our blacksmith, whom your Kingship loves so. . . ."

Like the wolf loves the lamb . . . just let me get my claws on him. . . . The King made a wry face. "Yes, yes, dear Captain," he said, "I'm listening."

"My long-lived King," began the captain, "from the information that I have been able to gather about the pirate who came to your Palace and seized the poor blacksmith, I have come to the conclusion that he must be from Cyprus. The Cypriots, my King, have an interest in keeping us from using iron. Who would buy their copper otherwise? They have no other major source of income than from their copper mines, and we're their best customers. . . ."

The King looked at Kaphisos sharply. It was obvious from the look in his eyes that he had not thought of this possibility. *Of course! That was it! This captain's brain was sharp . . . what he said made sense. They had seized the blacksmith, not to learn to work iron themselves, but to keep others from learning . . . this way they could keep on selling their copper. . . .*

Kaphisos smiled. *So far so good. The bait was working.*

"But then," declared the King, after pondering in silence, "our poor blacksmith is in danger. They'll kill him."

The foxy captain shook his head. "They must have killed him already," he allowed, pretending to wipe away a tear.

The King was growing testy. "Forget the tears," he said, "and

101

tell me, did you get to Cyprus? Did you learn anything out there?"

"My King," replied Kaphisos, "you are aware that I travel regularly to those parts, and I know Cyprus well. I know the merchants there, and the nobles and the people. I have many friends in Cyprus, and the minute I received your orders, I set sail at once for that beautiful island. I had good winds and arrived there in a few days. My friends all came and welcomed me, and the merchants came and took me to their warehouses to show the copper that they wanted to sell me. But I had my little plan ready. I looked at the copper and pretended to laugh. 'What do we want with copper?' I said. 'We have iron now in Crete. We use iron now to make our weapons. I've merely come to see my friends and say good-bye since I'll not be doing business here in Cyprus any longer. I'll be traveling north now,' I said, 'transporting IRON back to Crete.'

"When they heard this they all turned pale. They scattered, in a terrible state, all except one man, a nobleman who owns the island's richest copper mines. He waited around after the others had gone and was looking at me mockingly and smiling. 'Come and dine with me at my mansion,' he said to me. 'I have something to tell you.'

" 'With pleasure,' I said to him, thinking there might be something to be learned from him.

"We walked together to his mansion—the doors are made of gleaming copper; even the tiles on the ground in the courtyard are copper—the slaves polish them every day and the whole house glitters like gold. We sat down, we ate, we drank, and when we finished, the man raised his cup to me: 'My friend,' he said, 'everything you said about iron has thrown the poor merchants here into shock. But I have no fears. I'll be selling copper to you for many years to come. Your ships will continue coming to Cyprus and loading up on our copper. This I swear to you.'

"I pretended to smile.

" 'Don't laugh,' he said, 'I know what I'm saying. Do you want to hear my secret?'

" 'Sure,' I said

" 'You have iron,' he said, 'but you don't have a blacksmith.'

" 'Yes we do,' I said, 'and one who's the best craftsman in the world!'

" 'Who?' he said.

" 'Aristidis,' I answered.

"He laughed. 'How long have you been away from Crete?' he said.

" 'Several months,' I lied.

" 'Eh, then you don't know,' he said. 'You had him once, but you no longer have your Aristidis.'

" 'What?' I shouted, pretending surprise. 'Has he died?'

"He burst out laughing again. 'I don't know what's happened to him,' he said, 'but this I know for sure; he no longer is in Crete!'

" 'Was he abducted by pirates?' I said.

" 'I don't know, I tell you,' he said. 'Don't ask. He may have been abducted, he may have been killed, I don't know, but little by little, the same will happen to all your blacksmiths, whoever they may be. So do yourself a favor, my dear Captain Kaphisos,' he said, 'buy the copper that I have in my warehouse and go. I'll sell it to you cheap, so you can make a profit, too.'

"This is what he told me, my King. He probably knows something more, but try as I would, I couldn't get another word out of him. I kept filling his glass, but nothing! I figured, though, that what I learned was important, so I hurried back to tell you."

The King had been listening attentively. The news was certainly important, but he had been expecting something better.

Kaphisos eyed him cautiously. He could sense the King's dissatisfaction and quickly he resumed talking, to temper the disappointment. "My King," he said, "what I have found out is most important. Now we know that the blacksmith did not go away to betray the secret. He was seized by force, and we can be sure that whoever is holding him will never allow him to work the iron, or teach others to work it." The cunning seaman sighed. "He's in danger, though, my King, your beloved blacksmith is in danger of being killed."

The King thought for a while. He pondered and pondered. *What should he do? Declare war on Cyprus? He had no stomach for that. Better to get a new blacksmith and guard him more carefully. Fortunately, it was not what he had feared . . . the blacksmith had not been seized by his enemies to learn from him how to make iron weapons. . . .*

"Very well," he said aloud. "Thank you, Captain Kaphisos. You have accomplished something worthwhile. Of course, it would have been better if you had delivered my beloved blacksmith to me; but the news that you have brought will be enough for the present. Go now, and when I have confirmed that all you have told me is true, I will reward you for your trouble."

The captain raised his arms, saluted, and retreated backwards through the door, his face still turned toward the King.

Outside the door Ikaros was waiting for him. He was stubbornly determined to find out what was going on. As soon as the captain emerged, the youth approached him. "Welcome, Captain Kaphisos," he said. "I am Ikaros, a friend of Haris's."

"Not here!" said Kaphisos curtly. "Go back to the olive tree where you were sitting, and I'll find you there."

A short while later, the captain was strolling past the olive tree, making his way back to the harbor. He glanced at the tree and, with a barely perceptible nod at Ikaros sitting beneath the shade, signaled the youth to follow.

Ikaros, convinced now that Captain Kaphisos had some important secret to reveal, waited until he had gone a safe distance, then casually rose and followed after him.

When the captain reached the harbor, he headed quickly for his ship and went aboard. There he waited in the stern and before long, Ikaros, looking unobtrusive in the crowd, appeared alongside the ship and leaped quietly aboard.

Inside the stern Kaphisos held out his arms and greeted him warmly. "Where's Haris?" he asked in surprise. "Why isn't he with you?"

"He's not in Crete," answered Ikaros and began at once to relate the details of all that had happened: how Haris had been sent away by the King, how the letter had come from Athens, how the Princess had read it. . . .

The captain listened to the boy's story and rubbed his hands with glee. *He had managed it well with the King . . . now he'd be sending all his ships to Cyprus. . . .* He chuckled to himself, shrewdly refraining from confessing his secret.

When Ikaros had finished, the captain went to the hold of the ship and opened a chest from which he removed a spidery woven veil covered with beautiful embroidery. "I brought back a small gift from Cyprus," he said presenting it to Ikaros. "It's for Krino. Greet her for me, and tell her to wear it and remember me." He took Ikaros's hand. "Go, now, my lad," he urged, "go, so that they don't see us talking together. And listen well to what I am about to say to you: all will end well! Do you hear? Tell this to Krino. All will end well!''

20

Captain Kaphisos was sleeping easily in his ship, his mind content. But man's mind entertains one thing, and Fate another.

It was raining and cold, and the King, sitting in his room, was warming himself next to the fire. His mind was far away, on past glories when he was young and waging wars and returning triumphant and victorious to his people. . . . He was shaking his head sadly. He had grown old . . . and so had his kingdom. He could feel the end coming. There was only one consolation left to him: his iron. But where was he to find craftsmen to work it? Aristidis was yet to be heard from. "They've probably killed him by now," he sighed aloud, "and I thought. . . ."

But his thought was interrupted by a commotion as the door to the royal chamber swung open and a messenger burst in.

"My King!" The messenger fell panting at the old monarch's feet. "I bring you a letter! From Athens! From Captain Tylissos!"

The King sat up. "Summon the scribe to come here at once!" he commanded the two guards at the door.

In a short while the frail old scribe with the long gray hair appeared before the King.

"Read!" commanded the King.

The old scribe reached for the letter and began to read aloud the curious-looking symbols:

To the King of Kings: His humble slave, Tylissos, writes:

I carried out your orders, my King. I delivered your letter to the King of Athens, and after he read it he said all would be done as you commanded.

Starting tomorrow, my King, I shall go fishing with the bait you gave me. As soon as I catch the two fish that you ordered, I will write you.

I kneel and kiss your royal feet. I, Captain Tylissos, the humble slave of the King of Crete.

The King smiled. "He's clever," he thought to himself. "He'll manage it. If the two fish are in Athens, they'll see the bait and bite. But . . . I'm afraid they may be far away in Cyprus."

When the scribe had gone and the King was alone he rose from his throne and stood for a moment staring at the walls with their murals of lilies and exotic animals, then wearily he dragged himself to the threshold and looked out. It was raining. The sky was dark with clouds, and the trees were stripped bare. Ida, towering over the spine of Cretan mountains, was covered with snow. He shivered. Winter.

He walked back to the huge brazier that was burning next to his throne and held out his withered old hands to warm them. "I've grown old," he sighed. He thought of his youth again, and how he used to sport with the bulls; how he used to go hunting and kill wild boars, and how once, when Lato rose up in rebellion, he had taken his army and leveled the city to ashes in three days. And now? It was all he could do to hang on to what he had. He could no longer raise an army, let alone wage war. He had no heir. A galling bitterness, this not having an heir. He had sired two daughters. But no son. Who would inherit his Kingdom? Sons-in-law . . . strangers. . . .

The halls beyond the royal chambers echoed faintly with the voices and laughter of the Palace nobles. Seated on their soft pillows around glowing braziers in their apartments, the lords and ladies were amusing themselves, wiling away the winter hours with games and food and drink. Toward nightfall, the plaintive tones of the santouri carried softly, along with the sound of maidservants singing.

In the Palace cellars below, the slaves were returning to their quarters for the night. They had finished their day's labors— sweeping, washing, kneading, baking, cooking, chopping wood, hauling water, toiling in the workshops or out in the muddy fields—and were gathering in the cellars now to eat a crust of bread and talk with one another before settling down, exhausted, to their night's sleep.

A burly giant among them was grumbling loudly. He was a northerner, with a blond beard, brought to Knossos from the lands up north and sold as a slave to the King. He was grousing to another slave beside him, a broad-nosed Cypriot who, like himself, had been brought to Knossos along with others from his country, and sold into slavery. "This is no life!" he was muttering bitterly. "Do you call this living?!" He had begun to raise his voice and the Cypriot was looking at him uneasily. "What's eating you?" he whispered, casting a nervous glance at the door.

"We're not men!" the blondbeard shouted angrily. "We're yoked animals!"

A hush fell over the cellar. The chatting ceased abruptly and the slaves lowered their heads, averting their eyes. No one dared speak. No one dared voice an opinion, all fearful of the spies in their midst who might betray them to the King.

One among them, a lean rawboned slave with fiery eyes, lifted his head in the cowed silence and looked at the blondbeard. "A foreign ship arrived the other day," he said, "and brought strange news. Do you by chance know something about it?"

"I know about it," grunted the blondbeard. "I've already talked with the captain."

The lean one kept his piercing eyes on him. "And what did he tell you?"

The blondbeard didn't answer.

"You're not saying?"

Still the blondbeard didn't answer. He sat for a while without speaking, looking at them soberly—all friends, all comrades. He rose and closed the door. "The captain of the foreign ship is from my village," he said at length. "He's from up north, near the Danube, where I come from. My countrymen have taken to their ships and are heading down our way. Their land is too small to hold them, and they've set out for new territory to settle in. They've already taken over the smaller islands north of here—Thasos, Samothraki, Skyros, Skopelos—and are heading south . . . thousands of them. They've just taken over Euboia—that's where the ship has come from now. . . ." He paused, looking at them as if uncertain whether he should tell them more.

"Are they coming here?" the lean one rasped.

"I don't know."

"Didn't he tell you anything more?"

"Nothing more!" The blondbeard turned away abruptly.

The slave was following him with his piercing eyes.

For a while, the other stood looking into the fire. "Why don't you bring out some beans," he said, to change the subject. "Let's roast some beans, and pass the time."

"We can't; the storeroom's closed," the rawbone answered. "The guard has the keys."

"Then let's call it a night," shrugged the blondbeard. "Let's go to bed and dream in our sleep we're eating roasted beans."

"At least there we're free to do as we please," muttered the slave.

The blondbeard stretched out on the floor and lay staring at the ceiling. *That's not enough!* he growled silently, . . . *that's not enough!*

One by one, the slaves lay back on the tiles, wrapped their rags about them, and soon fell to snoring. The blondbeard lay awake, his blue eyes open wide. He was thinking of the foreign ship, of what the Captain had whispered to him, and his heart was pounding hard.

"Eh, Comrade!" he heard the lean one close beside him. "They're all asleep now . . . no one will hear . . . tell me, what else did the captain say to you?"

The blondbeard lay silent. A while went by. He turned, and in the dim light of the oil lamp he could see the other's huge black eyes burning. "Come closer," he said.

The lean one moved close, bending his ear to the other's mouth.

"Very soon now," hissed the giant, "they'll be coming to Crete!"

21

For days now, Captain Tylissos had been roaming the narrow streets of Athens, with Haris in tow. Up and down the streets he walked him, round and round the Palace. A holiday or festival did not go by that the two were not out among the crowds, with the captain pushing Haris conspicuously to the forefront.

Any time, now, Tylissos kept telling himself, the blacksmith was bound to appear. He was bound to see them and rush up to his son. Then, in the name of the King, he, Captain Tylissos, would nab him and carry him back to Crete in his ship.

The days were passing and there was no sign of the blacksmith. Who knew what dungeon he must be in! And the Prince . . . there was no sign of him, either. No telling how long he'd be away, chasing brigands in the mountains.

A week went by. Two. Captain Tylissos was growing nervous. To return to Crete empty-handed was unthinkable. That spiteful old King would have his head for sure.

108　　One day, word came that the Prince had cleaned out the bandits in the mountains and had returned to the Palace. Tylissos had an idea. Why not take the boy to the Palace and present him to the

Prince? He could watch their reaction and see if the two recognized each other . . . and this way he might even get a glimpse of the blacksmith hidden somewhere in the Palace dungeons.

He quickly called the boy to him. "Haris," he said casually, "I have a plan."

Haris looked uneasy. He was tired of all this roaming around the rustic streets of Athens; there was nothing to see here. Besides, he was wary of all the mystery . . . of why he was here. He suspected the captain had some evil purpose in mind for him.

"Don't be afraid," said Tylissos to reassure him. "It's something that will work for your good. Now listen closely. I have to return to Crete and must leave you; I can't stay here any longer."

"Take me with you," pleaded Haris.

"I can't," said the captain. "The King has commanded that you are to stay here. But I have a plan for you. I'm going to take you to the Palace and present you to the Prince. He is recruiting young men, to train for his army. If you prove yourself strong and good, if you obey orders, if you show yourself brave in danger, I'm sure the Prince will take a liking to you, and some day you could become great and powerful."

Haris listened without comment, weighing the captain's words. *He might be right*, he was thinking to himself. *Athens was his true country . . . why shouldn't he enter the service of his true King? And who knew . . . he might become a good soldier, and some day march against the Cretan Kingdom, and liberate his country . . .*

The captain was watching him closely. "How does the idea strike you?"

"Fine," said the boy.

The captain smiled. "I'll go to the Palace right away," he said, "and get permission from the Prince to present you. Wait for me here. I should be back within the hour."

Haris followed the captain to the door. Tylissos opened it and went out, but when he had gone a few steps a suspicious thought took hold and he stopped abruptly and turned to look back at the boy standing at the threshold.

"Don't go out!" he warned sternly.

"I won't," said Haris, and the captain turned and strode away.

As Captain Tylissos was hurrying to the Palace, the Prince at that very moment was in his room, reading a letter that had just arrived on a ship from some mysterious person across the sea: *To the Prince of Athens, the renowned Theseus,* the letter read. *The person writing this is someone you know, who must remain anonymous. Your young friend Haris, the son of the blacksmith, is in Athens with a Cretan captain. Find him and free him.*

Theseus was reading the letter and smiling. *What astounding good news! Haris was here in Athens! He would find Aristidis and tell him . . .* and he made at once to head for the cellar where the blacksmith was working, but almost instantly he stopped. "It would be better to find Haris before saying anything," he reflected. "I'll find Haris first, and surprise Aristidis with the boy in person!" and, thinking better of it, he turned instead and summoned his Officer of the Guard.

The Officer appeared at once, a sunbaked old man clad in bronze armor and a great helmet adorned with feathers.

"A Cretan captain has arrived here with a young boy," Theseus informed the Officer. "Have you seen them? Do you know where they can be found?"

"I do, my Prince," said the Officer who prided himself in knowing all that went on in the city. "I know of the Cretan captain and the boy. They have been walking around the Palace for fifteen days now. I have had them trailed. They're staying at the house of a Palace chef by the name of Demos. The captain, in fact, has already delivered a letter to your father."

"A letter? From whom?"

"From the King of Crete."

"What does it say?"

"That, I don't know, my Prince."

"Never mind . . . I'll find out," said Theseus. "Let's not lose time. Send two guards to the house where the boy is staying and have them bring him to me at once!"

"You'll have him here in minutes, my Prince," declared the Officer, ". . . that is, of course, if he's there at this hour." He saluted, strode out the door and disappeared. But barely had he left the room when he appeared again. "My Prince," he laughed, the Cretan captain is outside, waiting in the anteroom, and he says he wants to see you."

"Is he alone?"

"He's alone."

"Then the boy must be at the house now. Go! Send the guards

immediately to bring him. And tell the captain to come back to-morrow. I'm busy today.''

The Officer hastened out on the run, and in a few minutes two soldiers were making their appearance at the house of Demos, where Haris, still standing at the threshold, was waiting for the captain to return.

The soldiers approached him. "Are you Haris from Crete?" they asked.

"I am," said Haris.

"Come with us!" they said. "You're wanted at the Palace!"

And Haris, thinking the captain had sent for him, stepped down from the threshold and followed the soldiers to the Palace.

Theseus, meanwhile, was pacing the floor in his room. Strong emotions were stirring beneath his breast. He had guessed who sent the letter and was envisioning the golden-haired Princess, remembering ever so vividly that late afternoon in her Palace . . . how she smiled at him . . . how she spoke to him . . . *Theseus, take this ring and if you ever are in danger, don't forget me.* He walked back and forth across the room. Would the guards find Haris alone in the house? Would they reach him in time before the captain returned? He preferred to snatch the boy away quietly like this, rather than have the captain raise a hue and cry. The Athenians weren't ready for war just yet. Their time had not yet come to tangle with the King of Crete. . . .

The door opened and the Officer entered.

"They've brought him?"

"He's here!"

The Officer turned and signaled.

Haris stepped across the threshold and entered the room.

"You can leave us now," said the Prince to the Officer.

Haris stared. He opened his mouth to speak, but nothing came out.

The Prince smiled. "It's me, Haris. Don't you remember me?"

"*YOU?*" managed the boy. "*YOU!*, the Prince of Athens?"

"Every inch of me!" laughed Theseus, opening his arms wide to his small friend. Haris stared, dumbfounded, then with a jubilant cry, was in the Prince's arms. *What good fortune! What incredible good fortune!* He could hardly contain himself for joy.

"An even greater joy is waiting for you," said Theseus, embracing his young friend warmly, and when the boy had caught his

111

breath, and calmed himself somewhat, he took him by the hand and led him from the room. He escorted him down a corridor to a dark stairwell where they descended to a lower level of the Palace. Haris could dimly make out guards snapping to attention here and there as the Prince went by. He could distinguish bronze weapons hanging on the walls and as his eyes grew more accustomed to the dark he could see them clearly—suits of armor, swords, lances.

They walked on, and now the sound of clanging could be heard—a loud clanging like iron beating against iron—and they could see flames from a lit fire at the other end of the corridor. They were coming to a workshop where a man, his back to them, was standing before a fire, raising and lowering a hammer over an anvil. Alongside him a fair-skinned Negro, was fanning the flames with the bellows. As they approached they could hear the blacksmith with the hammer. "Faster!" he was urging the man with the bellows. "Faster!"

Haris started at the voice. His heart was pounding. They were at the threshold of the little workshop now and Theseus stepped in front of him, hiding him. "Eh, Master!" he called to the blacksmith. "Turn around and look at us!"

The blacksmith turned. "Welcome, our Prince!" he exclaimed, laying down his hammer and wiping his hands on his apron to greet him. But hardly had he time to take the situation in, when Haris, who by now had recognized his father, tore out of the shadows, shouting *Father! Father!* and flung himself into the blacksmith's arms.

While Haris was rejoicing with his father and the Prince at their reunion, the captain was returning to the house of Demos to find his young charge gone.

"Two soldiers from the Palace came for him," old Demos told him. "Weren't you the one who sent for him?"

"Me?"

"Who, then?"

The wretched Tylissos slumped on a stool. "I'm lost!" he groaned. "They've stolen him from me!" He sat exhausted on the stool, pondering the situation, and as the horror of his predicament sank in, he dragged himself to his feet and hastened back to the Palace. But the Prince had given orders to his guards that no one was to disturb him. "Come back tomorrow," they told him. "We have orders, he's not to be disturbed today."

"But it's urgent!" the captain pleaded.

"Tomorrow! Tomorrow!" was all they would say and would not let him in.

The Officer of the Guard came out, too, now, demanding to know what the commotion was about.

"They've abducted the boy that was with me," shouted the captain. "Soldiers from the Palace abducted him. I want justice!"

"Stop shouting!" commanded the Officer. "I'll look into it."

"I protest!" screamed the captain. "In the name of the King of Crete, I protest!"

"The King of Crete is far away," sneered the Officer. "The King of Athens is near; take care that he doesn't hear you or, I promise you, you'll be sorry!"

"You'll pay!" raged the captain. "You'll pay for what you've done to me!"

The Officer turned away. "Take him to his ship," he said to the two guards, "and see that he leaves! Give orders that he is not to be allowed to step ashore here again."

"I'll return to Crete," shouted the captain, "and report you to the Great King!"

The Officer laughed. "You don't dare return to Crete, poor wretch!" he said. "You don't dare. You know what death awaits you there."

The captain's shoulders sagged; the Officer was right.

"Let's go!" the soldiers ordered, and grasping him by each arm, they led him away.

22

What good fortune it would be, Haris was thinking, if people had wings and could fly like birds over mountains and plains and seas. How he wished he had wings now to fly to faraway Crete and drop down on Krino and tell her he had found their father. But people don't have wings, and Haris was obliged to write a letter and wait—God only knew how long—for the opportunity to find some ship sailing to Crete. He longed to know how Krino and

Ikaros were faring out there; he knew how concerned they must be about him.

And true, Krino and Ikaros were sick with worry. It had been a long time since Haris had written, and their minds were suspecting the worst.

The Princess Ariadne, too, was all anxiety. Had Theseus received her letter? Had he guessed who sent it? Had he been able to free Haris?

And the King. He, too, was filled with his own tormenting thoughts. The captain was long overdue in returning with the blacksmith in chains. The sleepless winter nights were endless. His lone diversion now, the only consolation left him, was playing chess with that fat, cunning dream interpreter. But now and then his sly old eyes would light up; spring was bound to come, he'd tell himself, and like it or not, the King of Athens would have to obey his command and send him the Prince for the Minotaur to eat.

He was feeling a strong compulsion these days to see the Minotaur. For a long time now, the beast had been groaning ceaselessly beneath the Palace, and wouldn't let him sleep. He had an uneasy feeling that it wanted something.

One night he descended the stairs to the subterranean foundation below the Palace and headed for the Labyrinth. He had to see the creature, to stop its groaning. It was keeping him awake. Carrying a flaming pine torch to light his way, he entered the underground maze, exulting in the knowledge that no one could enter those dark convolutions and come out alive—only he, and one other—Daidalos, who had designed them. The air was thick and suffocating down there, smelling of dank earth. He held his breath. A bat flew past his head and here and there a snake hissed at him as he stumbled through cavernous passages that twisted and turned like those circles in a whirlpool that keep getting shorter and shorter until nothing is left in the center but the vacuum that sucks one down.

Suddenly a frightening roar reverberated from the tunnel's depths, an eerie, groaning roar, full of savagery and pain. The old King stopped. His teeth were chattering and cold sweat was running down his face. He paused to ease his breathing. It was a frightful monster, this Minotaur. Rarely did he come down to visit it. He had found it imprisoned here in the Palace from ancient times—a monstrous creature with the body of a man and the head of a bull. Come spring, they had to bring it a meal of seven youths and seven maidens. It would toy with them for a while, playing a game of cat and mouse, and when it tired of the sport, it would eat them.

The King could feel the beast's hot breath as he approached. For a terrifying instant, he thought of turning back, and indeed, he was making to retreat when, without warning, a gigantic hairy body blocked his way. With a cry of horror, he realized he was already in the monster's den. Arms spread wide, its enormous mouth open in a ghastly toothy grin, the Minotaur was towering before him. Shuddering, the old man leaned against the wall, his eyes riveted on the grinning beast. It was looking down at him and laughing, holding out its arms as though to keep him from leaving, but as the King stared back at it with dread, he could see two giant tears spilling from the creature's eyes. *The Minotaur was crying!*

And indeed, the Minotaur kept looking down at him, baring its teeth in that ghastly grin, and two fat tears were rolling down its monstrous cheeks. *Why was it crying?* The King drew in his breath uneasily. *Something was wrong. . . .*

"Are you hungry?" he croaked, addressing the beast tremulously.

The Minotaur opened its mouth wider and groaned.

"What did it want?" The King looked at it in bewilderment. "Be patient," he ventured, taking hold of himself. "Spring is coming. Soon I'll be bringing you seven handsome youths and seven beautiful maidens. It won't be long now, you'll get your fill."

The creature's toothy grin widened. A reddish spittle ran down from its mouth, and one could sense it understood the words spoken to it, though it could not answer.

The King took courage. "Satisfied?" His raspy voice was steady now, entreating. "I've come to quiet you," he soothed. "Why have you been groaning these many nights and keeping me awake?"

A sound like a sigh, heaved from the Minotaur's lips.

The King looked at it uneasily again. *What was wrong with it? What did it want?* The creature had turned its eyes on him with a look of profound anguish and was moving its mouth strangely, opening and closing it over and over again, trying desperately to bring forth something like a human sound. But it couldn't. And two new tears spilled from its eyes.

The old man watched it with growing apprehension. *What did it want to tell him?* He had learned from his father and grandfather that the Minotaur was a holy monster that safeguarded the Kingdom of Crete, and every Cretan King was obliged to grant it its every wish, to keep it satisfied. If the Minotaur was not satisfied, the Kingdom would be in peril. He could see the Minotaur's agitation, and he was frightened. *His Kingdom was in peril!*

"Tell me what you want!" he importuned the beast. "I'll give you anything you ask for!"

Again that mournful sigh from the Minotaur.

"What do you want?" shouted the King in desperation. "I'm bringing you Theseus! the King's only son! What more do you want?!"

The Minotaur let out a groan, as though someone had stuck a knife in its heart. It thrust out its tongue and bit it, spurting blood all over the King's bald head.

"What's wrong with you?" shrieked the King in panic. The Minotaur had dropped its arms to its sides now and was leaning against the wall, barely able to stand. *What did it want? If only it could talk and tell him what it wanted! His Kingdom was in peril!* The old man girded his heart and cautiously put out a hand to pet the creature. "There . . . there . . . ," he purred nervously. "Calm yourself . . . in a month, spring will be here, and the ship with the black sails will moor in our harbor, and the seven youths and seven maidens will come ashore—and the first among them will be the King's son, Theseus. . . ."

The creature groaned again, like an animal being slaughtered, and the foundations of the Palace shook from the tremor.

The King shrank back in horror. The Minotaur had rolled on the ground now and lay motionless. Trembling, the old man nudged it with his foot, but the creature wouldn't budge. "It must be asleep," he rasped, shaking with dread. "I'll leave now, while I can," and backing away stealthily, he turned and fled through the twisting corridors until he reached the subterranean entrance where his guards and slaves were waiting to carry him up to the Palace.

It was past midnight when he dragged himself, exhausted,

116

across his bed. *Something was wrong with the Minotaur!* And he trembled for his Kingdom.

23

The day broke bright and clear. Spring had arrived in Athens, the time of year when the choicest blossoms of her youth were to be plucked and sent to Crete to be devoured by the Minotaur.

The mournful city was gathered at the Agora, where the King and his twelve elders had convened since dawn, to draw the lots and choose the sacrifices.

Haris had come among the first and was standing near the elders who were assembled on the steps below the stone throne where King Aigeus was addressing his people:

"Men of Athens! my beloved countrymen!" the old King's voice shook with the terrible awesomeness of the moment. "The dreaded day has arrived. All the peoples of the earth await spring with joy. Athens awaits it with dread. Before we draw the lots, let us raise our arms to our patron Goddess and pray.

"Oh Virgin Athena! Goddess of strength and wisdom," he intoned, "hear our prayers: Your beloved city is enslaved to the King of Crete. Raise your lance, Oh Goddess, and help us liberate her!"

He spoke, and the people cried out in one voice: "Liberate her, Oh Athena!"

The prayer over, the first of the elders rose and gave the command: "Let the youths and maidens come forward!"

The crowd made room and an aisle was opened through which a procession of glowing youth, the choicest of Athens, came forth. In the lead, handsome and strong, came Theseus, the King's own son. The youths were clad in short chitons and their bronzed athletic bodies glistened lean and hard in the morning light.

Alongside the youths walked the maidens, regal and lovely in long veils, their hair plaited and wreathed with the first flowers of spring. A murmur of anguished admiration for the doomed loveliness rippled through the crowd.

The youths and maidens approached the steps, and the first of the elders addressed them: "Welcome, our noble youth! Fourteen of you must be sacrificed for our country. Do you choose this of your own free will?"

"We do!" the words came as one from the youthful lips.

"Let us commence, then!" commanded the King, rising from his throne.

The lots were brought forth, some forty little wooden pieces, each with the name of a youth or a maiden, and dropped into a bronze helmet.

They were ready to draw the first lot when the King stepped forward again to speak. He paused, leaning on his tall royal staff. For a moment, his eyes rested on his son standing erect among the youths, then quickly he looked away. "I have a request to make," he announced, and his voice trembled. "I ask that my son be among the seven chosen, whether or not his lot is called!"

A gasp went through the crowd. The King was asking that his son, his only son! be sent away to be killed! The elders rose in consternation.

"King," said the first, "it is not right for your son to go, if it is not his lot. You have no other son, no other heir!"

"It must be so!" replied the King.

"Why so?"

"I have orders. From the King of Crete!" The withered lips of old Aigeus pronounced the royal edict heavily, and the words hung like naked swords over the silenced crowd.

There was a stir among the youths, and Theseus stepped forward from the ranks. "O men of Athens!" he called aloud for all to hear. "I go to Crete of my own free will! The time has come! Even had there been no command from Minos, I would have gone of my own volition!"

Cries went up among the crowd. "You'll be killed!"

"I am not going to Crete to be killed!" shouted Theseus. "I am going there *to kill!*

"The Minotaur?! That dreadful monster!" The people trembled for their Prince and for their country.

Theseus raised his voice above the cries. "With Athena's help," he shouted, "I will kill the Minotaur!"

Old Aigeus looked down at his son proudly, and his eyes filled with tears. The handsome Prince, bathed in the morning light, glowed like a god in the center of the agora. Haris, at the forefront of the throngs, was near to bursting with awe and admiration. "Long may you live!" he shouted fervently with the cheering crowd.

118

The King turned to the elders. "Begin the drawing!" he commanded.

The elders shook their heads. "Let your will be done," they murmured.

A child was summoned from the crowd, and the lots were brought forth. The child plucked out a lot from the helmet and handed it to the elders.

"Androkles! son of Timokrates!" read the first elder aloud.

"Present!" shouted a youth, leaping from the line and going to stand alongside Theseus.

The child pulled out a second lot.

"Demokritos! son of Theagenes!" read the elder.

"Present!" from a dark-haired youth with burning eyes who bounded forward and went to stand alongside Androkles and Theseus.

The child pulled out a third lot, a fourth, a fifth . . . until the seven youths were called, and then the seven maidens, and when the last name had been called, the old King rose and addressed the fourteen youths and maidens.

"I give you three days to say your farewells to family and friends," he said. "The storerooms of my Palace will be open; the tables will be spread for you. Come to my gardens and eat and drink and ask any favor you wish. You are sacrificing your lives for your country, it is only right and just that you ask for whatever you desire." His old eyes misted again. "In three days," he continued hoarsely, struggling to keep his emotion under control, "the ship will put up black sails and you will set out. May her grace, the Goddess, allow you to see your country again!"

He spoke, and the mournful ceremony was over.

The youths dispersed among the crowds and the King, leaning heavily on his royal staff, stepped down from the throne. His knees were unsteady, buckling under him, and Theseus, coming to stand alongside him, gave him his arm.

"My son," the King whispered, taking the Prince's arm and keeping his voice low so that no one could hear, "come with me, I have something to tell you."

Slowly father and son returned to the Palace, and when the two were alone in the Throne Room, old Aigeus dropped wearily on his throne. "Come close," he said quietly, "no one must hear us."

He held out a withered old hand and bade Theseus sit at his feet. His heart was unbearably heavy. His son, his only hope and joy, was going away, perhaps never to be seen again. For a brief spell he was silent, looking about him at the colossal stone boulders that made up the Palace walls.

"Your grandfather was a giant," he began, stroking his son's curly head. "He built this Palace with his bare hands. He lifted these huge rocks single-handed, to build these walls. When he set out for war, or when he set out to hunt, he struck terror in all he came up against. Beasts in the forests and men in the battlefields cowered in fear before his giant sword."

"I know," said Theseus.

"Yes, the whole world knows," said the King. "But what I am about to tell you now, nobody knows, not even you."

"I'm listening, Father."

"Up at the Akropolis, at the foot of the bronze statue of Athena, is an enormous rock."

"I know it," said the youth.

"Did you know that hidden beneath this rock is the giant sword that belonged to your grandfather?"

"No, that I didn't know," confessed the Prince.

"Now hear the secret," said the King, lowering his voice. "There is an old oracle that says *he who lifts this rock and takes the sword will be invincible.*"

"*I'll* lift it!" said Theseus, leaping to his feet.

"Ten men can't lift it!"

"But *I* will!" declared Theseus. "With the help of Athena, I will lift it!"

The King looked at the gallant youth, and for a moment a glint of awe lit up his tired old eyes. "Will you be able to, my son?" he murmured.

"I will!" said the Prince, all impatience to get at it. "Let's go!" and he made for the door.

"Not yet!" said the King, calling him back. "We mustn't be seen. Come back at midnight, and we'll go when it's dark. Now hear me carefully," he whispered, when the impatient son had settled at his father's feet again, "you sail in three days, and according to tradition, your ship will unfurl black sails. If, with the power of Athena, you return victorious, unfurl the white sails on your ship. I shall be sitting on the high cliff overlooking the open

120

sea, watching for you. I want to see the sails from a distance, to know if I should rejoice, or if I should jump into the sea and drown. . . ." He faltered, choking on his tears.

The Prince pressed his old father's knees. "I'm going to be victorious," he said. "You'll see the white sails in the distance, and your heart will rejoice!"

"May her grace, Athena, so will it," said the King. "And now, my son, go meet your friends. The tables are spread in the Palace; invite your companions to eat and drink and at midnight, return to me."

Theseus kissed his father's hand and hurried out.

At the door, young Haris was waiting for him to emerge. "My father sent me," said the boy. "He said it's important that he see you."

"We'll go to him at once," said Theseus. He, too, was anxious to see Aristidis on an important matter of his own, and he hastened now with Haris down the steps to the forge beneath the Palace.

They could hear the pounding of the blacksmith's hammer and see the glow from the blazing fire well before they approached. The Negro was fanning the flame with his bellows, and the blacksmith, standing alongside, was pounding away when they drew near. At the sight of the pair approaching, the blacksmith spoke to the Negro, who put down the bellows and took off his leather apron. "Come back this afternoon," he called after him as the Negro disappeared into the dark corridor from where Theseus and Haris had emerged.

The Prince strode near, and with buoyant step crossed the blackened threshold. "I'm here!" he called out jovially to Aristidis. "You wanted me?"

"My Prince!" The blacksmith hastened to greet him warmly. "I've prepared something for you. . . ."

"Let me guess!" laughed Theseus. "I'll bet it's an iron dagger . . . a double-edged iron dagger."

"Yes and no," smiled the blacksmith, going to a secret cabinet hidden in the wall and taking out a broad double-edged dagger.

"See, I was right!" exclaimed Theseus, eyeing the broad dagger. "I was absolutely right!"

"Not quite," laughed the blacksmith, holding out the weapon. "What do you suppose this dagger is made of?"

121

"Iron, of course."

"It's something more than iron," said the blacksmith. "That's the secret of my craft. It starts out pure iron, but as we keep working it, the iron becomes steel—a metal many times stronger.

"When we heat the iron," he explained, "and it reaches the point where it turns white, we dip it in water, and that increases its strength many times over. With a dagger like this, you needn't fear a beast in the world. Take it," he said, handing the dagger to Theseus, "and with the power of Athena, plunge it deep into the Minotaur's neck."

Theseus grasped the coveted dagger and attached it to his silver belt. He pressed the blacksmith's hand gratefully. "Now, what favor can I grant you?" he demanded.

"None," said Aristidis. "Go with Godspeed! Kill the man-eating monster and return. I will remain here and prepare more daggers of steel and swords and lances for the great campaign."

"What campaign?" laughed Theseus, feigning innocence.

"You know very well, my Prince," winked back the blacksmith. "The great campaign for which you took me from Crete and brought me here. Am I right?"

"You're right," answered Theseus, and he pressed his faithful ally's hand again. Turning now to his young companion, "let's go," he said to Haris, "my friends are waiting."

When they had gone some distance, he looked down at the boy walking beside him. "And you," he said, "don't you have a favor to ask of me?"

Haris blushed.

"Aha," said Theseus. "You do have something you want."

Haris looked up shyly and went to say something but stopped.

"Speak up," smiled the Prince. "Don't be afraid."

The boy took courage. "Take me to Crete with you," he said softly.

Theseus tousled the youngster's hair.

"You'll take me?"

"How can I refuse?"

Haris let out a whoop. Now he would see Krino again! He would see Krino and Ikaros again! He whooped aloud and could hardly contain himself for joy.

Theseus smiled. *He, too, would see the blonde Princess again.*

. . .

They took the steps two at a time and came out at the main courtyard where the tables were spread and Theseus's friends were waiting. When the youths and maidens saw him coming, they raised their arms in welcome. "Our hero!" they shouted. "Welcome, our great hero!"

"Not so fast!" laughed Theseus, taking his place with Haris at the table. "Let me kill the Minotaur first!" and he patted the handle of the new dagger hidden in his belt.

They ate and drank well into the evening, but with the approach of midnight, Theseus rose, and leaving the youths and maidens to continue with their banquet, he hurried back to the Palace where the King was waiting.

"Ready?" The old man was standing at the door.

"Ready, Father."

They slipped out a rear exit of the Palace and by midnight were making their way up the hillside to the Akropolis. Athena's giant statue at the summit gleamed softly in the night. Old King Aigeus approached and pointed to the gigantic stone that lay at the Goddess's feet. "There it is," he whispered.

Theseus bent down and studied the stone.

"See if you can lift it!"

Theseus girded himself and bent over the stone again, grasping the thick bronze ring at its center.

"Power to you!" murmured the King.

The youth gave a tug, and the stone barely budged, its edges separating slightly from the earth.

"You can do it!" exhorted the King.

Theseus widened his stance, bracing his feet firmly apart against the ground, and pulled the ring with all his might. The veins protruded in his arms, the blood rushed to his head, and the rock groaned and lifted slightly.

"A little more!" prodded the old man who was on his knees now, bending over the earth, examining the rock anxiously.

Theseus summoned all his strength. For a second, the statue of Athena seemed to move and, lo, with one last mighty heave, the gigantic stone broke loose and stood on end.

The aged King leaped to his feet. "Bless you, my son!" he shouted. "Your grandfather is resurrected!"

123

Theseus wiped the sweat from his brow and paused to catch his breath.

"Now search for the sword!" commanded the old man. "You must find the sword!"

Theseus thrust his hands into the earth and dug deep with his nails. He felt something hard. "I found it!" he shouted, and pulled from the soil a colossal sword encased in a protective lead scabbard. He removed the lead sheath, and the awesome bronze blade lay gleaming before them.

"You are invincible, my son!" cried the jubilant King clasping the Prince to him. "Now I fear nothing. Nothing!" and the tears flowed copiously from his aged eyes.

24

The almond trees had blossomed, and the morning air was fragrant with the early scent of spring.

Ariadne had not yet wakened, though the sun's warm rays had long since filtered through the closed window above her bed. She lay in that deep sweet sleep that comes with the first balm of spring, a smile on her face, dreaming of cool sea breezes and distant voyages. She was a mermaid, standing at the prow of a fast ship, and the wind was blowing her hair, and the sea was parting before her, letting her swift ship cut through its foaming waters. . . .

"My Lady! My Lady!" Krino was bending over her mistress, holding a small papyrus roll in her hand, calling to her softly. But the Princess, her blonde hair spread across the white pillow, her smooth forehead flushed with dreaming, continued to sleep.

"My Lady!" Krino called again, shaking her mistress gently.

Ariadne opened her eyes and saw Krino bending over her. She sat up reluctantly. "You interrupted my dream," she mumbled half awake, "I was traveling. . . . "

Krino laughed, holding up the letter to her mistress. "Your dream might come true, my Lady!" she cried, handing the letter to the Princess to read.

Ariadne reached for the papyrus and unrolled it quickly. It was from Haris! She read aloud eagerly. *I, Haris, son of Aristidis the blacksmith, to my sister Krino: Where shall I begin? Everything is like a dream. I found Father! And I found the handsome foreigner who came to the Palace last summer. . . .*

The Princess's voice shook.

. . . you'll never guess who the foreigner is! The son of the King of Athens!

"Poor Haris," laughed Krino, "he thinks we don't know."

Ariadne read on: *How good he is I cannot begin to tell you. But I'm terribly afraid for him. Prince Theseus (that's his name) wants to come to Crete with the seven youths who are coming in the spring to be fed to the Minotaur, and I tremble. . . .*

The letter fell from Ariadne's hand.

Krino looked at her mistress anxiously. "Don't worry, my Lady," she said, "the King of Athens will never let his son put himself in such danger."

"But if he, himself, wants to come?" Ariadne was pale and her voice shook.

"Why should he?"

"To rescue his country from this terrible slavery . . . to rescue the youths and maidens who come here to be eaten by the Minotaur!"

"But no one can battle such a monster!" exclaimed Krino.

"That's exactly why he'd want to battle it!" answered the Princess. She rose from her bed and went to the window. The sky was blue and cloudless. The first swallows had arrived and were pecking at the air, chirping giddily. Down in the garden the trees were already in bloom. Spring was here. In a few days the mournful ship with the black sails would be sighted on the horizon, bringing the seven youths and seven maidens. *My god! what if he's with them!* she thought. *I must write to him not to come!*

She turned from the window. "Find Ikaros!" she said to Krino, "and bring him here!"

Krino hastened out, and Ariadne moved away from the window with its dreaded portent of spring. Her eyes lit on the small statue of the goddess that she kept on a niche in the wall. "Great Goddess," she murmured, "don't let him come! don't let him come! . . . but if he does, help me save him!" She stood for a long time before the little statue, her arms clasped over her bare bosom. At last the door to the room opened and Krino returned with Ikaros behind her.

"Go down to the harbor," she said quickly to the youth when he had entered. "Find out if there is a ship leaving for Athens and come back and report to me!"

125

Ikaros left on the run, and Ariadne went back to pacing the floor again, distraught. Would she reach him in time? Would her letter get to him in time? She looked across the room at Krino, who had withdrawn to her corner and was watching her mistress uneasily. "Stand guard at the door," she said to the girl, "don't let anyone in." Then sitting down at a low stool, she began to write.

Krino took her place at the threshold and stood vigil, her eyes on the corridor. Doors on either side of the long hall were opening and closing, slaves were coming and going, bringing the morning meal to their mistresses. A door nearby opened and Phaidra, wrapped in a fuzzy robe, brushed past on the way from her bath.

"Is your mistress up yet?" she called, spotting Krino.

"She is, my Princess."

"Tell her I'll be in to see her," and Phaidra disappeared into her room.

How beautiful she was, thought Krino. Her own mistress was not quite so beautiful; but she was ever so much nicer. She continued her vigil at the threshold. Five, ten minutes went by. The adjoining door opened. In a flash, the faithful maid slipped back into her mistress's chamber and signaled the Princess. "Phaidra!" she whispered.

Ariadne jumped to her feet. Quickly, she hid the letter she was writing and picked up a mirror.

"Sleepyhead!" laughed Phaidra, breezing cheerily into the room. "Aren't you dressed yet? And here I come, bringing you important news."

Ariadne held up her mirror, pretending to arrange her hair. "What news?" she murmured casually. Phaidra's news didn't interest her much. She had probably come to tell her about some new dress that she was having made, or some new hat.

"Spring has arrived," said Phaidra, putting on a solemn face.

"I know," from Ariadne. "Is that your news? That spring has arrived?"

Phaidra smiled good-humoredly. "When spring arrives," she purred, "you know what else arrives."

"The swallows," snapped the younger Princess, impatient for her sister to leave so that she could finish her letter.

"Yes, the fourteen swallows," said Phaidra giggling. "You know about them?"

126

Ariadne looked at her sister sharply. "I know," she said. "A barbaric custom. Shame on us!"

Phaidra laughed. "The most important news I haven't told you yet," she said. "I found out last night from Father. Guess who will be coming among the seven youths this year?"

"Who?" Ariadne's heart stood still.

"The King of Athens's own son!"

Ariadne leaned against the bed.

"Aren't you well?" Phaidra put an arm out to her sister. "You look pale."

"It's nothing," murmured Ariadne, and she picked up her mirror, pretending to arrange her hair again.

"Well, then, I must be going," said Phaidra, bending down to embrace the younger Princess. "I'm expecting the seamstress this morning," and kissing her sister good-bye, she hurried from the room.

When she was gone, Ariadne flung the mirror down and turned to Krino. "You see?" she cried. "See? He's coming! to be eaten by the Minotaur!"

Krino looked at her in awe. He was coming to battle the Minotaur! "My Lady!" she cried, falling to her knees and clasping her mistress's feet. "Help him!"

"How?"

"I don't know. Help him!"

Ariadne looked down at the girl in despair. How? How could she help him? No one had ever been able to enter the Labyrinth and come out of it alive!

A soft knock sounded at the door. Krino opened. It was Ikaros, back from the harbor, breathing hard.

Ariadne took a quick step toward him. "Well?" She waited tensely for him to enter.

"My Princess," said the youth. "The ship with the black sails has been sighted!"

25

Trumpets blasted from the watchtowers, heralding the news.

From his vantage point on the highest terrace looking north, King Minos smiled a triumphant smile. *The black-sailed ship was on its way!* "Marshall the army in the central courtyard!" he commanded, "and dispatch a horseman to the harbor to see if the Prince of Athens is among the seven!" He rubbed his hands together, his feeble eyes glittering with anticipation. "Prepare the Throne Room! Bring out the ceremonial dress!" And having set his subjects scurrying to carry out his orders, the King retreated to his bedchamber to don the regal vestments.

The Princesses, too, put on their finest raiment. Phaidra, clad in her new dress, came out to stand on the terrace, accompanied by two slave girls who were holding plumes over her head to shade her from the sun. The King's dream interpreter came out, too. Carefully shaven, his mustaches neatly groomed, the pomaded, perfumed patriarch glistened like an old white bull in the dazzling sun. "Had the Princess dreamed good dreams?" he smiled cordially.

Before she could reply, Phaidra's eye caught sight of her sister emerging on the terrace, aglow in pearls and gold. "I dreamed," she laughed aloud, turning to answer the fat old courtier, "that the Prince of Athens was coming. . . ."

"And I," said Ariadne drawing near, "dreamed that our dear Minotaur was sloshing in blood." Her rouged cheeks were flushed, and never had Phaidra seen her looking more beautiful.

"In his own, or in the Prince's blood?" Phaidra mocked.

"I don't know yet," said Ariadne.

Her sister sneered. "You don't know?" She looked at Ariadne testily. "So you think. . . ."

"I think nothing," answered Ariadne. "We'll see."

The foxy dream interpreter was smiling, listening to the sisters argue. He knew their differences. The one, dark Phaidra, was all passion and coquettishness. The other, fair-haired Ariadne, suppressed an inner restlessness, a yearning for distant travels, adventures, and heroics.

In the royal bedchamber, meanwhile, where the King was dressing, slaves were putting azure seashells about his neck and a royal crown on his bald head, a crown with silver lilies and seven peacock feathers. They put red sandals on his feet, and in his hand they placed the sovereign staff with three gold lilies.

A breathless guard approached the royal presence. "My King," he gasped. "The ship has anchored! The fourteen are on their way! The son of the Athenian King is with them!"

The King smiled. "Have them appear before me the instant they arrive!" he commanded. He summoned Malis. "You're to remain with me when the Athenians come in," he instructed the former chief, "and see if you recognize the Prince. See if he's the stranger that you stupidly allowed to get away last year."

"As you command," the humiliated former Officer replied and retreated shamefaced to a corner of the room to wait.

Out in the streets a clamor of anticipation had begun to fill the air. The workshops were closed and all Knossos was preparing for the momentous occasion. Houses everywhere were bedecked with flowers, and the city reverberated with the din of festive throngs spilling into the streets to celebrate the Cretans' ancient victory. For nights now the people couldn't sleep from the roaring of the hungry Minotaur that shook the foundation of the Palace. "The beast is hungry!" they would murmur terrified and press their ears to the ground to hear. "Listen to how it groans!"

Many were running down to the harbor now to watch the ship come in and be among the first to see the fourteen bodies that would sate the hunger of the dreadful monster. All were emerging from their houses, filling the streets, lining the broad main road from the harbor, to stand and wait.

Ikaros, too, had hurried to the harbor to be among the first to see the Athenian ship come in. He was standing on the quay, watching the black-sailed ship approach, and a curious turbulence was pounding in his breast, an eerie presentiment, as though he were expecting to see someone he knew.

The ship drew near. It dropped its sails, came to anchor, and Theseus leaped ashore.

Ikaros let out a cry. *The foreigner!*

An old woman standing nearby gasped softly.

"Yes . . . what a pity to throw away such manhood on a beast!" murmured her neighbor.

"Shh!! They'll hear you, poor thing, and bury you in the pits!"

The escort guard approached. The youths and maidens came ashore. The trumpets sounded. The fourteen fell in step, and the procession was under way.

Ikaros scrambled from the pier to follow. He wanted to walk alongside the foreigner, to admire the splendid youth from up close. But as he was making his way down the wharf among the crowd, a sailor who had spotted him from the black-sailed ship,

129

leaped ashore and ran after him, grasping him by the arm. He was clad in sandals and the short chiton of an Athenian and was smiling behind a curly blond beard and mustache. Ikaros looked at him in bewilderment. "Did he know him? Who was he?" But the sailor kept smiling behind the curly blond beard and tugging at his arm, pulling him toward the ship. "Where was he trying to take him?" Ikaros disengaged his arm. He had no wish to let the procession get away without him, and he turned from the sailor so that he could head back with the others to the Palace.

"*Ikaros!*" the sailor whispered then, addressing him by name.

Ikaros stopped short. He knew that voice! He had heard it before. But where?

"Ikaros!" the sailor whispered again, pulling urgently at his arm. "Come with me!"

Ikaros hesitated. He looked curiously at the mysterious sailor. "He must have some secret to tell me," he thought to himself, "a letter perhaps, or some message from Haris in Athens . . . ," and trusting his instinct, he followed the sailor to his ship.

The crew were all on deck at the ship, staring at the famous Cretan harbor with its endless wharfs and warehouses, its bronze double axes glinting atop the tall pikes, its towers that spired to the left and right. . . .

The sailor leaped aboard, Ikaros close behind, and the two descended to the empty galley below. Alone, in the dimly lit hold, the sailor turned to Ikaros. "Don't you recognize me?" he laughed, pulling off the blond beard and mustache.

Haris! For an instant Ikaros's eyes bulged in disbelief. "Haris!" he shouted, pouncing on his friend and embracing him in a delirium of joy.

"Shh!" whispered the boy, quickly putting the beard and mustache back on. "No one must know!" He looked about him cautiously. "Now let's go up on deck and talk." He was clamoring to learn about Krino. Was she well? Did she get his letter?

She was fine, Ikaros assured him, still gazing at his friend with elation and disbelief. "And your father?"

He, too, was well, Haris told him. He was working in Athens, making iron weapons. The two sat on the open deck, exchanging their news, listening avidly to one another's every word. "Soon now," Haris whispered confidingly to Ikaros, who hadn't stopped

staring and murmuring his surprise, "we'll be coming to Crete—
to free our country. . . ."

Ikaros sat up, fairly bursting to hear.

"But for now," cautioned Haris, "you mustn't tell anyone that
I'm here."

"Not even Krino?"

"Only Krino. I'm going to hide until. . . ," he hesitated.

"Until? . . . ," Ikaros prodded eagerly.

Haris leaned closer. He could hardly contain his excitement.
"Until our Prince Theseus kills the Minotaur!"

Ikaros gave an incredulous cry. "But nobody. . . ."

"Have faith!" beamed Haris. "My father has made him a dagger
of steel that can go through the fiercest beast." He jumped to his
feet, all impatience now to get to Knossos. "Let's follow them," he
urged, looking out at the procession that by now had covered
some considerable distance, having reached the main road to the
countryside.

Ikaros scrambled to his feet. The two friends leaped ashore and
raced down the deserted wharf. They sped past the great shipyard
with its myriad stocks, past the warehouses with their vast treasures from distant lands, past the central agora of the noisy city that
served as the commercial port of Knossos, until they came to the
broad main road where they caught up with the procession.

The seven youths and seven maidens were walking briskly side
by side, looking about them at the pastoral green landscape. How
beautiful the country looked in the first bloom of spring! The
fecund earth was bursting with budding growth. White and yellow daisies shimmered golden in the brilliant sun. Tender violets
and red anemones peeping from the soil swayed gently under the
soft caresses of the cool spring breeze.

Theseus was walking ahead, striding tall and proud past the
curious crowds. Throngs of people had lined the road to the left
and right of the procession, jostling to get a glimpse of the Athenians as they went by. A few compassionate souls were shaking
their heads . . . *what fault was it of these innocents?* Here and
there some whispered mumblings could be heard . . . *this
wasn't right, to kill such splendid youth . . .*

*. . . but if they didn't feed the Monster, he'd bring down the
Palace!*

131

. . . then someone should kill the MONSTER!
Who?!
To this no one replied.

The towers and tall terraces of the Palace were finally in view. They could see the bronze double axes atop the black columns gleaming in the sun. "Like the palaces in the myths," whispered Androkles to Kleo walking beside him. The youths and maidens stopped in awe to gaze with admiration at the marvel.

Theseus turned. "Come, comrades," he prodded gently. "Don't stop now."

They resumed the march. Theseus opened his stride, picking up the pace. Now and then his hand would move to the dagger beneath his belt, as though to make sure it was still in place.

At last, the Palace loomed before them. A few more strides, and they were at the main north entrance. They crossed it, climbed the great stone staircase, and entered the grand courtyard where the giant horns spired above the altar.

There beside the altar, surrounded by his elders and nobles, sat King Minos on his throne, dressed all in gold, a smile of malice on his face. Beside him, arrayed like peacocks, sat the two Princesses; and all around, crowding the tall Palace windows that overlooked the courtyard, sat the regal ladies of the Court dressed in their finery, leaning out eagerly to catch a glimpse of the youths and maidens now approaching.

Theseus, tightly girded, in his short blue chiton, entered first. As he strode forward, head held high, a crimson band of ribbon in his hair, a gasp went through the courtyard.

Ariadne blushed a violent red.

The King narrowed his eyes and searched the crowd for Malis.

Malis saw. He approached the King. "He's the one," he murmured, kneeling at the old man's feet.

Phaidra looked at Ariadne who was blushing furiously now. "You like him?" she whispered mockingly.

The younger Princess looked away. "Who?" she murmured, trying hard to sound indifferent. But she could hardly utter the word for the pounding in her breast.

Phaidra smiled amused. "You needn't pretend," she laughed, "you're red as a poppy. I saw your face the minute he walked in."

"Don't be silly," said Ariadne, "it's the rouge," and she turned her back to end the conversation.

A hush fell over the courtyard. The King had lifted his arm to speak, and his thin voice shrilled across the open courtyard. "Are you the son of my subject, the King of Athens?" he called to Theseus.

"I am the son of the King of Athens!" answered the Prince, striding forward with his proud mien, and as he raised his right hand in greeting, a large gold ring glinted on his forefinger.

Ariadne's heart leaped in her breast. *The ring she had given him!*

"My subject!" the angered King reiterated, stamping his foot in pique at Theseus's omission. "Say it!"

Theseus remained silent.

"Say it! Why don't you say it?" shouted the King. "Aren't you my subjects?"

"We are free people!" answered Theseus.

"Then why," sneered the King, curling his spiteful lip, "do you send me seven youths and seven maidens every year in tribute?"

Theseus flushed. *Caution*, he thought silently. *Athena, my protectress recommends prudence here as well as valor.*

Ariadne looked admiringly at the proud youth. *She would not let him be destroyed*, she was vowing silently, . . . *she would help him . . . but how?!*

"Great is the power of my Kingdom!" crowed the King. "Everyone bows to me! Woe to anyone who dares lift his head. The double ax of my god will fall on him!" He turned to an Officer. "Take them to the Palace," he commanded, "and put the yellow wreaths of death on their heads! But first, have them bathe and eat and drink. In three days, bathed and well-fed, they are to appear before the Minotaur. I have spoken!"

A venerable old noble standing behind the throne shook his head. *What a strong gallant youth*, he was thinking. *If only they were blessed with such an heir!*

"YOU!" shouted the King, thrusting out his royal staff and jabbing Theseus as the Athenians filed past the throne. "YOU are to remain!"

He turned to the others in the courtyard. "Everyone leave!" he commanded. "I want to be alone with this arrogant one!"

The courtyard emptied quickly.

Ariadne, still seated, turned to her father. "Can't I stay?" she whispered, giving him her most endearing look.

The King glowered. "No! Everyone must leave!"

Ariadne rose. She looked at Theseus, her face impassive. The King must not suspect.

Theseus looked back at her, his face betraying nothing. For an instant, his eyes flashed the barest flicker of acknowledgment as he lifted his hand and ever so casually touched the gold ring to his lips.

The ostrich fan dropped from Ariadne's hand and clattered to the ground.

Theseus stooped to retrieve it. The Princess, too, bent down to pick it up. Their faces met. Theseus touched her fingers lightly and handed her the fan.

"Ariadne!" The King was striking his staff impatiently against the tiles.

The Princess straightened. She hesitated one last instant and turned and left the emptied courtyard.

Alone now, the King confronted the proud youth. "Well?" he hissed.

Theseus didn't answer.

"What do you think of my Palace?" the King asked mockingly.

"It's big," said Theseus. "Big and rich."

"Is this the first time that you're seeing it?"

Theseus remained silent.

"What? The proud one doesn't dare speak the truth?" the old King jeered.

"I've been here before," answered Theseus.

"When?"

"Last summer."

"What brought you here?"

"I was traveling, and I came to see the Palace that kills the flower of my country's youth."

"Did you come inside?"

"I did."

"Did you speak with anyone?"

"I did."

"Who?"

Silence.

"You'll talk!" said the King. "You'll see!"

"There's nothing you can do to me," said Theseus. "I've committed my life already, so I have nothing more to fear. All you can do is throw me to the monster. So throw me!"

"I'll throw you," said the King. "You'll have your wish but not so fast. I have one more thing to ask you. What did you do with my blacksmith?"

"I took him with me. He's at my Palace, working."

"Preparing weapons?" The King's voice shook.

"Yes."

"What do you plan to do with them?"

"Free my country, if I can."

The King laughed. "I'm unbeatable," he roared. "Can't you see?"

"You're an old man—excuse my saying so," said Theseus. "When you're gone, who will mount your throne? Your daughters? They're women, they're no match for me. Your sons-in-law? They'll fight among themselves. So you see, I can afford to wait."

"For me to die?"

"Yes."

"You forget one thing."

"What?"

"That you're going to die before me. In three days."

"Perhaps," said Theseus. "But now let me ask one thing of you."

"Ask."

"If I kill the Minotaur, will you give me your word that you won't set your army on me to kill me?"

"You have my word," the King said laughing, "but you'll never kill it. And even if you do, you'll never find your way out of the Labyrinth."

"We'll see."

The King didn't answer. His mind was working. *This fearless prince was dangerous. If he was to get his blacksmith back— before he armed all those Athenians out there with iron weapons—he'd have to use a ruse. He'd have to trick him into bringing back his blacksmith . . . then he'd kill him.*

"Listen, my young man," he said, changing his tone and putting on a benevolent face, "do you want to save your life?"

"Are you making me an offer?" said Theseus.

"Bring me back my blacksmith, and I'll spare your life."

135

Theseus remained silent.

"Well? What is it?" pressed the King. "Yes or no?"

"No," answered Theseus.

"Take care! You're condemning yourself to death!"

"I have faith in my Goddess Athena," answered Theseus.

The King sprang from his throne. "Guards!" he shouted. "Take him to the Palace and put him in a room apart from the others! Put guards outside his door to see that no one goes near him!" He glared at Theseus mockingly. The noble youth returned the look, unflinching.

"Are you satisfied now?" jeered the King.

"I am," said the Prince and turned to follow the guards into the Palace.

26

Ariadne was standing at her window watching the night approach. She was searching her mind desperately for some way to help Theseus. "Think, Krino," she murmured to the girl sitting quietly at her feet. "Help me think of something. . . ."

The unhappy maid raised her eyes to her mistress. "What can I tell you, my Lady," she answered. "I tried twice to get into his room today, but the guards sent me away. 'They have orders,' they say, 'from the King'."

Ariadne continued to gaze out the window. The sun had just set and the west was brilliant with color. A cool breeze was picking up and the birds that had begun to fill the trees were warbling drunkenly out along the riverbank. *How beautiful the world was! She must think of something to help the doomed youth! Even if he succeeded in killing the Minotaur, how was he going to find his way out of the Labyrinth? She must speak to him . . . She must see him. . . .* She turned to Krino again. "Help me, Krino," she pleaded. "Help me find a way!"

"Strange things are happening," said Krino, shaking her dark curly head. "Just now as I was coming back from trying to see Theseus, I met Ikaros in the hall. He came up to me in the dark and told me to expect something tonight—some great joy, he said—but before he could explain, he saw Malis coming, and he hurried away, terrified."

"Some great joy?" The Princess sat down on the couch and

closed her eyes. "Sing me a song," she said presently, "something to quiet my soul."

"What song shall I sing, my Lady?"

"That new one . . . that wild one that the ships have brought in from the north."

"The one about Herakles—the hero who roams the earth and kills wild beasts?"

"That one."

Krino raised her slender throat and began to sing. She sang a simple song with primitive words and a slow heavy beat.

"It's barbaric," said the Princess when the maid had finished. "But I like it."

Krino didn't answer. She sat up suddenly, listening hard.

"What is it?"

"Someone's at the door," whispered the girl.

"I didn't hear anything. . . ."

"Someone's out there," insisted Krino, rising and tiptoeing to the door. She stood and listened. She could hear breathing on the other side. Cautiously, she opened, and standing at the threshold was a blond-bearded youth in strange clothing. Before she could speak, the youth had pushed his way into the room and was closing the door quickly behind him.

"Who are you?" Krino exclaimed drawing back in alarm. "No one enters here!"

The youth laughed. "*I* do!" he said, and putting his hand to his face pulled off a fake beard and mustache.

Krino let out a cry. "Haris!" she shrieked, and fell into her brother's arms.

Ariadne was on her feet.

"Shh!" Haris cautioned, pressing his sister close and embracing her warmly. "Don't let anyone hear! No one must know that I'm here! If the King or Malis find out, I'm lost!"

"We'll hide you!" Ariadne said quickly. "Here in the next room where Krino sleeps."

Haris released Krino and entered the room to kneel at the Princess's feet.

"Come, sit here," said Ariadne, taking his arm, "sit on this stool, and tell us everything! How did you get here?"

Haris sat on the stool and began hurriedly to tell them all that had happened. . . .

137

"And Theseus?" prodded Ariadne, when he had finished. "How is he?"

"I haven't been able to see him since we've been here," said Haris looking worried. "But before we came ashore, he told me to give you this." And taking from his bosom a small object wrapped in red cloth, he handed it to Ariadne.

The Princess reached for it eagerly and unwrapped it. She let out a moan.

"What is it?" asked Krino anxiously.

"The seal of the ring that I gave him," said Ariadne with a catch in her voice. "I had told him that if he was ever in need of my help, he should send me this seal." Tears welled in her eyes. "And now? Look at me. I can't do a thing for him. I can't even get to see him!" She stood up and began pacing the floor. "Oh, what can I do? How can I save him?"

"Why don't you go to your father and beg him. . . ," offered Krino hopefully.

"That would be worse!" groaned the Princess. "That would doom him all the more!" She stood for a moment before Haris. "You're clever," she said in desperation to the boy. "Think of something!"

Haris looked at her and wished with all his heart that he could think of something for his Princess.

Krino, too, was watching anxiously, her heart aching.

Suddenly the boy jumped to his feet. "I have an idea!" he said. "I have a friend who works down in the kitchen—he carries the meals up to the lords and ladies, and to all the foreigners in the Palace. I'll ask him to let me carry the trays for him tonight. He'll be glad to be rid of the bother. . . ."

Ariadne looked at him, a ray of hope in her eyes.

" . . . I'll dress in his clothes . . . I'll wear his white cap and apron," said Haris, warming to the idea, "and take Theseus's tray to him. The guards can't stop a kitchen servant from bringing the foreigner his food. . . ."

Krino let out a jubilant shout. "Splendid!" she cried, flinging her arms about her brother. "How clever! How clever!" And she hugged him to her.

The Princess, too, drew Haris to her and embraced him warmly. "You are, indeed, a clever boy!" she declared looking at him with kindled hope.

Haris flushed. "What should I tell him when I see him?" he asked, bursting to get on with his idea.

"Tell him that I'm thinking of him," said Ariadne, "and that we must meet. Ask him if he can find a way. It's important that I see him!"

"Consider it done!" declared the boy. "I'd better hurry now. I should get over there; it's getting dark and they'll be taking up the trays soon."

For an instant Krino held him to her. "You're ever so clever and brave!" she whispered, regarding him proudly.

"Take care," said the Princess. "Good luck! And hurry back!"

"In half an hour!" the boy assured her and hastened from the room.

It wasn't long before a cook's assistant, dressed in a white cap and apron, and carrying a large tray laden with food, appeared before the door where Theseus was imprisoned.

"Open!" he shouted to the guards. "I'm bringing his food!"

"We hear you!" grumbled the two guards at the door. "You don't have to yell!" and unlocking the door they sullenly motioned him in.

Haris entered. No lamps had been lit. Theseus was sitting in a corner, in the dark. At the sound of the door, he jumped to his feet.

"Who's there?" he called out.

"Your food!" said Haris, disguising his voice.

"I don't want food!" declared Theseus from his corner in the dark. "Take it away!"

"Your food," repeated Haris, drawing closer.

"I told you, I don't want it!" Theseus's voice rose angrily.

Haris drew close. "My Prince," he whispered almost inaudibly as he set down the tray, "it's me, Haris!"

There was silence as Theseus strained to see him in the dark. "You sly old fox!" he laughed softly, grasping the boy's hand. "You fooled me!"

Haris chuckled. "There's no time to talk," he said hurriedly, keeping his voice low. "The Princess wants to see you—to tell you how to find your way out of the Labyrinth. Even if you kill the monster, she said, you'll never find your way out."

139

"I want to see her, too," whispered Theseus. "But how?"

"Give it some thought. I'll be back tomorrow night with your tray. In the meantime, we'll try to think of some way, too. . . ."

"Hey, in there!" The guards were at the door, peering inside. "What's taking so long?"

"I can't find a lamp to light," said Haris aloud.

"Never mind, we'll take care of the lamp!" they called back churlishly. "Get going!"

Haris picked up the empty tray and hastened out.

Back in the Princess's apartment, the girls were waiting anxiously.

"Well?" they cried when Haris returned. "Did you manage it?"

"I managed it!" laughed Haris.

"You saw him?"

"I saw him! At first he didn't recognize me and ordered me to leave. . . ."

"What did he say to you?"

"He, too, wants to see you, my Princess. But he hasn't figured out how. He said he'll think about it, and tomorrow night he'll tell me."

"Did he seem worried?"

"I couldn't tell, my Princess. From the sound of his voice, he seemed to be angry with the King."

"You must be tired," said Ariadne. "Now go to bed, and tomorrow night you'll take the tray to him again." She turned to Krino. "I'm tired, too," she said. "Prepare my bed, and you, too, get some sleep. Maybe the Great Goddess will give us good advice in our dreams."

27

The hall through which she was walking was long and dark . . . an endless corridor, somewhere in the Palace. She was walking barefoot, stalking, following the sounds of song and laughter that were echoing from its depths. She followed the sounds to a door, where two sentries were standing guard. They were holding an enormous pitcher between them, lifting it to their lips and drinking drunkenly. They drank and drank and began to sing. Suddenly, the door opened and a youth came out. He looked at the sentries and laughed. Then he blew at them and they keeled over. "Ariadne!" the youth called. "Ariadne!"

Ariadne wakened with a start. Someone was calling her. She sat up and looked about. No one. The candle was flickering quietly in front of the little statue of the Great Goddess. She listened. Nothing but stillness echoed from the sleeping Palace.

She rose from her bed and went to stand before the candle. "Great Goddess," she whispered softly, "you know my pain. Help me!" In the flickering light of the candle the little statue seemed to smile at her.

She went to the window and looked out. The moon was casting its pale light on the gardens and terraces. "It's only past midnight," she murmured. "When will day break!" She went back to her bed but sleep wouldn't come. For a long time she lay thinking. There had to be a way to see him! What could she do to see him? All night she lay thinking, listening to the warbling of the nightingales that carried from the ravine.

Out toward the east, the sky began to lighten. One by one, the stars grew dimmer, the crow of a rooster sounded, the eastern sky turned red . . . dawn at last!

She rose. Today she would find a way to see him!

Krino came to the door. "You're up, my Lady?"

"I couldn't sleep. I thought someone was calling my name, and I woke up."

"It must have been a dream," said the girl.

"Yes, a dream," murmured the Princess. "I remember walking down a dark corridor . . . there was a door somewhere, with two guards outside, drinking and getting very drunk . . . then a young man opened the door and came out. He laughed and blew at the guards and they fell down . . . that's when I heard someone calling my name and woke up."

"That's it, my Lady! That's it!" cried Krino, clapping her hands excitedly. "The Great Goddess sent you a dream, showing you the way!"

"What are you saying?"

"Me? Nothing, my Lady. The dream is saying it all! It's telling us that we must find a way to get the guards drunk . . . then Theseus can open the door and come to you!"

141

Ariadne pondered the idea in amazement. *Of course! The girl was right. The Great Goddess had sent her the dream.* . . . *that was why she had smiled at her behind the flickering candle last night!* . . . She smiled, hugging Krino to her.

"Is Haris up yet?" she asked presently.

"He's still sleeping, my Lady."

"Have him come to me as soon as he wakes up." *His mind is sharp,* she reflected. *He'll find a way.*

There was a knock at the door. It was Ikaros, come to see his young friend.

"Haris is still asleep," said Ariadne when he had entered and bowed to the Princess respectfully.

"I must see him," said the youth, starting impulsively toward the door of the room where Haris was hidden. "May I wake him?"

"What must you see him about?" Ariadne's eyes were dancing playfully. Her mood had lifted, and she was beginning to feel that all would go well.

Ikaros hesitated. "Forgive me, my Princess," he said, "it's something important."

"Ah, a secret! In that case," laughed Ariadne, "since it's something important, you may go in and wake him."

Ikaros opened the small door and went inside. Krino's room was simple and spotless. It had a small window overlooking a little garden, and on the windowsill was a beautiful earthenware pitcher decorated with a big black octopus that covered the entire surface with its tentacles. The walls, too, were decorated with large white lilies and butterflies. A small black kitten lay on a straw mat in a corner of the room.

Ikaros went up to the mat where his friend was sleeping and shook him gently. "Haris!" he called urgently.

Haris wakened. "What is it?" he mumbled in alarm. "What brings you here so early?"

"Early!" laughed Ikaros. "The sun's two lance lengths in the sky already. Wake up! I have news for you."

"What news?" Haris lay back again and rubbed his eyes.

"The experiments worked!"

"The experiments? I don't understand."

"You forgot already? Didn't I tell you that my father. . . ."

"Oh . . . the wings."

"Yes, the wings! My father tried them out last night and they worked! He flew from the Palace all the way across to the hill! NOW do you understand?" Ikaros beamed down at his friend triumphantly. "It means we can fly away to freedom!"

Haris yawned.

"I see you're not impressed."

"I'll tell you," said Haris, sitting up. "This trip has changed me. I see things in a different light since I've been away. I've found another way to freedom."

"What way?" snapped Ikaros, nettled at his friend's indifference to his astounding news. He looked at Haris uneasily. There was something different about him since he had gone away; he had a strange new air about him, as though he had grown up overnight.

Haris stood up. "I'm not going to put on wings and fly away from the tyranny here," he said soberly. "I'm going to stay right here and fight it!"

"Alone? How? You're only one person."

"I'm not alone. There are more like me. We're all going to join together and fight."

"With what?" laughed Ikaros scornfully. "Do you have weapons? Do you have a leader?"

"We have weapons. My father's making them right now, out there in Athens. And we have a leader, too. You know him."

"The Prince of Athens?"

"Yes. He's strong and wise and just. You should go to Athens, Ikaros, and see how the people live out there."

"Don't they have a king?"

"They do, but they're not his slaves. They're free citizens. They live and work and think in freedom."

"That may be so," said Ikaros impatiently, "but I can't wait."

"You'd fly away," said Haris "and leave all the others behind, as slaves?" He shook his head. "That's not right, Ikaros. Doesn't it seem a little . . . cowardly?"

Ikaros reddened. In his soul he knew his friend was right, but his heart was set on flying away to freedom, and nothing would shake him from his purpose. "I have to be going now," he said, avoiding Haris's eyes. "I have to help my father."

Haris reached out and grasped his hand. "Ikaros," he said, looking closely at his beloved friend, "there's something I must ask you."

"Go ahead, ask."

"If anything should happen here at the Palace, are you going to help us?"

"What could happen?"

"I don't know yet, but *if* something happens, I want to know if we can count on you to be with us."

Ikaros was silent. "If it happens soon," he said at last. "Yes, I'll be with you. But if it takes long. . . ."

"You're in that much of a hurry?"

"I'm in a hurry."

Haris looked at him thoughtfully. How was he going to convince his friend of something that he, himself, had only just now begun to understand? If only he could show him what he had seen in Athens—how they all worked together out there, like brothers, like a family, with the King their father. "We don't need wings on our shoulders, Ikaros," he said softly, "we need wings in our souls."

"Fine," said Ikaros, moving toward the door. "We'll talk about it later."

"When will you be back?"

"When I finish my work."

"I'll be here."

<h1 style="text-align:center">28</h1>

When Haris had ushered Ikaros out the door, he found the Princess and Krino waiting for him.

"We've been waiting since dawn for you to wake up," they cried when they saw him. "How did you sleep?"

"Like a mole," laughed Haris.

"Come and sit here, we need your advice," said the Princess. "We've solved half the problem and want you to help us solve the other half," and hurriedly she related her dream and the interpretation that Krino had given it.

" . . . So you see," she concluded, "we know we should get the guards drunk, but we haven't figured out how."

"That's easy," said Haris, reflecting a moment. "If you'll order me a big pitcher of old wine and a tray of roasted meat from the kitchen, I'll take care of the rest."

"What will you do?"

144

"I'll take the wine and meat to the guards, before I bring The-seus his tray tonight, and I'll tell them that the Princess is celebrating her birthday and greets them with this gift of wine and meat to toast her health. Then I'll bring Theseus his tray and tell him the plan. As soon as the guards get drunk and fall asleep, he'll open the door and walk out . . . and I'll be hiding nearby to bring him here."

"Splendid!" said the Princess pleased. "Now go back to Krino's room and keep out of sight. Don't let anyone see you; and try to sleep again, you're going to be awake all night."

"And you should get some sleep, too, my Lady," said Krino to the Princess when they were alone again. "You'll be up all night, too."

"How can I sleep?" declared the Princess. "My mind can't stop thinking. What will I tell Theseus if he comes tonight? How can I describe that tangled web of a Labyrinth to him?" She stretched out on the couch and rested her head on the pillows. "I must find a way," she fretted, her eyes staring at the ceiling. "I must find a way. . . ."

Krino took out her sewing basket and settled down on the mat to work on her embroidery. The two women were silent, each lost in her thoughts. From the half-open door, Krino's little kitten wandered in, its tail upturned, its green eyes aglow, and bounded across the room to nuzzle against its mistress's arm.

"Welcome, Psipsika!" laughed Krino, dropping her ball of thread to caress the pampered little fluff purring at her arm. No sooner had she reached to touch it, when the kitten, spotting the great blue ball, pounced on it and began pulling at the thread with sportive delight.

Krino chuckled and put out her arm to scoot the frisky little pet away, but it had grasped the ball firmly in its tiny claws and was running off with it. "No! . . . no!" scolded Krino playfully, swooping to retrieve it.

Ariadne leaned forward on her couch, watching the pair amusedly. The kitten was romping with the blue ball, reveling in the uncoiling strands, rolling on its back, getting its four little paws hopelessly ensnared in the unruly threads. "How are you ever going to get her out of that tangled web?" she laughed at Krino who had finally caught the squirming kitten and was pulling at the snarled thread in exasperation.

"What a labyrinth she's made of it!" the girl moaned, pretending to spank the little mischief maker.

Ariadne sat up. "Krino!" she cried, startling the maid. "That's it! You've given me the answer!"

Krino looked at her in bewilderment. Ariadne had jumped from her couch and was fairly dancing up and down. "Now I know what to tell Theseus tonight!" she exclaimed, her face aglow with excitement. "Now I know how I can help him! I'll give him a ball of thread! and tell him to tie one end to the entrance of the Labyrinth and carry the rest with him as he goes through the twisting tunnel, unraveling it along the way. Then, when he reaches the Minotaur and kills him, he can pick up the thread again and follow it back to the entrance!"

Krino stared at her mistress in awe. "How simple!" she murmured, " . . . how simple it was, after all."

The Princess nodded. "All great ideas were simple," she smiled, " . . . all great ideas!"

29

When night descended over the Palace and the corridors were filled with darkness, white-clad Haris, with his tray of meat and a great pitcher of wine, approached the two guards standing watch at Theseus's door.

"You're in luck, my good fellows!" he laughed, holding out the tray before the guards. "Tonight you'll be living high!"

The guards glowered. "Get going!" they snarled, eyeing the roast resentfully. "Take that to the masters and stop waving it under our noses."

"Tonight *you're* the masters, old chaps," laughed Haris again, setting the tray down at their feet. "This god-sent feast is yours."

"Talk sense!" threatened the shorter of the guards, grabbing Haris by the arm. "Talk sense before we let you have it! We don't put up with jokes!"

"It's yours, my brave fellow! All yours!" protested Haris, feigning a frightened look. "Our Princess sends it to you, with her greetings—to toast her health. It's her birthday today, and she remembered you."

The guards stared in disbelief. A look of pleasure had begun to creep across their churlish faces.

"Come . . . sit on the doorsill here, and fall to," urged Haris. "No one will see you. Pick up the tasty lamb . . . empty the pitcher . . . and drink to our Princess's health."

The guards approached the tray warily. The shorter of the two reached for the pitcher. "To her health, then!" he laughed, taking a nip.

"And to yours, my lad!" laughed the other, his face all smiles now. "To yours, too!"

Haris chuckled, and, turning on his heel, sped back to the kitchen to get Theseus's tray.

When he returned with the tray, the guards were already settled comfortably on the tiles outside Theseus's door, eating away at the roast and drinking heartily from the pitcher.

"I'm bringing the poor foreigner his, too," said Haris, " . . . his last, before the Minotaur swallows him whole tomorrow. . . . He might as well eat something, too, and go to Hades well fed."

The guards wiped their mustaches and got up good-humoredly to open the door.

Haris entered. Quickly he crossed the room to where Theseus was waiting in the dark. "Cheer up!" he laughed softly, drawing near. "Why so sad?"

Theseus was looking dispirited. "I couldn't come up with anything," he whispered gloomily, " . . . except to kill the guards and. . . ."

"No, you'd never get away with it," said Haris, "but it doesn't matter. We've thought of something," and quickly he explained their plan to Theseus.

The Prince took Haris's hand. "If I kill the monster and get back to my Kingdom," he whispered with deep emotion, "I'm going to make you a great lord in my Palace!"

"Don't worry about me," answered Haris. "Let's get our country liberated." He glanced nervously at the door. "I'd better go now, before they get suspicious."

Theseus pressed his hand. "I'll be waiting for you at midnight."

"I'll be here," and Haris picked up the tray and hurried out the door. "Good appetite, my friends!" he called cheerily to the guards who had fallen to eating in earnest now, tearing at the roast and drinking from the pitcher greedily. "Drink your fill! To our Princess's health!"

147

"To our Princess's health!" laughed the two, lifting the pitcher to their lips.

Keep drinking! smiled Haris, hurrying away down the long hall. *By midnight, you'll be out cold.*

He returned the tray to the kitchen and sped back to the Princess's room where the two girls were waiting anxiously.

"Everything's going well!" he reported. "It won't be long now; our guards will be in seventh heaven!"

The hours passed. The night wore on. Now and then Haris would steal from the room and go down to check on the guards. Then he'd return to report their condition. "Now they're in their cups!" he'd announce with glee. "Now they can barely stand." Finally, near the hour of midnight, he hurried from the room and went to take up his post behind a column, opposite Theseus's cell.

The guards were dead to the world, sprawled across the tiles to the right and left of the threshold. Haris, still clad in his kitchen uniform, hid behind the column and waited. *Theseus would hear their snoring now and open the door . . . any minute, now, he'd be coming out.* He waited, watching the door and darting furtive glances down the hall. The guards were snoring blissfully. He stood waiting, counting the seconds, when suddenly the blood in his veins ran cold. Down at the other end of the corridor, beneath the light of a burning lantern, he saw Malis. The ex-Chief was coming toward them! *If he passed the door and saw the drunken pair on the floor . . . it would be all over!* Haris cowered behind the column, paralyzed, his eyes glued with dread on the door where Theseus would be coming out any second now. What to do? Quick as thought, he sprinted from behind the column where he was hidden, pulling low the white cap over his forehead, and began racing desperately down the hall toward Malis.

The ex-Chief looked up, startled.

"Fire! Fire!" yelled Haris, racing past.

Fire?! Where? Malis stopped dead in his tracks.

"Behind the storerooms!" shouted Haris, disappearing down the hall.

With a groan of dread, Malis whirled around and followed after him toward the storerooms.

148   Theseus, meanwhile, was opening the door to his cell and pulling it shut behind him when Haris, panting furiously from his decoy chase, came rushing back. "Hurry!" he gasped, grabbing

Theseus by the arm, and before Malis could return, the two were speeding through the corridors on wings. Up the stairs they flew, toward the women's quarters, and in minutes they were entering the Princess's chamber.

Ariadne, wrapped in a violet shawl, was waiting at the door.

"Welcome, Prince of Athens," she said and her voice shook.

"Well met, my Princess," Theseus said and he bowed and kissed her hand.

"We must hurry," whispered Haris. "Malis is wandering the halls!"

"My Princess," said Theseus, coming directly to the point, "I sent you the seal of your ring because I need your help."

"I know, and I intend to keep my word," answered Ariadne. "I, too, am in need of your help."

"Speak, my Princess," said Theseus. "Whatever you ask of me you shall have!"

Ariadne smiled. "I'll tell you later," she said softly. "After you kill the monster and come out of the Labyrinth."

"I'll need your help for that," said Theseus. "Help me find my way out and ask whatever you wish of me."

Ariadne reached down into Krino's sewing basket and pulled out a thick ball of thread. "Take this," she said, handing it to Theseus. "It will show you the way."

Theseus looked at the thread with dubious surprise.

"Take it," laughed Ariadne, "and when you go into the Labyrinth, tie one end to the entrance and as you proceed inside, unravel. . . ."

The Prince's face broke into smiles. "Let me kiss the hand that's rescued me!" he cried, the light of understanding glowing warmly across his countenance.

Ariadne gave him her hand. "Come back victorious!" she said.

Theseus took the small white hand.

"It's time to leave!" called Haris urgently from the door. He had just returned, breathless from running through the corridors, snuffing out the lanterns. "Hurry! before Malis notices!"

The Prince held Ariadne's hand. "I will return victorious!" he said, pressing her fingers to his lips. "And then . . . you have my word, I will do whatever it is you wish of me."

"Godspeed!" said Ariadne, and her breast heaved inside her from the pounding in her heart.

149

30

The next morning the King was seated on his throne surrounded by his councillors. He had summoned his Elders and was gravely reviewing the week's news. For many days now, his ships had been returning from distant lands, all with the same disturbing reports: his colonies around the world were rising in rebellion. One by one, from the islands of the Aegean, the lands of Anatolia as far as Palestine, and west as far as the Iberian peninsula, the faithful colonies of his ancestors were beginning to rear their heads.

Centuries of commerce with these conquered lands, under the rigid rules imposed on them by the Cretan Kings, had enriched Crete, making her the wealthy Kingdom that she had become. And now, for the first time in their history, the colonies were challenging the Cretan King, agitating for their freedom. They chafed under their slavery and wanted to control their own lands, they said, and their own commerce, for their own interests.

"If we allow that," murmured the Elders gravely, "what will become of us?"

An aged Elder rose to his feet. "It's time that we gave up some of our luxuries," he counseled. "The colonists out there have awakened. They've built ships like ours, and they've raised armies. They've grown strong. How long will we be able to keep them subdued?" The Elder sat down, and a few aged heads nodded in agreement.

But others began to mutter angrily. "How will we live?" Loudest among them was a wealthy merchant whose myriad ships trafficked the high seas and hauled in all manner of treasures from the colonies abroad. "How will we live?" he shouted vehemently.

"We'll fall back on our own island," answered the Elder. "It's big enough to sustain us. We can plant trees and cultivate our fields and fish in our own waters. . . ."

"We can't survive alone!" shouted the wealthy merchant. "We need things like copper from Cyprus and ivory from Arabia and monkeys from Egypt and all the rare fruits that Crete doesn't grow. . . ."

"We can live without rare fruits and monkeys!" snapped the aged Elder angrily.

150

"Enough!" The King struck his staff against the tiles. "I summoned you here to get your opinions, and from what I am hear-

ing, we have two opposing views: either we send our army and
fleet to force the colonists to submit, or else we allow them their
freedom and concentrate ourselves on our own island and live as
best we can."

"Retreat and let's have peace!" shouted half the Elders.

"Arm the ships and break their heads!" shouted the other half.

A venerable Elder who had been silent until now, rose to speak.
"My King," he said, "as you can see, we are divided. Give us your
opinion, and we will abide by what you decide."

The King looked at him angrily. "You're the first among
Elders," he answered. "I've heard the others speak, except your
lordship. Why? What's on your mind?"

"If I were to tell you what's on my mind," replied the Elder
shaking his head, "I fear you'd all rise up and tear me limb from
limb."

"It's your duty to tell us," said the King. "Now speak! Enlighten us."

The Elder rose reluctantly to his feet. "Neither the one opinion
nor the other seems correct to me, my King," he began. "If we fall
back on our own island, we won't be able to survive; and if we
declare war, we won't be able to win." He hesitated. "There is
only one solution. . . ."

"Well?" prodded the King. "What's the solution?"

Still the Elder hesitated.

"Speak!" commanded the King. "You've always been a sensible
councillor. Now speak! I won't allow anyone to harm you."

"And you, yourself, my King? Will you give me your word that
you won't turn on me?"

"You have my word," said the King. "Now speak! I command
you!"

"Hear my solution, then," said the Elder. "Let us become rec-
onciled with the Athenians! Let Crete and Athens unite and become one Kingdom. You, my King, are advanced in years, and you
have no heir. What will happen when you die? If we unite with the
Athenians, we will have a splendid youth to succeed you. . . ."

The King glowered.

An angry murmur went up among the councilmen.

". . . the Prince of Athens," continued the Elder, "is strong
and wise—strong enough to wage wars and win. He can raise our
declining Kingdom back to its former glory and wealth."

151

The King laughed contemptuously. "A foreigner?" he sneered. "You propose a stranger to sit on my throne?"

"Make him your son-in-law," answered the Elder. "Give him one of your daughters for his wife."

"Never!" thundered the King. "I'm throwing him to the Minotaur tomorrow!"

"You asked my opinion," said the Elder, "and I'm giving it to you. Our Kingdom is in grave danger, and the gravest of all has not even been told you yet: the blond barbarians up north, the Dorians, have been assembling, and now they're on the move. They've taken over Thrace and Macedonia and are spilling into the plains of Thessaly. Their fleet is sailing southward, taking island after island, and advancing toward us. If they descend on us tomorrow, with their thousands of ships and their armies, what will we do? What King will rush forward and fire up the people and take the lead to drive them out?"

"Enough!" shouted the King, his jaw quivering with rage. "You've said enough!"

"I've said the truth," said the Elder. "If what I've told you isn't done, we'll all be lost!"

"Silence!" thundered the King. "If I had not given you my word, traitor, I'd banish you from my Kingdom!"

"I'll banish myself," said the Elder. "I'll go live in another land. Here I see catastrophe approaching."

"Ill-omened bird! Owl of doom!" shrieked the old King, "so now you're playing the prophet!"

"Yes, my King. There are times when the mind of man is capable of prophecy," answered the Elder. "And I say to you, the day is going to come when your Palace will be reduced to ashes."

The King raised his staff menacingly. "Go!" he bellowed. "Get out of my sight and don't ever let me set eyes on you again!"

"I'm going," the Elder answered quietly. "I'm taking my children and grandchildren, and by tomorrow I'll be sailing away in my ships." He looked at old Minos one last time. "Farewell, King!" he said sadly. "I hope I'll be proved wrong, but I'm afraid that everything I've said will happen. And soon."

31

Night fell. The third and final day was over.

In the darkness, Ikaros and Haris had stolen out to the riverbank to talk in private, away from prying eyes. It was the eve of the momentous day, and Haris could barely contain his anxiety. In a few short hours, Theseus and his thirteen companions would be walking into the Labyrinth. Would he come out of it alive? Hidden among the clumps of blooming myrtle that grew wild along the river's edge, Haris was voicing his concern to Ikaros. "Would Theseus really be able to defeat the terrible monster? Would he be able to find his way out of the Labyrinth? And if he did succeed in coming out, wouldn't the crowds fall on him and tear him to pieces? . . ." These were the things the two friends were weighing uneasily when they became aware of voices coming from behind an old plane tree not far from where they were hidden.

. . . the people are up in arms . . . a man's deep voice was saying. *. . . They found out what you said to the King at the council meeting this morning and they're. . . .*

"Malis!" cried Haris under his breath. "I know that voice well!"

"Shh . . . let's listen!" whispered Ikaros.

An elderly man's voice was answering: *What are they saying? . . . what are the people saying?*

That you've been bribed by Theseus and that you're betraying your country.

I've never talked with Theseus. I saw him once, when they all arrived from Athens. He impressed me. I liked his pride and noble manner, and I thought to myself, if only we, too, had an heir like him. And I say it again—a king like Theseus would save our imperiled Kingdom. That's my opinion.

That's my opinion, too, old man. What do you suggest we do?

I told you. I'm putting my children and grandchildren on the ships tomorrow, and I'm leaving. You should leave, too—especially after the way the King has treated you.

There was silence. Then Malis's voice sounded again. *Shouldn't we see Theseus first?*

No. They'll say we were bribed, and that we're in league with him to start a revolution.

But if we really believe this is the only way our country can be saved? . . .

For a long while there was silence from behind the plane tree. The boys waited.

153

At last the old man's voice was heard again. *The best thing for our country is what I recommended to the King this morning—to have the King give one of his daughters to Theseus. . . .*

The two men were moving away from the plane tree now. Their footsteps could be heard thudding softly in the earth, until they disappered beyond the riverbanks.

"Did you hear?" Haris gasped.

"I heard!"

They scrambled to their feet. "We'd better be getting back," whispered Haris. "It's almost time for me to be taking Theseus's tray to him."

"Are you going to tell him what you heard?"

"Yes."

"And the Princess, too?"

"You think she doesn't have it on her mind already?" laughed Haris.

The pair hurried back in silence, pondering what they had heard. "Would you believe," murmured Ikaros, " . . . would you believe the day would come when we'd think of terrible Malis as our friend?"

They reached the Palace and separated. Haris put on the white cap and apron again and raced down to the kitchen. In a few minutes he was standing with his laden tray before Theseus's door.

The two guards greeted him good-humoredly. "Hey, there!" they laughed, "what did you do to us last night? It's a good thing no one came by to find us out!"

"What?" pretended Haris.

"That was some wine you brought us—enough to knock a man out cold!"

"Why?" chuckled Harris. "Did you pass out and start snoring?"

"Who, *us* pass out?" They twirled their mustaches cockily. "You don't know us!" they scoffed. "We stood up like rocks!"

Haris laughed. "Fine," he said, "now open up for me to go inside. I'm bringing him his last, poor guy."

They opened for him and he entered.

Theseus was standing at the small window, looking out at the night. At the sound of Haris entering the cell, he turned and waited for him to draw near. "The last meal," he murmured, pressing his young accomplice's hand. "Who knows where we'll be eating tomorrow?"

154

"On the ship," whispered Haris. "On your white-sailed ship!"

"I think so, too," smiled Theseus. "And you'll be sitting beside me, to my right."

"To your left," corrected Haris teasingly. "Another will be sitting at your right, my Prince!"

Theseus flushed. "Perhaps," he murmured.

Haris put the things down from the tray and eagerly related what he and Ikaros had heard at the riverbank.

"Her father will never agree," said Theseus when he had finished.

The door to the cell opened and someone strode in. "Get going!" a voice commanded brusquely. "Take your tray and get out!"

Malis! Haris grabbed up the empty tray, lifting it hastily to his head to hide his face, and scooted out.

The ex-chief closed the door and came to stand before Theseus. "I am an Officer of the Palace," he said. "I have something to discuss with you."

"I hear you," said Theseus with regal courtesy.

"What I have come to suggest is not out of love for you," said Malis, "but out of love for my country."

"All the better," answered Theseus. "This way I'll be certain that you're telling the truth."

Malis let the comment pass. He came up close and lowered his voice. "Our Kingdom is on the decline," he began, looking carefully at Theseus. "Our colonies are in revolt . . . the Dorians are on the march, heading our way, and our people, in all their wealth and luxury, have forgotten how to fight. Our King is old and has no son. . . ."

"I know all this," said Theseus. "What's your point?"

"I propose that we join together in friendship with Athens," said Malis, "and that you take one of the King's daughters in marriage, and thus mount the throne of Crete lawfully."

"The old King will resist," said Theseus. "Who will help me?"

"You have secret friends in the Palace and in the city," replied Malis.

Theseus didn't answer. For a long while he remained silent, reflecting on what Malis proposed. At last he spoke. "I must say no for now," he answered. "Let me perform my duty first. Let me wrestle with your monster. If I win, it means that God is with me. After that, we'll see."

"But even if you kill the monster," said Malis, "how will you find your way out of the Labyrinth?"

"That need not concern you, my friend," smiled Theseus. "Athena, my goddess and protectress, will show me the way."

32

When morning dawned, Theseus fastened the steel dagger securely inside his belt, hid the thick ball of thread beneath his bosom, and strode out of the cell into the great courtyard where the thirteen companions were waiting for him.

The youths looked leaner in the early morning light, the maidens paler. The newborn day was unfolding before them in glorious splendor, and their hearts were crying out to live!

Theseus strode resolutely toward them. "We must be prepared to welcome death without fear!" he said sternly. "There is no greater shame than fear." The maidens blushed and kissed his hands, and all gathered round him.

The courtyard had begun to fill with people. A small crowd was already forming, Ikaros and Haris among them. The Palace nobles, too, had wakened early to see the young Athenians preparing themselves for death. One by one the tall windows overlooking the grand courtyard were opening and lords and ladies could be seen emerging to sit and watch the spectacle below. At a lofty, gold-embellished window in the women's royal wing, a slender girl had come to stand.

Theseus glanced up. For an instant, he let his gaze fall on the slight figure at the royal window, his face expressionless, then quickly turned to his companions again. "The moment has come," he said quietly, "for us to show if we have brave souls. Let us show ourselves courageous and not shame our country."

The youths' and maidens' eyes flashed proudly. "We're not afraid to die!" they said.

"Gather close," said Theseus. "Let's pray now to the goddess who protects our nation."

The companions gathered round him and all lifted their arms toward heaven.

"Athena, Goddess of power and wisdom!" Theseus called out loudly. "We are here at the Palace of the King of Crete! We are going down to the foundation, to battle the man-eating monster, the Minotaur! Raise your lance, Athena! Help us!"

The Palace guards were approaching now. With Malis at their head, they made a circle round the fourteen young companions. Malis, who had been stripped of his rank and relegated to this lesser role of Guard to the Minotaur, threw Theseus a covert questioning look.

"Is it time?" said Theseus, ignoring the look.

Malis drew closer. "Is that your answer?" he said under his breath.

"It is."

An angry glint flashed through the ex-Chief's eyes. Without another word he lifted the double ax that he was carrying and gave the command. "Forward!" he shouted and commenced the march toward the Labyrinth.

Theseus and his companions followed. The crowd, too, surged after them, following close on their heels. The young Athenians began to chant softly, marching with unfaltering step toward the Labyrinth, their voices chanting the hymn to Athena.

When they reached the entrance, Malis halted. "Everyone stay where you are!" he shouted, motioning to the crowd to fall back. "YOU!" he commanded the fourteen, "step forward and collect your torches!"

The crowd hushed. A frightening roar had begun to rumble from the foundations of the Palace.

"The beast smells its food!" mumbled an old man to his wife.

The old woman pulled back. "Let's go," she whispered. "I'm afraid. . . ."

"It's tied in chains," he laughed, "it can't get loose. . . ."

"I'm afraid," shuddered the woman and tugged at his arm to leave.

Malis was looking at Theseus now, his lips twisted in a taunting smile. "It's all yours!" he laughed, nodding toward the door. "You may enter!"

Theseus turned to his companions. "With Athena's help!" he said firmly, "forward!" and thrusting his right foot across the threshold, led the way into the Labyrinth. Pale and silent, the thirteen followed.

When the door to the underground closed behind them, the fourteen stood in mute darkness. For a moment, Theseus waited, gathering his bearings, then his voice rang in the cavernous stillness. "Light your torches!"

They ignited the pinewood torches and in the dim illumination they could make out what seemed an endless cave, with a dark stone stairway visible back along its black depths.

Theseus took out the ball of thread that he had hidden in his bosom and began fastening one end to a rock near the cave's entrance. When he had tied it securely, he commenced unraveling it and, directing the companions to follow, proceeded to enter the cave, unwinding the thread as he advanced.

The companions followed cautiously. The ground beneath their feet was slippery and they tread with care, holding on to one another. No one spoke. They followed Theseus in solemn silence, their hearts beating hard within their breasts. Theseus walked ahead, unraveling the thread. When they reached the stone stairwell, they descended slowly to the level below, and here they followed the twisting corridor where they continued along a slippery footpath that kept twisting and turning in dizzy convolutions until they were completely lost.

Theseus led on, carefully unwinding the ball of thread. The roaring in the depths was growing louder as they advanced, resounding against the walls, and before long a new din arose to strike terror—the clamor of clanging chains. "Courage!" murmured the youths, taking the trembling maidens by the hand, and resolutely they pressed on. On and on they walked along he twisting footpath, penetrating deeper and deeper into the maze.

Suddenly a heavy odor began to permeate the air, assaulting their nostrils as though they were entering a stable. Theseus opened his stride. Quietly he unsheathed his knife, proceeding cautiously, widening the distance from his companions. He was stalking forward, blade at the ready, searching out the monster's lair that was verging on the imminent now, judging from the smell in the air when, without warning, a hot foul breath swept down against his face. He raised his torch, straining to see, and for a paralyzing instant icy horror gripped him. There before him, mouth agape like some monstrous chasm, loomed the Minotaur.

With a shudder, Theseus recoiled. "STOP!" he shouted to the companions, his gaze riveted on the ghastly beast. It was looking down at him through red, blood-saturated eyes. In the flickering light of his torch, which was beginning to die out now, he could see the glint of two horns protruding through the hair on the creature's head. Its gigantic body, in the shape of a man's, was greenish and bloated, and two thick chains were clamped around its swollen feet. Theseus stared, and for an instant hesitated, his blade poised in the air. *This poor wretch was neither animal nor man! This was the dreaded monster?! This sickly creature? . . .* He stared at the beast and a wave of compassion welled up in him.

Androkles, meanwhile, had broken from the others and was rushing up behind him. "Theseus!" he was calling anxiously, "do you need help?"

Theseus continued to scrutinize the Minotaur. "Stay back!" he answered sharply, his eyes riveted on the creature.

Androkles retreated and went reluctantly to stand with the companions outside the lair. They could hear Theseus's torch sputtering, ready to go out—but no sounds of wrestling. What could he be doing? They waited, their ears pressed against the damp wall, listening with dread.

"He's *talking* to it!" whispered Kleo with a startled gasp.

And indeed, "Oh frightful monster," Theseus was saying, "can you speak?"

A low deep groan rumbled from the creature in response. A grievous, mournful groan, and they could hear the sound of teeth grinding.

"Talk to me!" Theseus was coaxing the Minotaur softly. "Say something . . . unburden yourself and get some relief!"

Again, that desolate, inconsolable groan.

Androkles stood listening with mounting agitation. "Stop talking to it!" he shouted, beside himself. "Kill it!"

"Quiet!" called back Theseus, and there was anger in his voice.

The companions hushed. Pressed against the wall, they waited uneasily. They could hear the final sputterings of Theseus's torch—then silence, as the flame died out. They were huddled together, their ears glued to the wall, when all at once the shattering sound of clanging chains erupted and the grinding of jaws and scuffling of savage wrestling filled the air. "Athena! help him!" they cried softly, their blood running cold.

The cave was reverberating now with the din of violent battle.

159

The foundations shook and a desperate savage groan rent the air. Then suddenly a thud—a thunderous thud of a heavy body collapsing.

Androkles broke from the group and rushed into the lair, the trembling youths and maidens following behind. A cry tore from their lips. Theseus, his dagger dripping thick black blood, was standing pale and upright in the dusky light. The thirteen youths and maidens fell on him. Wild with triumph and relief, they embraced him, clinging to their Prince with sobs of joy. Blood, mingled with sweat, was rolling down his chest. "Was he wounded?" They all clamored in concern, examining his heaving chest.

The exhausted Prince brushed away the sweat. He was breathing hard. "Come," he said, when he had gathered back his strength. "Let's not waste time," and picking up the ball of thread, he led them out.

Buoyant now, they retraced their steps, briskly following the thread back through the tangled corridors, along the twisting slippery footpaths, up the dark stone steps, until they reached the door. They could hear the courtyard on the other side, throbbing like a vast sea.

It was nearing noon, and the crowds that had gathered there since early morning were growing restless. The King had come down, too, to wait with the expectant throng. Every year the ritual was the same. As the allotted hour approached, the King would come to wait outside the Labyrinth, and if by noon no one came out the door, the King would offer sacrifice to the Great Goddess, and the festival would be over.

"What are we waiting for?" someone muttered among the crowd. "They've all been eaten by now."

Ariadne had come to stand beside the King, looking very pale. Haris, Ikaros, and Krino, too, were among the waiting throngs, leaning nervously against a column, their eyes fastened on the dreadful door.

"They're late," Haris was whispering uneasily to his sister.

But Krino wasn't answering. Her eyes were on her mistress who had moved slightly away from the King and was leaning now against the Labyrinth door listening.

Malis, watching from nearby, was laughing to himself. *Our little Princess has been widowed,* he was snickering with evil glee, *. . . widowed before she could become a bride.*

A stir began to rustle through the crowd. With a gasp, all were on their feet. The door, it seemed, was moving! The King, too, half rose from his throne, staring with bulging eyes. He had turned pale. The door to the Labyrinth was opening, and blood-splattered but erect, Theseus strode forth!

Ariadne let out a cry and ran to grasp the hero's hand. But the King had already lunged down from his throne and was pushing her aside in his haste to get to the Prince.

"Did you kill him?" he demanded in a strangled voice.

"I killed him."

A roar went up among the crowd. The King wheeled around. "Kill him!" he shouted, pointing to Theseus with murderous rage.

The people surged to grab him, but Ariadne, moving quickly, stepped forward and stood between them. "Father!" she cried. "You gave your word!"

The King looked at her sharply.

"You gave your word that you wouldn't harm him if he killed the Minotaur!"

The King was silent.

"Did you or did you not?" persisted Ariadne.

The old man still kept silent.

"Father!" said Ariadne sternly. "A King doesn't break an oath!"

The King lowered his head. He turned to the people. "Release him!" he ordered. "I gave him my word." And having said this, he turned to Malis who was standing by with his men. "Disperse the crowds!" he commanded. "Take the guards and leave!"

The crowds dispersed, the guards with Malis retreated from the courtyard, and Ariadne and the fourteen Athenians remained.

The King sat on his throne again and motioned Theseus to draw near. He was trembling, trying hard to control his rage. "I gave my word," he said, "and I won't go back on it. But I want you out of here! Get in your accursed ship and leave!"

"That's my wish, too," said Theseus, and turned with his companions to go.

But the King held up his hand. "Not so fast!" he barked. "I want you to take this lance and bring it to your father. It's my

161

declaration of war! Tell him that the summer won't pass before I march on his city and make rubble of his Palace and scatter its ashes to the four winds. I have spoken!"

Theseus grasped the lance. "I accept your war," he said. "I'll be waiting for you!" He looked at the King ironically and a smile played on his lips.

"What are you laughing at?" snarled Minos.

"Take care, old King," said Theseus, "take care that I don't come first and make ashes of YOUR palace."

The King didn't answer. A tremor of foreboding seized him and he slumped back in his throne. He turned to Ariadne. "Call the guards," he said weakly, "I want to go back to the Palace."

The guards arrived. They took the old King in their arms, carried him into the Palace, and laid him on his bed. Phaidra and Ariadne followed anxiously. Inside the bedchamber, they bent over him, smoothed his pillows, fanned his withered old head.

Out in the courtyard, Theseus turned to his companions. "I have some unfinished business yet inside the Palace," he told them. "You go ahead to the harbor and prepare the ship. I'll join you later."

The youths looked at him uneasily, reluctant to leave without him.

"I'll be with you before dark," Theseus assured them. "Now go."

They left, and Theseus crossed the courtyard and went inside the Palace. Guards in the corridors moved aside for him to pass, all looking at him with awe and hatred. Now that the fearsome monster in the foundation of their Palace had been killed, it seemed as though the great pillar that supported it had collapsed; as though Crete, the mistress of the seas, was foundering, and was about to capsize.

At a turn in the corridor, as he was approaching the stairwell to the women's quarter, he caught sight of Malis. The demoted Chief waited for him to approach, he, too, eyeing him with begrudging awe. "There's still time," he said coldly as Theseus drew near. But Theseus strode past. What they wouldn't give him willingly, he would take with the sword.

162　At the head of the stairs he came upon Haris hurrying toward him. The boy grasped his hand. "The Princess sent me to find you!" he whispered urgently. "Come!"

They hastened past the perfumed narrow halls of the women's

quarter, reached the cypresswood door with the white lilies, and entered.

Ariadne was waiting. The Princess looked at Theseus and didn't speak. She, who was so bold and brave, stood before him now, pale and mute.

Theseus crossed the room. "I've come for you to tell me what favor you want of me," he said, and bowed and kissed her hand. "I won't forget that I owe my life to you."

The Princess dropped her eyes. Krino had fallen at her feet and was crying. Haris stood watch at the door, looking on uneasily.

Theseus waited, and still the Princess didn't speak. "What favor do you ask of me, my Princess?" he said again. "Speak. I must be on my ship and sailing before nightfall."

Ariadne lifted her gaze and looked directly at him now. "Take me with you," she said quietly.

Theseus grasped her hand. His heart was beating hard. "Come!" he said. "I could ask for no greater honor!"

"When night falls," answered the Princess. "I must leave in secret. When night falls, I'll be at your ship. Wait for me."

"I'll be waiting, my Queen!" declared Theseus warmly. "I'll leave Haris with you, to help if you should need him." He kissed her hand again. "Until tonight!" he whispered, and left.

His heart was soaring. He strode out into the sunlight, past the courtyard, past the terraces, the towers, the work shops, past the storehouses crammed with all the world's rich yield. When he had gone some distance, he turned for one last look at the renowned Palace. *This empire of Crete had done all it could do. It had accomplished great things, built cities as far as the ends of the earth, conquered a whole world with its ships and its trade, built magnificent palaces, created a great civilization. . . .*

But now it had finally spent itself. It had nothing more to give. It stood in the way of the young and kept them from creating great works of their own. It had to be destroyed. He, with the help of Athena, would destroy it!

" 'Til we meet again!" he murmured, waving farewell. " 'Till summer, when we meet again!" He opened his stride, plunged into the main royal road, and hurried toward the harbor.

33

King Minos, alone with his daughters, raised his head from the pillows. "Did he leave?" he rasped.

"He's on his way," said Ariadne. "He'll be sailing tonight."

The King's eyes filled with tears. He half sat up and looked around. "Are we alone?"

"No one else is here, Father."

"I have a secret to tell you," he whispered, looking about the room. "But first you must swear you won't give it away. If word gets out, my army will lose its strength and the people will abandon me."

"You have our word," the Princesses assured him. "Tell us your secret, Father. Unburden yourself."

The old King motioned them to come close. He looked ashen, and his voice shook. "There's an oracle, my children, . . . an old oracle that no one knows about."

Phaidra stroked her father's forehead. "What oracle, Father?" she murmured soothingly.

"The one that says: *whoever kills the Minotaur will take the Kingdom!*" The old man's voice broke and he fell back on the pillows.

The two sisters looked at one another. A flush of anger spread across Phaidra's face, contorting her brow. "Traitor!" she hissed in Ariadne's ear.

"It was written, Phaidra," protested Ariadne softly. "It was the will of Fate. . . ."

"Quiet!" Phaidra silenced her. "I know everything!"

"But Phaidra. . . ."

"Quiet!"

The younger sister held her tongue.

Old Minos opened his eyes. He raised himself slightly. "I'll resist!" he rasped. "If it's written that I'm to be the last King of Crete, I won't shame my race. I'll die with sword in hand!" He lifted his voice defiantly, as with a sudden surge of strength. "Call the Elders!" he commanded. "Call Malis and my generals and my captains! I want to speak to them!"

Ariadne started for the door, but Phaidra grasped her by the shoulder. "*I'll* go!" she said, and hastened out to summon them.

Ariadne looked down at her father. Two great tears spilled from her eyes. The old man put his hand up and caressed her cheek. "Why was she looking at him that like that . . . as if she were saying good-bye?"

Ariadne didn't speak. Gently she bent down and kissed him.

"You're crying," the old man murmured.

The Princess looked at him mutely. *I'm leaving, Father . . .* she wanted to cry out, *. . . I'm never going to see you again! . . .*

The old man shook his head. "We mortals," he murmured, "we're nothing but toys that Fate plays with."

Phaidra returned. "They're coming," she announced.

"Go now!" The King sat up. "Leave us men to decide what we will do."

The councilmen entered. They sat around the King, and the two Princesses withdrew.

Out in the corridor Ariadne took her sister's hand. "Phaidra," she whispered, "I must talk to you."

"Don't touch me!" Phaidra's eyes blazed angrily.

"Phaidra. . . ," pleaded Ariadne. "It's not my fault. . . ."

Phaidra turned stonily away.

Ariadne looked at her entreatingly. "Phaidra, listen to me," she said, " . . . listen to what I have to say. Look after Father. Don't leave him alone . . . he's old. . . ." Her voice broke.

Phaidra turned. Her lips were trembling. "You're leaving?"

"I'm leaving."

"With him?"

"Yes."

Phaidra stared in silence. For a moment neither sister spoke. Then Phaidra shrugged. "All the better!" she said bitterly. "You have no place here any longer. You betrayed your country. Go!"

Ariadne turned without another word and went to her room. Krino was sitting quietly waiting for her. "Gather my things," she told the girl, " . . . my dresses, my jewels, whatever I have."

The faithful servant wiped her tears. "I've gathered them, my Lady," she murmured, and pointed to two heavy chests that she had filled.

"Where's Haris?"

"He's gone to get slaves to carry the chests down to the ship. And to say good-bye to Ikaros."

Ariadne cast a last look around the room. Her heart was crying silently. She looked at each familiar object—the doors, the window, the little statue in the niche against the wall. She picked the statue up and put it in her bosom. *Come with me, my little Goddess.* One by one, she caressed all the beloved possessions. *Farewell . . . Farewell. . . .* Her eyes lingered over them, taking in

165

the room for one last time. Krino was watching her in wretched silence. *Her beloved mistress was going away . . . and she would never see her again!* Ariadne crossed the room and took the tearful maiden's hand. "Krino," she said softly, "will you come with me?"

The loyal slave fell at her feet. "My Lady!" she sobbed. " 'Till death, and even beyond!"

Night approached. The evening star appeared.

The door opened and Haris entered. Behind him came four slaves. They picked up the chests and carried them out. The boy looked at his sister, questioning her with his eyes. *"I'm coming too!"* the joyful girl communicated.

They held open the door. "Ready, my Princess?"

Ariadne stepped across the threshold. Her devoted maid and Haris followed close behind. Out in the courtyard she looked back at the Palace for one last time. "May you fare well, Father!" she cried softly.

" 'Till we meet again!" murmured Haris. " 'Till we meet again this summer!"

34

A gentle breeze was blowing and the sea waved joyfully at the ship cutting through its waters. The thirteen young Athenians were plying their oars northward and in each young breast a heart was fluttering like a pigeon in its eagerness to reach its homeland. Ariadne, leaning over the prow, was looking at the foam the waves were making against the ship. Krino, sitting at her feet, was thinking her own joyous thoughts, anticipating how soon she would be in her father's warm embrace. Haris, stretched out on deck with the Athenians, was thinking of his friend Ikaros whom he had left behind in the dreadful Palace. And Theseus, standing watch at the helm, was thinking how he would have to prepare an army and how he would have to find ships. It was not enough that he had freed his country from the terrible monster. He would have to expand it now and bring glory to it. That was his duty. He looked up at the sky. Venus was glowing brightly. The larger stars, too, had come out—stark white Jupiter, glittering like a diamond, and Mars, reddish like the god of war. He stood erect at the helm, thinking, and watching the night unfold.

The night advanced, it filled with stars, and the youths and maidens lay down to sleep. Krino spread out her mistress's bedding and Ariadne, too, lay down to rest. She had been through much that day, she had been through great elation and great sorrow, and she was tired.

Theseus, standing at the helm, watched her as she slept. He looked down at the slumbering Princess and deep emotions for her stirred in his breast. *He owed his life to her. When they reached Athens he would make her his wife . . . he would elevate her to the throne. . . .*

The night came to an end, the sun rose from the waves, and the youths and maidens wakened. For an instant the sea turned crimson, like some enormous rose, and the waters rang with youthful voices raised in joyous hymns to the emerging sun.

As the new day was dawning, back in Crete old King Minos, too, was gazing at the reddening sea. He had come to stand on the highest terrace of his Palace, looking northward, and Phaidra, who had come out to keep him company, was standing at his side.

"She's gone," the old King was lamenting. "She's gone. . . ."

"You could have stopped her if you wished," murmured Phaidra. "You could have sent ships out to capture them."

The old man shook his head. "I can't go against Fate," he said. "The Minotaur's been killed. The Kingdom's lost."

"And yet, yesterday you were ready to mobilize an army and go to war against Athens," Phaidra reminded him.

"Yes." The old man's eyes blazed. "It's what I must do! Fate has decreed that we'll lose, but we shall fight like men! We'll fight! To save our honor and not shame our ancestors!" He looked out at the sea. "There's something higher even than life, Phaidra my child," he whispered. "Honor!" He fell silent, still gazing at the sea. *It was their wealth, the sea. Crete's ships in the thousands had sailed it to the ends of the world. They had brought back all the earth's riches to her shores. Her flag flew over every harbor in the world. She was Mistress of the seas.* "Was," he reflected sadly, . . . *now she had grown tired . . . her colonies were rising in rebellion . . . and a mere youth, from some humble land, had come and killed the Minotaur. . . .* He sighed. "We've come to the end!" he murmured.

167

35

While the old King of Crete was sighing and mourning the twilight of his Kingdom, Theseus's swift ship was continuing on its
northward course toward Athens.

By morning of the second day, a lush green island had come
into view. A brisk wind was blowing, bringing with it the scents
of pine and mastic and thyme that grew on the island's mountain
slopes. Standing alongside Theseus on the deck, Ariadne was sniff-
ing the sharp sweet smells and looking at the island longingly.
"How charming!" she was murmuring. "What do they call it?"

"Naxos, my Princess," answered Theseus.

"Can we stop there for a while?" Ariadne, after a day of sailing,
was pining to set foot on land again.

"Tired of the sea already?" smiled Theseus.

"I am," confessed the Princess. "I'd welcome getting back on
land for a while."

Theseus turned to the companions. "Lower the sails!" he called
to them. "We're going into the harbor!"

They lowered the sails and directed the ship toward the harbor.
Ariadne leaned forward eagerly on the prow and watched as the
little island grew bigger. She could see trees and cliffs and little
white houses as they drew near. "Like a dream!" she murmured,
looking on with delight. Some sunburnt fishermen were sitting
along the sandy beaches, mending their nets. They lifted their
arms in welcome to the ship as it approached, and Ariadne too,
waved back.

They reached the beach, dropped anchor, and went ashore. The
friendly islanders came out to greet them, and when they had welcomed them, they took them to a shady pine tree where they laid
out food for them—wheat bread, olives, fish, dark wine.

When they had eaten, a kindly old man, an archon most likely,
began to question them. Where were they from? Where were they
headed?

"We're from Athens," Theseus told him. "We're just returning
from Crete."

"Merchants?"

"No," laughed Theseus, "travelers. We're going around the
world. To get to know new lands and people. To get our fill."

The old man shook his head and smiled. "Man never gets his

fill," he said. "Why travel? There's nothing sweeter than one's own country."

He turned to an old blind man sitting beneath an olive tree, his sunbaked forehead thrust forward to catch every word of the conversation around him. "Old bard," the archon said to him "strangers have come to our land. We've laid out food for them, we've given them all we have; now bring your lyre and sing something to please them."

The old bard reached for a lyre that was hanging from the tree. He caressed it for an instant, bent his ear to it, and began to strike the chords. "What do you want me to sing?" he asked, raising his sightless eyes to the guests.

"Whatever you wish," said Theseus.

"I'll sing the song of that great ingenious traveler who also wandered over the world and found rest only in his own country," said the man. "I'll sing you the song of the renowned Odysseus!" He struck the chords of the lyre, raised his snow-white head, and began the song:

> *Tell me, goddess, of that most ingenious man*
> *who buffeted about for years, after sacking Troy's holy citadel,*
> *and knew the lands and minds of many people*
> *and suffered myriad adversities at sea seeking*
> *to return with his companions safely to his own country.*
> *But them he could not save, despite his pains.*
> *For they died of their own offense, the impious ones,*
> *having eaten the cattle of the heaven-coursing Sun God,*
> *and thus deprived by Him of that day's return.*
> *Begin the song from somewhere for us, too, goddess, daughter*
> *of Zeus. . . .*

For a long time they all sat listening to the famous song. They put aside eating and drinking and listened while Odysseus, as in a fairy tale, rose before them, and island after island of his legendary sojourns came to life. They were all familiar with the tale. From early infancy their mothers and their grandmothers had rocked them to sleep crooning the saga of that much-wandered traveler, and they never tired of listening to his adventures . . . how he returned to Ithaca . . . how, dressed in rags like a beggar, he returned to the Palace and slew the suitors. . . .

"I've heard many men sing the travails of Odysseus," said The-

169

seus when the old bard had hung his lyre on the olive tree again, " . . . but none had your sweet voice, old man. What can I give you in return to please you?"

"You've already pleased me," answered the bard. "You've given me your kind word."

"Ah, but that's not enough," smiled Theseus. "I'm going to give you a gift that you can hold in your hands and remember me by. He turned to his companion Androkles. "Go to the ship," he whispered, "and bring me my gold goblet."

Androkles ran, and in a short time was back, holding a heavy goblet that was exquisitely engraved with an intricate scene.

Theseus took the goblet and approached the blind man. "Old bard," he said, "I'm giving you a gold goblet, for you to drink your wine. It's been made by a famous goldsmith in my country." He took the old man's hand and placed the goblet in it for him to feel. "The etchings on it," he explained, "depict an ocean full of tossing waves. And over the waves there's a sky with heavy clouds from which a giant trident is leaping out and striking at the waves, making lightning bolts all around. Between the ocean and the sky is etched a tiny ship that's sailing fearlessly with torn sails. And in the little ship, old bard, standing erect and holding the rudder firmly in his hand, is a man—Odysseus."

The old man grasped the gold goblet. He felt it carefully with his fingers. He felt the ocean, found the trident, felt the little ship. His face lit up. "I see!" he said. "I see. . . ." He held out the goblet joyfully. They filled it with wine and the old man raised it high. "To your health, my noble youth!" he said. "May you, too, perform great deeds to glorify your country! And after many years, may other blind bards come along like me and sit beneath olive trees before lordly feasts and sing your song!"

The day ended and the young travelers returned to their ship to sleep. In the morning when they wakened, the sea was frothing, and dark heavy clouds were hanging over the world. A loud rumbling had started in the heavens, and lightning was streaking across the sky.

The companions looked out in dismay. Haris, who couldn't wait to see the shores of Athens again, fairly groaned with disappointment. God only knew when they'd be able to put up sails again!

But Ariadne could not have been more pleased. Captivated by the charming little island from the very start, she was jubilant at the delay, racing barefoot on the sandy beach, calling gleefully to Krino to join her. The air was ringing with her laughter as she played with the frothing sea, now plunging into the waters to chase after the receding waves, now retreating, shrieking, to the safety of the pine trees when the foaming surf surged back to grasp her. All morning she cavorted with the ebb and flow of the raging sea, flushed and heady with her newfound freedom.

Finally around noon the clouds began to scatter. The companions watched the darkness lift and cast hopeful eyes at the sea. Theseus, too, was looking at the waters that were still thrashing angrily. Ordinarily, he would be embarking, despite the raging sea. But he was not alone this time. There was the Princess to consider. She was racing up to him now, flushed with play.

"We'll wait," he said. "We'll leave tomorrow."

Ariadne fairly danced with joy. Another day on her enchanting island! Already a new adventure was leaping in her head. "Would he let her? Would he let her take Haris and Krino and go for a long walk on the beach?" She was looking at him most entreatingly, eyes shining, cheeks flushed.

"Of course," he said. He'd stay behind and repair the ship. He watched her race off happily. "Enjoy yourself!" he called after her. "But don't be gone too long!"

"I won't!" she promised. "I'll be back before dark!"

He smiled, his eyes following her adoringly as she sped away frolicking with her companions along the water's edge, past the promontory and beyond, until she was lost from his view.

The three explorers ran and ran along the stark white beach, their hearts fluttering like birds. The sand was filled with tiny shells, deposited there by the sea. "Let's gather seashells!" shouted Ariadne, stooping to pick one up. They gathered seashells, enough to fill their fists, and continued on. On and on they ran along the stark white beach that kept stretching endlessly before them, and soon a little hut came into view. A man came to the door to watch them—an old fisherman, with a long harpoon that he used to gather sea urchins. He stood watching them, and as they drew near he called out to them, wanting to know where they were going.

171

"For a walk!" Ariadne called back merrily.

The old man stepped down from his threshold. "Don't go any farther!" he said coming toward them. "A foreign ship is anchored up ahead behind the cove. It arrived this morning with some strange men aboard—blond-bearded and blond-mustached. I don't like the looks of them!"

"And if WE like them?" laughed Ariadne.

The old fisherman shrugged. "Do as you wish," he said. "I've warned you. I've done my duty," and so saying, he turned back to the hut.

"Let's go!" said Ariadne. "What do we have to fear?"

"It would be better if we headed back, my Princess," protested Haris.

But Ariadne was racing ahead. "Afraid?" she taunted, laughing.

"Of course not!" and young Haris followed after her.

Krino was running ahead, too, full of joy at seeing her mistress so happy. Never, in that magnificent Palace of Crete, had she seen her in such high spirits. There, she was like a bird imprisoned in a gilded cage; and now, look at her! The door had opened and the bird was singing and soaring freely in the air!

Ariadne raced on, with Krino and Haris close behind. They reached the cove that the old fisherman had cautioned them against, and what should they see! There, in a round bay where the storm could not reach, was an exquisite three-masted ship. Trellises of vine leaves and branches adorned each mast, and in the prow stood a broad throne upon which sat a most handsome youth. The youth had golden hair, crowned with a wreath of vine leaves, and at his feet lay a pet leopard. Next to him stood another throne, this one empty.

Ariadne stopped short and stared in breathless wonder. Her golden hair, fallen loose about her shoulders, was blowing in the wind, and her flushed cheeks glowed crimson.

Seeing her, the youth rose to his feet. "Welcome to my ship!" he smiled, greeting her most cordially with a princely bow. "Won't you come aboard and allow me to offer you some refreshment. We have just arrived from the distant lands of Anatolia and have brought exotic fruits with us."

As he was talking, seven blond men with ruddy skin emerged from the gunwale of the ship.

172

"Take the rowboat," the princely youth commanded, "and help her Ladyship aboard."

Ariadne was staring and rubbing her eyes. She turned to Krino beside her. "Do you see it, too, Krino," she whispered, " . . . or am I dreaming?"

"I see it!" said Krino, staring open-mouthed.

"Could we both be dreaming?" murmured Ariadne. "Could we both be dreaming that we left Crete and came to an island and walked along a beach and gathered seashells and are standing in front of this fabled ship? . . . "

The little rowboat was approaching. Two men inside were rowing swiftly. The boat touched shore, banked in the sand, the men leaped forth, approached the Princess, and held out their powerful arms to her. "Allow us to carry you, noble Mistress," they said, " . . . so that the waves don't get you wet."

Without a thought, without an instant's hesitation, as in a trance, the Princess moved toward them—a feather in a dream and two men were lifting her in their strong arms and carrying her to the boat.

"My Lady!" Krino's voice was strident with alarm behind her.

"Princess!" Now Haris's. "Where are you going?!"

"Don't be afraid," she turned a smiling face on them, "the rowboat's coming back for you, too."

"My Lady!!" Krino's voice was shrieking.

Don't shout, my little Krino . . . it's a dream . . . a beautiful dream. Don't shout, you'll waken me!

The rowboat reached the vine-trellised ship. The golden youth inside was putting out his arms, lifting her. . . . "Welcome, my Princess," he was saying. He took her hand and led her to the empty throne. "This throne's been waiting for you," he smiled, and nodded to his men. The men reached over the side, brought up the anchor, and raised three huge triangular red sails on the masts. "Forward!" the princely youth commanded now. "Ariadne has arrived. Our purpose is fulfilled."

"My Lady!!" A heart-rending cry pierced the air from the shore. "Princess!!" Another.

But a strong wind had come up, scattering the voices, and the ship sailed off into the sea, shimmering on the waves like a giant open-petaled rose, and disappeared.

36

Theseus stood motionless in the center of his ship looking at the sea, not seeing it for the tears that were blinding him. Krino and Haris, dumb with grief and terror, were crouched at his feet. No one was speaking. Theseus kept his stricken gaze out on the sea where the night was falling over the waves.

Haris stirred, "My Prince," he murmured and held his breath.

Theseus looked down. He had forgotten the two children weeping silently at his feet. "Get up," he said, stooping to take them by the hand.

The wretched boy and girl rose trembling to their feet and hung their heads.

"Don't cry," said Theseus not unkindly. "You're not to blame. You couldn't have done differently." His voice broke and he turned away to hide the tears. "From what you've told me, it must have been the new God Dionysos who took her. That's how he cruises around the islands—with vine leaves and red sails, and a pet leopard at his feet." He fell silent, staring at the sea. *Let His will be done.*

The wind had fallen. The companions were standing by, waiting silently. He turned to them. "Prepare to sail!" he commanded.

They lifted anchor, unfurled the sails, and the ship embarked.

Theseus stood at the helm looking out at the night. His heart was aching terribly, and his eyes kept filling with tears. He stood in silence, holding the rudder firm, the ship thrusting forward through the waves, into the open sea. The brisk sea breezes blew against his face. He took deep breaths, inhaling the clean crisp air. Night advanced. His mind took hold. Gradually it began to tame his pain. *He was the leader of a people . . . he had responsibilities. The King of Crete was no doubt rabid by now, preparing to sail to Athens to sack his country. He couldn't let that happen. He had to hurry home and prepare for war!* He thought of his father, and how his old heart must be pounding, waiting for him to return.

174   And in truth, the King of Athens couldn't sleep for worrying over his son. As the days went by, he had begun to fear that the monster might have eaten him. Every morning he would go down

to the shore, to a tall cliff that jutted out into the sea, and there he would climb and look out at the horizon. He'd stare at the waves and tremble, waiting for the sails to appear. Would they be white? Or would they be black, for death? "Athena," he would pray, "help my son return alive and I'll build you the most beautiful marble temple the world has ever seen!"

Such were the promises that old Aigeus was making as he paced back and forth on the cliff, his eyes riveted on the sea.

One day he climbed the cliff and vowed not to come down until he beheld his son's ship. That night he had a dream. "Without fail, he'll be coming today," he murmured when he wakened in the morning. He sat motionless, facing the south, watching. The hours passed, the sun rose in the sky, noon arrived. The sea stretched out deserted. In the stillness and the silence, the old man nodded, fell asleep, and soon a voice came to him in his dream. "Open your eyes and look!" it prodded softly. He sat up with a start. The sun was inclining toward the west; Hymettos had taken on a soft rosy tint. The King looked toward the south. He looked again! "Athena!" he cried, "Athena! what do I see?" A ship—his son's—was approaching on the waves, a billowing black sail on its mast.

Old Aigeus staggered to his feet. "They killed my son!" he screamed. "They killed my son!" He stood trembling on the edge of the cliff. Down below, the surf was groaning, pounding against the rocks. "My Theseus!" the broken man cried out, "I'm coming down to you in Hades!"

From his ship, Theseus was looking at the cliff. He could see a man pacing back and forth on the rock. "It must be my father," he guessed, watching the lone figure pacing back and forth. "It's my father, waiting for me."

"Father!" he shouted, waving to him from the prow. But the wind and the pounding of the surf drowned out his voice. He watched the man come to the edge of the rock and call out something. "He's caught sight of me," he thought, "he's calling to me." But before he could raise his own voice to answer, he saw his old father spread out his arms and plunge headlong into the sea.

"Father!!" his voice tore from his throat. His breath caught, he raised his head for air, and for the first time now he saw the sails on the mast. The black sails, that in his haste and jubilation to embark from Crete, he had forgotten to take down!

175

37

It was dark when the ship finally entered the harbor and moored. Barely had it touched shore when the news sped forth. It spilled over the quay, took the main road on the run, reached Athens, darted into house after house, into workshop after workshop, climbed joyously to the Akropolis and there, for Athena's pleasure, fires were lit to announce to the surrounding towns that Theseus had returned.

And in a short while, what a spectacle! Fires ignited on all the mountains of Attica, on Aigaleos, on Hymettos, on Pentelikos, on Parnes.

The news reverberated across the land. *Theseus had returned!*

The people spilled into the streets; the mothers who had sent their sons and daughters to be eaten by the monster danced with joy; the city Elders put wreaths of roses on their heads and, with the people in tow, set out to meet him.

They walked briskly, carrying blazing torches to light the way, and before long they spotted him coming up the main road from the harbor. Clad in white chiton, the double-bladed dagger hanging at his side, behind him the jubilant companions, Theseus approached.

The Elders raised their arms and greeted him. "A thousand welcomes to our hero!" they shouted.

And the mothers fell on him and kissed his hands.

But Theseus remained silent. He bit his lip. His father had not lived to celebrate his victory, and the bitterness cut deep.

When they reached the city he went directly to the Palace where the Elders followed, escorting him into the Throne room. There, with heavy heart, he picked up the royal staff and mounted the steps to his father's throne. "The King is dead! The King is dead! Long live the King!" the Elders chanted in solemn unison, and one by one the faithful councilmen passed before the throne and bowed, saluting their new King.

Early the next morning Theseus went up to the Akropolis together with his people, to pay homage to the Goddess Athena, and to thank her for his victory. He stood between the columns of the temple, soberly watching his people come. The day had been proclaimed a holiday, to solemnize his victory and his elevation to the throne, and the crowds had been coming since dawn, climbing the sacred hill to thank the Goddess for their deliverance. Bright youths, astride handsome horses crowned with laurel, were leading fatted cows for sacrifice; maidens, carrying baskets, were bringing fruits and flowers; others were bringing doves or vases filled with milk and honey. All were hurrying to the Goddess to present some offering.

The temple was a simple structure made of reddish stone, in the center of which stood Athena's great bronze statue. Her eyes, made of precious gems, looked out enormous and unmoving on her beloved city. She held a long lance in her right hand and in her left, a royal shield upon which was etched the head of Medusa.

In his people's eyes, Theseus, standing motionless beside the statue, might have passed for a god, himself. He addressed them now, as they gathered round him and hushed to hear.

"Men and women of Athens!" his voice rang with deep resonance. "What I did, I did with Athena's help. Man cannot achieve anything without her strength and wisdom. Strength without wisdom ends up destructive and barbaric. Wisdom without strength ends up futile. This is our Goddess—Athena—who combines both of these virtues."

He paused, looking solemnly at his people. "Celebrate today man's victory over the beast. Let each of you feel in his heart that there is a Theseus in him, slaying the beast within that has been tyrannizing him. Only in this way will my victory gain worth and you will be able to say that you have become liberated people."

The people listened, marveling. His voice, it seemed, resounded more deeply than they had ever heard it. Their minds, it seemed, expanded, and for the first time they were beginning to understand the worth of their Goddess and why they worshiped her. For the first time, they were beginning to understand the worth of man.

Theseus's voice rang out again. "Offer your sacrifices!" he enjoined them. "Eat and drink and celebrate. Today is a day of joy. On another day I will invite you back and tell you what I am going to ask of you!" He spoke, stepped down from the temple, and amid the people's cheers, made his way back to the Palace.

There were difficult decisions to be made, many plans to be worked out yet, and he needed to be alone, to think. Above all else, he would need Aristidis, to help him formulate his plans.

He reached the Palace and went at once to the blacksmith's

177

quarters. He found him in his room, sitting with Krino and Haris, celebrating a private reunion with his children. For a moment Theseus stood at the door, taking pleasure in the little scene. Krino and Haris were sitting at their father's knee, relating all that had happened back in Crete. First the one, then the other would describe how Theseus found his way out of the Labyrinth . . . how they had boarded the ship . . . how the Princess was abducted. But here Krino's voice broke and she burst into tears.

Theseus strode into the room. "Happy?" he called out jovially.

"Bless you, my King!" exclaimed Aristidis, rising quickly to his feet. "We owe everything to you!"

"I've left the celebration to come and find you," said Theseus. "We must put our heads together."

"At your service, my King!" declared the blacksmith. "I'm with you in life and death!"

"In life! In life!" laughed Theseus. "Forget death! That will come, too, in time. We have work to finish first!" He looked at Haris who had jumped to his feet to greet him. "And you, my friend?"

"I'm with you, too!" declared the boy, repeating his father's words.

Theseus smiled down at him. "From this day forward," he said, "you'll be with me always—at my side in war and peace. I'm appointing you my Adjutant. Will you accept?"

The boy grasped Theseus's hand. "In life and in death, my King!" he vowed, and bowing low, kissed his sovereign's hand.

"And Krino? What shall we do with Krino?" smiled Theseus.

The maiden dropped her eyes and blushed. "Whatever you command, my King," she murmured.

"I have a plan in mind," he smiled, "but I'll tell you later. He patted the young girl's head and turned to the blacksmith.

"Come," he said. "Let's get to work."

The next day Theseus summoned his trusted captains and instructed them to prepare their ships. They were to sail north at once, he told them, and bring back iron. They were to gather all the workmen they could find up north, all the laborers who knew how to work the iron, and bring them back to Athens. By persuasion, or by force, if necessary.

"We'll bring them!" the captains assured him, and hurried off to do his bidding.

When they were gone, Theseus summoned another captain, a daring, thrice-crafty adventurer, whose real name no one knew since everyone called him by the nickname Captain Fox. He was a short, dark man, all skin and bone, with eyes full of fire. Theseus knew him to be not only daring and courageous, but devilishly clever, too—just what he needed for the mission that he would be entrusting to him.

"Captain Fox," he said to him, "I want you to load your ship with cargo and sail south with it to Crete. When you get there, pretend that you're a merchant. Talk with the people at the harbor, make friends with the captains and the soldiers. Give them gifts and get them to talk. See if they're building up their navy. Find out how many ships they have and what kind of weapons. Go up to the Palace, too, and see if they're mobilizing an army. Make note of how big it is . . . how it's armed . . . find out all you can. Understand?"

"I understand," smiled the captain. "You want me to spy."

"Yes, I want you to spy. Our country is in danger."

"I'll take wine with me," said the captain. "There's no better cargo for the kind of work you want done."

"They don't call you Fox in vain," laughed Theseus. "Now go! Prepare to leave at once! I'll have your ship loaded with wine. Pick out a few good comrades to take along and go. There's no time to lose!"

The captain didn't move. He scratched his head and stood hesitant.

"Well?" Theseus looked at him impatiently.

"From what I can remember of the Palace in Crete," the captain said, still scratching his head as though to aid his recollection, "they have some stone chests hidden in the ground. . . ."

"So?"

"So, my King, when you sack the Palace, will you give me whatever is in one of those chests?"

"If you're successful," said Theseus, laughing, "I'll give you three of those chests! Does that satisfy you?"

"It does, my King!" beamed the captain, and putting on his cap askew, he hurried out.

179

Alone again, Theseus called to Haris standing duty at the door: "Have the woodchoppers come yet?"

"They are outside waiting," Haris reported.

"Have them come in," commanded Theseus.

Three colossal men came into the room and bowed.

Theseus looked them over, the thick strong arms, the fierce-looking faces. "Have you gathered many others?" he said to them.

"About two hundred, King," they answered. "All born and raised in the woods."

"Good! Now go into the forests of Parnes and Pentelikos . . . wherever you find trees, and chop them down. Set up the timber in piles and I'll send men to haul it to the harbor, for the work to begin. Now hurry, we must start getting ships on the stocks."

"We'll have the beach overflowing with timber," the men assured him.

Next, Theseus sent for the technicians who were to work on the ships. He sent for the weavers, to weave cloth for the sails. He sped to the harbor; he conferred with the shipbuilders; he supervised the dockhands who were putting up the stocks for the ships. . . . Night and day he worked, never stopping.

In a few days you could see the change in the city. No longer did the people stroll leisurely along the streets or stand about in the agora in idle chatter. All were caught up in the fervor of preparation—building ships, training, getting ready. You could see them in the public squares and in the fields, youths and men of every age, training for the army, learning how to march, how to throw the lance, how to wrestle, how to fight in hand-to-hand combat.

The women, too, and the children. All had organized in ranks, learning to defend themselves. Athens no longer was a city, but a training camp.

"It's the only way to save ourselves!" Theseus went about exhorting them. "Otherwise, the enemy will come and make ashes of us."

"God bless this enemy of ours!" an old man said to him one day. "He's quickened our blood."

"There are times when the enemy is more useful than the friend," answered Theseus. "He forces us to make ourselves strong."

180

In time, the captains whom Theseus had sent out to the north returned, their ships' holds filled with iron. They had rounded up some twenty blond-bearded craftsmen, who spoke a barbaric tongue, and no sooner had they landed when all were put to work.

The weeks passed. The heart of summer came, and finally Captain Fox, too, returned from his spying mission in Crete. Theseus had been growing anxious as the weeks were going by and had begun to fear that the Cretans might have caught him spying and killed him. But the cunning Fox returned at last and hurried with his news to Theseus.

He found him in the shipyards, prodding and supervising the workers.

"Welcome to the Captain!" Theseus called out in relief when he spotted him. "When did you arrive?"

"This very minute, my King. I sold all the wine at a good price!"

"Come at once and give me an accounting!" laughed Theseus, taking him aside. He could see that the captain had managed it well.

"I'll be brief and to the point," said Captain Fox. "I went to Crete as you told me, and the minute I landed I began hauling out the wine and offering free samples at the harbor. Some soldiers came to watch and I gave them some. They tasted it, and I opened another pitcher and offered them more. I opened another pitcher and another and kept giving them more wine."

"And what did you find out?"

"I'm coming to that. The soldiers kept drinking, and I kept offering them more. Then I slaughtered a young pig that I had brought along and roasted it and gave them appetizers with their wine. They kept drinking and eating the tasty appetizers and by the time night rolled around they were all in great spirits and I was sitting buddy-buddy with them, getting them to talk."

"And what did you find out?"

"I found out that they're preparing for war. Their King is in a rage. He wants to take revenge, they say, because the Athenians killed his house pet, his handsome Minotaur. They're repairing their ships, they're recruiting foreign sailors—the wealthy Cretans are tired of fighting, you see, and they pay foreigners to do their fighting for them—mercenaries, I think they're called. . . ."

"I know," Theseus nodded impatiently. "So what did you find out?"

"The next day I went up to the Palace. I found some old friends, old officers and nobles that I knew, and to make a long story short, my King, I got them drunk. 'I have a wine,' I told them, 'that can resurrect the dead,' and day after day I kept bringing them wine to drink, and they, in turn, would invite me to sit down and eat with them—as if that wasn't what I was aiming for. . . ."

"What did you find out, Captain Fox? That's what I want you to tell me!"

"I'm coming to that, my King, I'm coming to it now: I found out that they've gathered together three hundred ships. Each ship holds fifty soldiers. They're going to set out in early autumn, and they'll not be coming at us from our harbor here, but from behind, at Marathon. They're going to send a few ships here to trick us— some fifty, to put us off guard—and while we're fighting them here, their full force will be coming from the other road to Athens. Understand their cunning strategy?"

"I understand. Anything else?"

"What more do you want, my King? I told you everything— how many ships, how much of an army, from where and when. You want more?"

Theseus smiled. "No," he said. "I'm satisfied."

"So . . . the three Palace chests are mine?"

"All yours."

"That's settled, then," said the captain, his eyes dancing. "Now, we can get on with something that's even more important."

"More important?" Theseus looked dubious.

"You'll see, my King. But first, let's make a deal. Good bargainers, they say, make good friends."

"I'm listening."

"If you like this other piece of news that I'm bringing you, you'll give me three more chests, eh? . . . because this news wasn't in our original agreement."

"Fine, let's hear it."

The captain rubbed his hands. "One morning," he began anew, "as I was returning, a little tipsy, to my ship, who should I spot but an old friend of mine, a captain from the people up north. What haunches! what hands! like some monstrous giant— and such a beard and mustache! like gold! I took him to my ship, I opened a pitcher, we drank . . . eh, the blessed wine, what power it has! it opens every heart. What do you think my friend tells me? At a harbor that I know up north, out there in the Black

Sea, about five hundred ships and boats have gathered, filled with blond northerners and their wives and children. I asked him what they were doing up there. They want to come down south, he says to me, they want fields to cultivate, they want land, they're hungry. And where do you think they're headed, I kept after him. Who knows, he says, I've come ahead to scout, to see what Crete is like. . . ."

Theseus had jumped to his feet. The captain was rubbing his hands, smiling. "Well?" he said, "how does this news strike you? Is it worth three chests?"

"It's worth three and ten chests, Captain Fox!" Theseus declared. "When the blessed hour comes, the thirteen chests are yours!"

"Thirteen and three, my King," corrected the thrice-cunning captain. "The first three that you had promise me, and now these thirteen add up to sixteen."

"Thirteen and three!" laughed Theseus. He put his hand out to the captain. His heart was racing and he couldn't wait to be alone now. Having heard all that Captain Fox had to say, he took his leave of him and hurried back to the Palace, to calm himself and carefully evaluate what he had learned.

38

The weeks and months passed. By the end of summer all was in readiness. The Athenian storerooms were bulging with iron weapons, the Saronic was filled with new ships testing their sails, and the land was teeming with thousands of soldiers, trained and ready for battle.

Theseus had gone up to the Akropolis to think. It was past midnight and the air was cool and redolent with the scent of newly opened nightflowers. Athens lay sleeping peacefully beneath the blue darkness of an as-yet moonless sky. Above her, the bronze statue of armor-clad Athena stood erect and vigilant, guarding her beloved city. Theseus was sitting at the Goddess's feet, plunged in thought. For days now he had been trying to decide what course to take. Autumn was upon them, and the Cretans would be setting out soon with their ships and soldiers to bring war to Attica and profane her sacred soil. The responsibilities of King weighed heavily upon him. From his decision hung the deliverance or the ruin of his country. He sat pondering and weighing. Three roads were open to him. One was to wait and let the Cretans come and fight them on Attic soil. Another was to not wait but to go after them first and fight them on their own soil. And a third was to enlist the help of the barbarians who were assembled in the Black Sea looking for some island to plunder, and thus, together, they could be certain of tearing down the outworn Kingdom of Crete.

These were the choices the young King was struggling with, weighing one against the other. Now and then, he'd lift his eyes to the Goddess and his lips would move. "Athena," he would murmur, "enlighten my mind, show me which course to choose. . . ."

Midnight passed, new stars arose in the sky, others sank into the west, and still Theseus grappled with his thoughts. He stood up, leaned against a column, and gazed out at the sleeping city. A profound silence covered the world. Nothing could be heard but the faint sound of a night owl out among the olive trees. He raised his eyes and looked at the calm bronze countenance of Athena. He was tired, his eyelids were heavy; perhaps for an instant sleep overtook him. It seemed the bronze lips of the Goddess moved. In the stillness he heard a voice: *Theseus . . .*

I'm here, my Goddess. Command.

I, too, am here, above you. Speak to me. I shall answer you.

My Goddess, I must decide. Enlighten my mind. Shall I allow the King of Crete to come to our soil and fight him here?

It seemed the Goddess drew her brows together. *I don't want enemies profaning my soil . . . I don't want my army on the defensive; I want it on the attack. Defensive war is for the old. We're young and strong!*

Come in the lead, then, my Goddess. Lead us and we'll go to Crete!

The voice took long in answering; as though the Goddess were reflecting, as though she, too, were trying to decide.

Why don't you speak?

You know that I like strength when it is balanced with prudence, the voice was heard again, sober and measured. *I hate mindless, stupid heroics. The Kingdom of Crete has grown old, but no matter how antiquated, it's still big and rich and dangerous.*

184

Shall I call in the blond barbarians—the Dorians—and ask them to join with us and together attack Crete?

An agony of silence. Slowly, almost imperceptibly, the Goddess's lance appeared to move. The point, it seemed, passed through the temple's roof and glittered like a star in the night. *Yes,* the voice was heard again. *They are barbarians now . . . but in time their children will turn out better . . . and their grandchildren will become Greeks. Join with them and take Crete. I will march ahead and open the way for you!*

Theseus came to with a start. He moved away from the column and rubbed his eyes. Had he fallen asleep? Had he been dreaming? Was it really the Goddess's voice that he had heard? He looked up at her. She was standing motionless on her stone pedestal, her eyes of precious azure stones looking far out into the star-filled night. He bent and kissed the statue's feet. "You spoke to me, my Lady!" he whispered. "If for an instant sleep overtook me, still it was you who sent the dream and showed me the way. Let your will be done! It's my will, too. I see it now."

Relieved and lighthearted, as if a great weight had been lifted from him, Theseus moved swiftly. He knew what to do now, what course to follow. It was always difficult for him to arrive at a decision. His mind had to weigh everything carefully, examine every option, anticipate every consequence, and it seemed to take forever to decide. But once he was satisfied that he had considered everything, and had chosen wisely, he plunged ahead, lionlike, and there was no stopping him.

He summoned his councilmen. "We're going on the attack!" he told them. "Prepare!"

He went out among the soldiers. "In the name of Athena!" he thundered, firing them up, "we're setting out for war! We're not waiting for the enemy to come to us, to contaminate our soil! We're going out after them!"

Group by group, he went about firing up his people. "The moment has come for us to give up everything for our country!" he exhorted them. "Everything—our sleep, our comforts, our riches, our lives!"

185

The people cheered. Everywhere he went, the people cheered "Long live our King!"

When he had made the rounds, he returned to the Palace and summoned Captain Fox again.

"I'm sending you on another mission," he said to him. "This one is far away, but I have confidence in you. I know you'll manage it."

The wily captain's eyes danced. *Some profit was to be made of this, too . . . the sixteen chests would grow!*

"Now listen closely," said Theseus. "You told me that you know the harbor out there in the Black Sea where the barbarians' ships have gathered."

"Yes, my King. What do you command?"

"I want you to go to them and deliver this message: Tell them that the King of Athens sends you; that he knows of a land that flows with milk and honey; and that he, the King of Athens, invites them to join forces with him and together take the rich land and divide it between them. Tell them to come before winter sets in! Do you understand me?"

"I understand, my King."

"It's a difficult business."

"It's to my liking," said the captain. "I'll get them here. I know their language!"

"If you succeed, our country will be saved. Not only will it be saved but glorified as well."

"I know."

"Now what do you want as a reward?"

The captain reddened. He hesitated, and a struggle seemed to be taking place in his soul. "Nothing," he said at last.

"Nothing?" Theseus looked at him in surprise.

"I, too, have my pride," the captain answered. "All of you are giving your lives for our country; and you ask me to do something for my country and I say *pay me.* I'm embarrassed. I don't want anything!"

Theseus reached out and pressed his hand. "Go, now," he said. "And Athena be with you!"

The captain bowed and headed for the door. At the threshold he stopped. Some new battle seemed to be wrestling inside him. He turned slowly and looked back at Theseus. "If you need the sixteen chests, too," he said gruffly, " . . . take them!" and quickly he went out.

39

Not long after the captain had sailed away, Haris and Krino were sitting together on an upper terrace of the Palace, looking down on all the preparations and speculating on the impending campaign. The night before, a ship from the north had arrived at the harbor and had brought important news: the fleet of the barbarians had set out from the Black Sea and was on its way to Athens!

"Soon, now," Haris was predicting excitedly to his sister, "the Palace of Knossos will fall into our hands!"

"Aren't you afraid of the barbarians?" Krino shuddered.

"No. They're bringing us new energy" declared Haris. "They'll take root in our soil and in time they'll grow civilized and become Greeks." He looked out at the city. "If only we could live five hundred years," he sighed, "to see what glory this Athens of ours will take on!"

As the two sat on the terrace, talking, shouts began coming from the courtyards below, and people were gathering and looking up at the sky. Krino and Haris lifted their heads and what should they see! Something was flying toward the Palace. A gigantic bird was flying toward them, flapping its wings and descending. They stared. It had an aged face with white whiskers, and two arms were visible, raising and lowering the wings.

"Daidalos!" the children shrieked and began waving excitedly at the strange bird. They could see the old craftsman clearly, hovering over the Palace, descending slowly toward them on the parapet. Krino watched the approach and looked beyond for Ikaros. Where was Ikaros? Her heart tightened. Haris, too, was searching the sky for his friend, cold sweat breaking out on his forehead. Maybe he hadn't left Crete yet, he thought, but an evil premonition gripped him.

Daidalos was alighting now. Like a pigeon flapping its wings in midair, Daidalos came to a halt and landed on the terrace.

Brother and sister ran to him and embraced him and kissed his hand. "And Ikaros?!" they both cried looking up at the empty sky.

The old man shook off the wings. Tears were streaming from his eyes. He tried to speak. "Ikaros drowned . . . ," he choked and his voice trailed off.

The world went dim.

Old Daidalos tried to speak again. "He didn't listen to me," he said brokenly. "We were flying low over the sea . . . but he kept looking up at the sun and wanting to fly higher. I kept calling to him, begging him to stay low. But he wouldn't listen. He went crazy . . . he kept flying higher and higher, closer and closer to the sun until it melted the wax on his wings and he fell into the sea." The stricken man flung off his wings and stomped on them. His voice rose bitterly. "What do I want with wings!" he cried out shrill with grief. "I lost my only son!" He stomped on the offending wings and trampled them and made a thousand pieces of them.

With the coming of the winged man, all Athens turned agog. Some were saying that he was a god and had come to help Theseus; others that he was a seer; and others that he was a strange bird that resembled an old man.

In vain, Haris tried to tell them that he was the great architect Daidalos and that he had been able, with the power of his mind, to make wings for humans; but no one wanted to believe him. As so often happens, the people preferred the fairy tales to the truth.

Theseus took Daidalos into the Palace and gave orders that he was to be treated as if he were a King. Indeed, a man with such a brain, he believed, was a King! He had great plans for him. He would provide him with helpers, and all the material that he needed, and he would put him to work making wings for the youth of Athens. He would train his finest youth to fly and create an elite battalion of winged soldiers with which to conquer the world.

But when he approached Daidalos with his plan, the old artisan would hear none of it. "Never again!" he vowed. "The Gods have punished me. I raised my head too high. I wanted to surpass human limits and make man a winged creature. And look, they killed my son!"

In vain, Theseus tried to talk to him, to make him change his mind. But the old man was adamant. "If you want, I'll build palaces for you," he said, "palaces more splendid than those of Crete; I'll build temples so beautiful that people will come from the ends of the earth to admire them; I'll carve statues so lifelike, that you'll think they can walk and talk. But wings I'll never make!"

All that day, and well into the night, Theseus tried to convince Daidalos, but before the night was over he gave up. There were more pressing needs to turn to. Haris, looking ashen from grieving over the loss of his beloved friend, hurried to him with important news. "The sea is filled with ships!" he reported. "Ships, with burning red lanterns have been sighted and are approaching."

Theseus moved away from Daidalos now and hurried out with Haris to the courtyard where he had two horses waiting. Mounting the steeds, the pair sped toward the harbor.

When they arrived, they found the sea indeed was filled with ships—little single-masted ships with white triangular sails sporting strange red symbols. Each had a lantern burning at its prow, and the sea looked like a glittering city as far as the eye could reach.

Theseus leaped from his horse and quickly climbed the harbor tower. Dawn was beginning to break, and in the first faint glow of light he could see the crude armada approaching. In the forefront was a large, three-masted ship.

Captain Fox! he smiled, recognizing the three triangular red sails. *He's bringing the barbarians!*

The sea was billowing gently, and a balmy breeze was pushing the dense forest steadfastly toward the shore. All thoughts of Daidalos and the wings receded now from Theseus's mind. He had the blond barbarians. They'd be enough. He watched the ships approach. *Athena,* his heart prayed silently, *Goddess of wisdom and power . . . make Greeks of them!*

The sun, a round bright crimson face, rose beaming from the sea. The waters took on a winelike hue and the vast armada sparkled in the brilliant light. Men and women could be discerned now in the ships, lifting their faces to the sun and greeting it with wild cries.

Theseus and Haris hurried down from the tower and went to wait at the embankment. Captain Fox was entering the harbor. "I brought them!" he shouted, spotting Theseus at the pier. Behind him followed the largest of the barbarian vessels, a ship with red and black carvings on the prow. It approached, touched the pier, and a fierce blond giant leaped ashore. He was dressed in sheep-skins and had an iron hatchet in his belt.

"Their Chief!" called out Captain Fox to Theseus. "Talk to him!"

Theseus stepped forth and put out his hand. "I welcome you and your people!" he said to the Chief. "I am Theseus, King of Athens. My army and my ships are ready to set out for the rich land that my captain spoke to you about. We'll take it, and we'll divide it among us. Do you accept?"

The blond Chief put out his broad palm. "I accept!" His voice boomed loudly. "When do we leave?"

"Tomorrow."

The giant grunted and jumped back into his ship. For a moment Theseus stood watching him as he weaved in and out among the vessels, shouting out commands to his people. "What is he saying?" he called out to Captain Fox.

"He's telling them to stay in their ships," the captain answered. "That this is friendly land and they're not to harm anyone."

Theseus turned to Haris. "Come," he said, "let's not waste time," and mounting his horse, sped back to Athens, to prepare his people.

40

The King of Crete was sitting on the northern terrace of the Palace, resting his head against soft pillows. Slaves were moving about him quietly, bringing him refreshing drinks and fanning him with large ostrich-feathered fans. He looked pale and tired. For days now, he had been having bad dreams. He would dream that the sea was filled with seagulls, and as they'd touch the shore they would turn into hungry black crows; or he would dream that the Palace had vanished, that it uprooted itself and disappeared into the clouds, like a paper kite.

Oneirokritos, the dream interpreter, was sitting beside him, try-ing to console him. "Dreams are nothing more than reflections of our fears," he was telling him. "What we fear in the daytime, we dream at night."

Phaidra had come out to join them, looking very beautiful in her new fall dress, a black creation with large embroidered leaves of gold. "Father," she bent over him, taking his hand affectionately, "when are you going to order the games to begin? The full moon's here already; why are you delaying?"

The King turned away impatiently. "You women," he muttered, " . . . all you have on your minds are holidays."

"And why not?" smiled Phaidra sweetly, "life's a game. We might as well enjoy it."

"You're right, my Princess," the dream interpreter chimed in. "Life is a game. It only lasts a little while, why waste it fighting wars? That's what I've been saying to our long-lived King, here . . . don't pay attention to dreams, I've been telling him. . . ."

The King slumped back on his pillows and closed his eyes.

The sound of footsteps echoed on the terrace. The old man barely stirred.

"My King!"

Oh, bother! The King scowled and burrowed deeper in his pillows. *Why couldn't they leave him alone. . . .*

"My King!" It was Malis, his voice insistent. "The people are refusing to go to war! They've gathered in the marketplace and are throwing down their weapons!"

The old King opened his eyes. He glared at Malis. "What are they saying?" he snarled.

"They're saying that there's no need to go to war; that there's no need to go out and fight the Athenians just because their Prince killed the Minotaur. . . ."

The old man glowered.

" . . . They're saying that we don't need the Minotaur, that we have our trade and our comforts and our wealth—why should we go to war? We're not hungry."

"And if others who are hungry come and make war on us?" the old man shouted sitting up. "If others come and take our ships and our fields, and break into our storehouses? Did you tell them that?"

"I told them."

"And what did they say?"

"They said no one would dare step foot here."

The King closed his eyes again and leaned back on his pillows. "Go," he muttered wearily. "I'm tired."

Malis left and the slaves scurried forth again with refreshing drinks. Phaidra bent over him with a cup of cool rose water. "Don't pay attention to them, Father," she murmured soothingly, " . . . it's nothing. Give the order for the games to begin . . . to ease our hearts a bit."

As the old King lay there with his eyes closed, a figure appeared on the terrace, a stooped old man with long white hair approached, shuffled to a corner, and sat cross-legged on the tiles, as if waiting for the King to see him. Minos half opened his eyes. "Welcome, old Orphos!" he murmured. "You've come at a good time. Things aren't going so well here. Come and tell me a story, to pass away the time."

The old storyteller drew near. "As you command, my King. I'll tell you a tale to ease your mind."

"Closer," mumbled the King, slumping back on his pillows. "I can't hear you."

The old man dragged closer and settled at the King's feet. He looked embittered about the mouth and his voice sounded pained. "Good evening, all . . . ," he commenced, as though addressing an audience, "I begin the myth. Once upon a time. . . ."

"Night hasn't come yet!" interrupted the King from his pillows. "What are you talking about?"

Night has come . . . night has come . . . , mumbled old Orphos, shaking his head. "Once upon a time," he began again, "there was a great island in the center of the sea. It had thousands of ships and thousands of soldiers, and no fortress walls surrounding it as there was no fear of any enemy coming to attack it. In the center was a renowned palace where the King sat on a golden throne. The King was omnipotent. When he frowned the sun darkened, when he smiled the sea laughed. Now and then this King would go up to the mountaintop and talk with God. The King and God would talk as two old friends and the people down in the plain would hear them laughing. Once in a while they would quarrel, and then the mountain would shake and the earth would tremble and quake. One day the King said 'I can no longer fit into this island. I am going out to conquer the world.' He raised an army, armed his ships, and set out, and the masts of his ships filled the sea. He set out for the north, he set out for the west, he set out for the south. And when he returned to his island his ships were filled with gold and slaves and women, and all his sailors and soldiers were wearing crowns of gold. . . ."

A soft cry, like a whimper of an infant in its sleep, sounded. The old storyteller stopped. Minos had closed his eyes and was crying softly in his pillow.

Out in the west the sun was setting. The crests of Ida were turning red, and the light was rising high on its peaks, preparing to go out. The flocks in the pastures were returning from their grazing and the peacocks were gathering on the terraces, emitting strident cries and looking out with sleepy eyes at the twilight descending.

The lords and ladies sitting at their windows were watching the sun go down and throwing amused glances at their old King on the terrace. "Look at him, listening to fairy tales," they laughed. "He's grown senile, poor thing. Imagine, for no good reason, he wants us to go to war—leave our peace and quiet, our comforts and our pleasant conversations, and grab up swords and lances and run off to war! Poor dotard."

The ladies laughed and began talking about the winter fashions—what color would be in this year, what headwear would be chic, how the smartest would be wearing plumes of pheasant. . . . "My dear," they could be heard, "did you see Princess Phaidra's dress? Stunning! Black velvet, embroidered all over with leaves of pure gold!"

"And why not?" from some envious spinster. "She can have anything she wants! Especially now that she's an only daughter her father gives her anything she asks for."

"Ah, yes . . . what ever happened there? Does anyone know what's become of Ariadne?"

"Who can be sure, my dear? There are so many rumors. They say she was snatched by pirates and sold in the Anatolian bazaars!"

"I heard she threw herself into the sea and drowned—that she regretted having gone away. . . ."

"No, no, dear heart, they say Theseus killed her!"

"Curse him!"

Down below, the old Captains were emerging in the courtyards for their evening strolls. "Remember once in Cyprus . . . ?" you could hear them. "Remember once in Sicily . . . ?" They never tired of remembering the past. Nothing in the present seemed to interest them.

The chill of night moved in. The slaves appeared, closed the windows, lit the lanterns. They tended to the lords and ladies,

193

dressed them in their evening finery, set the tables, brought in the food. The lords and ladies, freshly painted, perfumed, and coiffured, sat at the tables, sniffed the food, went through the ritual of the evening meal. Not that they were hungry. They were never hungry, these lords and ladies; never without food and drink long enough to get thirsty or hungry. But what else was there to do? They toyed with the food; pushed it away; yawned.

"Open the window," someone drawled. "Let's see what's happening outside." They could hear the galloping of horses resounding in the courtyard and shouts and banging doors.

"What could be happening, my dear? It's only the slaves. They're always at something or other. Such energy! Like animals. . . ."

Horses' hooves were striking sparks on the tiles in the courtyard, and sweating horsemen were dismounting. "Where's the King?" The strident voice of one who appeared to be their leader rose above the clamor.

"He's eating," someone answered.

"He's sleeping," said another.

"Is he eating or is he sleeping?" the agitated horseman shouted.

"Both!" a third piped, laughing.

The horseman glared at them. "Laugh," he snapped. "We're drowning, and you're laughing!"

They escorted him to the threshold of the King's apartment, where he knocked and waited grimly. The door opened and Phaidra appeared, clad in her beautiful autumn garments.

"I must see the King!" The horseman's voice was loud with urgency.

"Quiet!" Phaidra frowned. "What could be so pressing that he should dare disturb them at this late hour?"

"My Princess, I must see the King!" the hapless messenger persisted. "It's urgent! The sea is filled with ships. . . ."

A sleepy voice trailed irritably from the bedchamber. "What is it, Phaidra?"

"Nothing, Father," and Phaidra went to close the door, but in a desperate move, the messenger pushed past her and burst into the room.

"My King!" he shouted, "we're lost! The sea is filled with approaching ships!"

"What ships?" The King sat up.

"I don't know, my King. It's night, we can't make them out. We can only see their lights! Thousands of red lights!"

The old man lay back. "Bring me some rose water," he said weakly.

What bother! . . . Phaidra hurried to get the rose water. *If this interfered with the bull sports tomorrow, she would die!!* . . . She sprinkled the reviving fragrance on her father's bald shiny pate, poured some on his wrists, rubbed his temples.

The old man sighed, refreshed.

"My King. . . ."

Ah, yes, the messenger. "Go get the officers and bring them here," the King commanded.

The messenger left on the run.

What bother! . . . *what weariness!* The King lay back and closed his eyes again.

Before long the door opened and the officers filed in. Some five or six of them, still clad in nightshirts, came straggling into the room. With them were three ancient captains.

"They tell me ships are approaching the harbor," Minos said to them. "Be good enough to run down there and find out what's happening."

The captains winced. "All of us?"

"You needn't all go." The King shrugged wearily. "Just send the younger ones; and if it's serious, come back and wake me. Otherwise, wait til morning."

It was almost midnight when the officers reached the harbor and climbed the towers to peer out at the sea. In the distance, the dark waters were shimmering with red lights. Boats in the thousands, with flickering red lanterns, were rising and dipping their way toward the shore. The startled officers stared. These weren't Athenian ships—Athens could never muster such a navy! "The barbarians!!" they gasped, and scrambling down the towers, they vaulted over their horses and sped back to the Palace.

Phaidra was sleeping soundly when the officers returned. She was dreaming that the bull sports had begun and she was sitting on a bull with golden horns. It was racing pell-mell toward the sea and she was grasping its horns and laughing as it went plunging into the waves.

195

In the adjoining room the shaken officers had wakened her father. "The sea is filled with ships!" they told him. "What should we do?"

The old King looked at them bitterly. *His ships were in the harbor, but they had no crews . . . his army was prepared but had no will to fight. . . .*

"You didn't want to fight when I was telling you to fight," he sneered. "You didn't want to fight for glory. Now, with the enemy at your door, ready to wreck your homes and empty your storerooms, we'll see how you fight!"

The officers looked at one another sullenly. "What do you want us to do?" they mumbled.

"Round up the army and rush down to the harbor! And die! All of you, if necessary!"

41

Out at the harbor the boats were approaching. Mast after mast, they came, pushing inexorably toward the shore. First among them came the fleet of the Athenians, and behind, the myriad red-lanterned boats of the barbarians.

Theseus, in the foremost ship, was leading the way, moving ahead of the others. His heart was pounding. *Whatever had rotted would fall . . . had to fall! so that they could pass! They were young . . . they would build a new world. . . .*

Haris was standing alongside him, holding an ax given him by the blond Chief. He was girding it about his waist and looking out at the dark Cretan shoreline that was approaching. His thoughts had leaped past the harbor to the sleeping Palace where his mind was envisioning the King in his bed, wondering what he was dreaming of at this moment.

"They're all snoring by now," smiled Theseus. "The lords and ladies, with their bellies filled with food, have all gone to bed."

"No, I know them well," laughed Haris. "They've hardly touched their dinner. They have no appetite, and they can't sleep nights."

Theseus threw a glance behind him, at the boats with the huge blond men and women that were following. In the glow of their red lanterns, the naked bodies pulling at the oars were gleaming hard and strong. "Look at them!" he laughed. "They have no problem eating or sleeping. Their stomachs aren't ruined. Did you see the new god they're bringing with them?"

"You mean Herakles?"

"Yes. Did you notice how much he looks like them, how coarse he is like them, and tall and gigantic? They claim he kills wild beasts and tames rivers and comes up from Hades and holds up the earth on his shoulders."

The huge blond men and women were paddling their crude vessels, shouting gleeful exhortations to one another. The din of their voices and the splash of their paddles filled the sea. Visions of plunder were propelling them forward—*jars, twice the size of a man, filled with honey . . . and wine . . . and oil! Chests filled with gold . . . and earrings . . . and bracelets! Clothes made all of velvet. . . .*

Ahead of them the lights of the harbor were coming into view. They could see the harbor lamps atop the tall towers flickering against the night Cretan sky. Behind the illuminated towers, the city lay in darkness.

"They're sleeping!" The blue-eyed giants looked out at the slumbering island and doubled over laughing. "Don't worry!" they shouted, patting their hatchets, "we'll wake them!" and the ships spurted forward rumbling with laughter.

"Quiet, lads! Don't let them hear us!"

"They haven't seen us yet," said Haris, peering anxiously at the harbor. "I don't see their ships coming."

"All the better!" muttered Theseus. "They're giving us time to capture them in their own harbor . . . Then, on to the Palace!"

"Are you going to kill the old King?" whispered Haris.

"No, why should I? He's no threat. When he stops being King, he'll be nothing but an insignificant old man. I'll give him a house and a bit of land and leave him alone to putter in his garden."

"I pity him," said Haris.

"So do I. But there's nothing more I can do for him," shrugged Theseus. "He's no longer needed in the world."

"Eh, King!" The three-masted ship of sly Captain Fox came up alongside the flagship. "Are we going to set it to the torch?"

Theseus threw him a look. "Don't be so hasty!" he said. Then chidingly. "Don't you pity all those gold chests going up in flames?"

"We'll empty them first!" laughed the captain.

"We'll see." Theseus turned away.

The morning star appeared. It winked gayly. The sky began to brighten, the horizon over lofty Ida reddened, and the harbor came boldly into view—the towers, the huge warehouses, the broad piers—all could be seen clearly now. Beyond the harbor, on the broad main road leading from Knossos, they could make out movement. Slight dark warriors with black hair, clasping lances and small round shields, were running past fields and vineyards, racing toward the harbor. Leading them was Malis, running ahead and shouting exhortations.

"Faster!" shouted Theseus to the oarsmen. "Faster!"

The ships spurted forward. By dawn they were entering the harbor.

Out on the road, the Cretans were coming. As they drew closer and caught sight of their sea darkened by thousands of ships, they stopped. Malis, waving his lance, lashed them on. He was a fierce fighter and, moreover, the chests in his storeroom were full. "On them!" he shouted "Kill them! They've come to plunder our wealth!" And taking courage, the dark-skinned soldiers rushed forward again.

Theseus had already leaped ashore and was nailing his iron-tipped lance into the earth. "In the name of Athena!" he was shouting, "I take possession!"

Behind him the Athenians were spilling from their ships, and behind them, came the blond masses. Holding their heavy shields before them, they raised their lances and rushed at the dark army coming at them. On the slope of the hill before the city, the two armies clashed.

"Herakles! Herakles!" the barbarians bellowed, surging behind the Athenians. Waving their hatchets and filling the air with a barbarous din, the blond giants, too, fell on the soldiers of the Cretan King.

The short-statured Cretans cowered. *These creatures weren't human! These creatures were monsters!* "We're lost!" cries went up among their ranks and they began falling back.

"Kill! Kill!" Malis shrieked, fighting valiantly to rally them. His eyes were pinned on Theseus who was charging ahead and he went to lunge at him, but before his arm could come down with his sword, Theseus thrust his own lance into the ex-Chief's heart and Malis fell dead.

"To the Palace!" Theseus shouted to his companions. All around them, the army of King Minos was scattering. The spoiled, emasculated soldiers caved in at the first clash, dropping their weapons and running—some up the hills to escape, others behind the river foliage to hide. Some made it breathlessly back to the Palace where the King was waiting.

The old King had wakened and was sitting on the terrace with his daughter Phaidra, looking out toward the south where the din of battle could be heard. He was listening uneasily, muttering to himself. The sounds of clashing metal and the screams of wounded men were echoing ominously over the plain. *What was taking his army so long? He had ordered Malis to return with a report . . . what was happening?*

The sun disappeared behind some clouds, and drops of rain began to fall.

"Let's go inside, Father," urged Phaidra.

"I have a feeling this is the end," murmured the King.

Two breathless guards approached. "The army has scattered!" they reported. "Malis is dead! The enemy has surrounded the Palace!"

"Who's their leader?" the King asked when he could speak.

"Theseus."

Phaidra, listening in ashen silence, rose suddenly and disappeared inside her room. She called her maidservants, picked out her finest garments, and bade them dress her.

Out on the terrace, old Minos leaned dazedly against a column and stared down at the central courtyard that had come alive now. Slaves and nobles were emerging, running in confusion, dogs were barking, monkeys screeching. Palace ladies were running to their windows, peering at the plain. "They're coming! They're coming!" they would shriek and roll their eyes to heaven for help. Some were dragging out their treasure chests, stuffing bracelets and precious trinkets in their bosoms. Lords were gathering up their treasures and running to the stables to find horses to flee. Some old merchants had bolted their doors and were burying clay tablets in the ground, hiding the ledgers upon which their debtors' accounts were recorded. In the storerooms below, slaves were dipping pitchers into jars of old wine, drinking greedily what had always been denied them. How they had ached for this old wine and never been allowed to drink. Now all was theirs!

In the royal wing, Phaidra, adorned and ravishing, emerged from her room. Weeping maidservants were following behind her. "Don't go out, my Lady!" they were wailing, "they'll kill you!" and they tugged at her skirts, trying desperately to hold her back. But she walked past them without a word. *If she showed fear now, all would be lost!* Numbly she walked down the steps of the women's quarter.

At the foot of the stairwell she could hear the din outside growing louder. Theseus, dripping with blood, was bursting into the grand courtyard. He was plunging his lance into the earth between the tiles and looking up at the Palace. "This Palace is mine!" his voice could be heard rising over the din.

Some younger lords, hiding behind bolted doors, felt shamed, and collecting what slaves they could, they opened the doors and surged at the enemy to defend the Palace. But they were no match for the Athenians and the barbarians who quickly surrounded them, and they fell dead.

"Heaven help us!" cries were erupting from the windows now, and down below blond barbarians were leering up at the shrieking women. "The ropes! the ropes!" they were shouting. "Bring the ropes!"

Phaidra stood at the door.

"My Lady, don't!!"

Dazzling, in all her beauty and royal splendor, the Princess opened and emerged on the threshold.

"Throw a noose around her!" someone bellowed. Hands reached out to grab her. "A noose!" the voice roared again above the clamor, and the Chief of the blond barbarians was seen surging toward her.

For an instant Phaidra stepped back, her eyes darting across the courtyard. "Theseus!!" her voice rose piercingly.

Theseus turned. He saw her standing on the threshold, opening her arms to him. "Theseus!" her voice was calling to him, "help me!" and in a bound he was at her side, holding out his hand in a gesture of possession.

"She's mine!" the blond Chief bellowed angrily and went to put his noose around her neck.

"She's mine!" said Theseus and stood between them.

The barbarian raised his hatchet.

Phaidra held her breath and watched Theseus pull out his dagger. *I hope they kill each other,* she was thinking to herself.

But as the barbarian was stepping back to get momentum with his hatchet, a hand grabbed it from his fist and Theseus saw Captain Fox grasping the Chief by the waist and speaking to him sharply.

The barbarian dropped his arm and looked sullenly at Theseus. "Take her!" he muttered and pushed past him into the Palace.

Quickly now, Phaidra grasped Theseus's hand. "Save my father!" she said. "Save me and the Palace, and everything is yours!"

"Lead the way," said Theseus, "before the barbarians get there!"

Phaidra hurried him inside. She led the way through the corridors that were groaning now with desperate shrieks and cries, raced up the stairs and arrived at the Throne Room. There they found her father sitting on his throne. The old King had put on his full ceremonial dress and was waiting for the end, clad in all his gold and pearls and precious royal feathers.

Theseus approached. "King of Crete," he said, "I have come back! Step down from your throne!"

"You'll have to kill me," the old King answered. "I'll not step down. I want to die a King!"

"You're weak and unarmed," said Theseus. "I don't want to kill you."

The old man didn't budge.

"Step down!" said Theseus, reaching to grasp him and unseat him bodily.

"Theseus!" Phaidra flew at him. "My dearest Theseus," she checked herself, "you're an Athenian. Don't behave like those barbarians!"

Theseus dropped his hold on the old King.

"Beloved friend," Phaidra now purred softly, taking his hand, " . . . the Gods did not mean for you to have my sister as your wife. But you can take me. With me as your wife, the throne will be yours lawfully, without barbaric force."

Theseus looked at her.

" . . . My father will resign," Phaidra held out coaxingly, "and you'll become the lawful King of Crete."

He hesitated. *What she proposed made sense . . . if he married her, he would have the throne lawfully and not have to resort to bloodshed. . . .*

"You're right," he conceded, "I'll marry you!" and taking her hand, he turned to the old King. "Step down and rest from the heavy burden, Father," he said, "my turn has come to sit on your throne."

The old King smiled a rueful smile. He rose now from his throne. "Bend down, my son," he said resignedly, and taking off the royal crown, placed it on Theseus's head.

Groans and screams were echoing out in the corridors, doors were breaking down, women were wailing, men were cursing. Smoke and frantic shouts were coming from the stairwell. "Fire! Fire!"

"The Palace! My husband, save the Palace!" Phaidra grasped Theseus's hands beseechingly.

Theseus bounded from the room and raced down the smoke-filled stairwell. In the cellars below, barbarians were setting storerooms to the torch. Flames were leaping from room to room, filling the corridors with smoke. In seconds, Theseus bounded up the stairs again "Come down!" he shouted to Phaidra from the stairwell. "Take your father and wait for me in the courtyard!"

Flames were licking the walls when Phaidra, dragging her old father behind her, fled choking from the room and took refuge out in the courtyard. There, amid the smoke and din, she stood against a column and watched the Palace burn.

Walls were creaking, canaries were choking, barbarians were breaking down doors, roping lords and ladies, dragging them swooning out into the courtyard and tying them by their nooses to the columns to be led away later as slaves. Down in the cellars they were smashing jars, spilling wine, oil, honey . . . setting everything ablaze. In vain Theseus formed water brigades with his men to battle the fires. In vain he tried to restrain the barbarians, to save the Palace from their mindless rampage.

"It's ours!" he shouted to them. "Don't destroy it!" But the Palace was beyond saving. A strong wind was coming up, helping fan the flames, and the fire spread quickly. It was soon roaring throughout the Palace, igniting everything it touched, setting doors and windows ablaze like gigantic burning candles.

Haris, whom Theseus had sent with soldiers to guard Phaidra, came to stand beside her. His eyes were filled with tears as he watched the Palace disappearing. Phaidra was looking on dry-eyed, her teeth biting into her lip, drawing blood. A wild look was in her eyes as she watched the splendid sculpted carvings, the peeling murals, the magnificent embroidered gowns, all going up in flames and becoming ashes.

The old King, his head dropped on his chest, was sitting on the tiles seeing none of this. Now and then, he would lift his head in all the din. "Phaidra," he would murmur, "what's that noise? What's that fire? What's burning?" Then he'd laugh softly. *All this was a dream . . . soon the cocks would crow and he'd wake up and all of this would vanish. And he'd summon his dream interpreter to ask him what it meant. . . .*

By nightfall most of the slaves had bolted and were racing drunkenly about the courtyard. Many had joined the barbarians and had taken up hatchets and were plundering the Palace. They were running in among the flames, lunging at the chests, filling their fists with jewels, darting away choking from the smoke, and running out to the courtyards to don the precious jewels, laughing and shrieking raucously.

"Slaves!" Phaidra watched them in disgust.

"It's their turn now," murmured Haris softly.

Theseus came to stand beside them. His hair was singed and his hands were covered with bruises. He had done everything he could. There was no saving it.

A gentle rain began to fall—as if the sky, too, were weeping for the beautiful Cretan Palace that was vanishing forever from the earth. All night the rain fell on the flaming Palace. By morning the fires were burned out.

When the smoke died down, Theseus took Haris and went in among the rubble. The seared tiles beneath their feet had crinkled like dry autumn leaves. Inside, a few charred walls still remained standing, but the thick cypress columns were reduced to ashes. Nothing was left of them but the stone bases upon which they stood. A few murals were still intact—a young prince with long plumes atop his royal crown; some frolicking partridges; some dolphins swimming in blue waters; a bull tied to an olive tree. . . . On one wall, the remains of a painting looked down unharmed—a girl, resembling Phaidra, with enormous eyes and curly hair tied back with a ribbon. Unharmed, too, were some tall jars, blackened by smoke. Here and there, were some skeletons—an old man clutching a handful of clay tablets, a charred woman holding a clay vase into which she had hidden her jewels—you could see the lumps of gold in the bottom, from the melted rings and earrings. Strewn about the ashes were bronze double axes, small clay statuettes, and protruding in the rubble, a chessboard, the King's splendid chessboard with its magnificent adornments intact. It had crashed down from the upper floor and lay among the broken jars.

Tears welled in Haris's eyes. *When would man ever again create such beauty?* He looked down at the rubble that had once been his home and the tears spilled from his cheeks.

Theseus took his arm. His heart, too, was aching, but he held himself in check. "Come, let's get out of here," he said. "Let's breathe some fresh air."

They walked back to the courtyard where old King Minos lay propped against a stone column, alongside Phaidra who had finally dropped off to sleep. The old man had wakened and was weeping, as though he had come to his senses. He was looking at the ashes of his Palace and the tears were streaming down his withered cheeks.

Haris's father was there, too. The blacksmith had managed to save the iron in the Palace cellars and, with the help of some slaves, had piled it in a corner of the courtyard and was looking for a wagon now to haul it down to the ships. He had managed to save his old tools, too, and was very pleased.

Theseus sat down beside his sleeping wife and her old father. *He had done his duty. He had destroyed the old. Now he would set foundations for the new.* He gazed at the white smoke that was rising from the Palace. A flock of crows were making circles over it, cawing and swooping down on the human carcasses that were strewn among the still warm ashes.

The Chief of the barbarians strode over from the riverbanks where his people had stretched out for the night. *Now begins the difficult work of peace,* thought Theseus. *Woe to him who wrecks only.* The barbarian Chief approached and sat down beside Theseus. His eyes were still red from the drunkeness of the night before, but his brain appeared alert. His was a simple brain, solid and straightforward. "King," he said to Theseus, "this land is to our liking. "It's rich, it has vineyards and olive orchards and plenty of crops. The natives look clever and hard working. Let's put them to work digging and ploughing, and let's get on with our own work, War. That's the custom of my tribe."

Theseus put his hand on the Chief's massive knee. "This land is mine," he said. "I brought you here, and together we conquered it. Now I want to return to my country. Let's take an oath of friendship. You remain here, and I'll return to my country, with the King's daughter as my wife. If anyone comes to attack you here in Crete, I'll rush to help you. If anyone comes to attack me in Athens, you'll rush to help me. Agreed?"

The Chief held out his giant paw. "Agreed!" he said, and rising to his feet, went back down the riverbank to tell his people.

The sound of the two men talking wakened Phaidra. She opened her eyes and for an instant looked around in confusion. Her father lay on his back beside her, his eyelids tightly shut. His face was waxen and yellow, and May flies were flitting about his nostrils. "Father," she called to him softly. The old King didn't move. "Father!" she bent over him anxiously. The old man lay rigid, his lips taut over clenched teeth. Phaidra touched his hands. They were cold. She put her palm over his heart. It was still. "Father!" she let out a pitiful cry and fell on him, weeping.

Theseus lifted her gently. "He's at rest," he consoled her. "He had nothing more to hope for in life."

They wrapped him in a sheet and carried him the short distance to the ancestral burial ground. A dark, well-built vault. They went down seven steps. The place was strewn with bones from all the bulls and sheep that had been sacrificed throughout the years. They bent the body of the old King, touched his knees to his chin, made a ball of him, and lowered him into the earth. That was the custom. The lords and ladies of the Palace, released from their captivity by the barbarians to attend the funeral, lowered him into the earth, and no one wept. Only Phaidra. "Father! Father!" she lamented, "how you've ended up! Thrown into the earth like a common slave, without a hymn, without a trumpet, without a sacrifice! Not even a small pitcher of water in your grave for your soul to drink!"

Theseus took her hand. "Come, it's time to leave," he said, not unkindly. "Say good-bye to Crete."

The reality burst upon her as though she had never seriously considered it until now. *They were leaving! . . . She was leaving*

Crete! Outside the burial vault she stood and looked about her. Now that the moment had come, how her soul fought against it! She went to stand before the Palace, to say good-bye. She stared, long and hard, dry-eyed, then slowly turned away and walked up the hill for one last look at the legendary land where she was born. Juktas was spiring from the plain like some brooding giant against the turbid sky. Beyond, Ida's peaks hid from her view, concealed beneath black clouds. No wind was blowing, the clouds hung leaden, and now and then a heavy drop would fall. The whole vast sky appeared suffused in tears, matching her soul.

Haris, too, had gone off to take his leave of Crete; to say good-bye to all the places where he and Ikaros had spent their boyhood years. All day, his friend had not left his mind. Seeing the familiar grounds where they had played together, where they had walked and talked together, wakened poignant memories. What plans they had made together, what dreams they had dreamed! *Ikaros! Ikaros!* his heart was crying, aching for his dead friend.

"Haris!"

He turned.

"Make your farewells quickly, and let's go!" It was Theseus.

Haris threw a quick last glance about him.

"Don't look back," said Theseus. "Look forward. Our work here is finished."

"I'm ready!" and Haris hastened after Theseus.

42

The sailors lifted anchor, hoisted the sails, and the ships of Athens embarked.

Phaidra, standing next to Theseus at the helm of his ship, was turned facing the shore, to look at Crete for one last time. She was crying softly, . . . *farewell . . . farewell . . .* holding her hand to her mouth to smother the sobs that were rising in her throat.

The barbarian women were rowing alongside the Athenian ships, escorting them out of the harbor. Good-byes were echoing all across the waters.

"Farewell!" the Athenians were calling back to them. The men were jubilant, their shouts reaching to the heavens. They had grabbed what they could from the renowned Palace—golden goblets, bracelets, rings, clothing, wine—whatever they could salvage; and now, loaded down with plunder, they were returning to their country.

Theseus's ship, too, was brimming with treasure—shields, lances, golden bracelets—a King's royal gifts for his city. Standing at the helm, he looked back at the harbor, watching it recede. The clouds were growing denser over Crete, the mountains and plains darker; now and then a distant streak of lightning would come tearing through and for a second the sky would light up, then fall back into darkness.

Phaidra stood beside her husband, sobbing softly. Her island was disappearing, vanishing, as in a dream. She watched it growing smaller, smaller, and when there was nothing left, she let out a desolate cry.

Theseus patted her raven hair. She had a right to cry, poor thing.

Haris, sitting in the prow, closed his eyes. He could not erase the memory of the renowned Palace heaped in ashes, the lordly masters tied in ropes, the pampered ladies dragging in the mud. All these days he could not get Ikaros out of his mind. Even as he rejoiced in victory, his heart kept filling with shadows. He remembered Theseus's words—*don't look back! look forward!*—and the darkness in his soul brightened.

He lay back. The wind was picking up, billowing the sails. He stretched out on the prow and gazed at the sea. The ships, tossing in the quickened waters, looked like giant seagulls. Their white sails flapping, their bellies bobbing over the waves, they looked like giant seagulls ready to take flight. His lids grew heavy. They closed. *A tall, sublimely beautiful girl was taking him by the hand, leading him through broad avenues. They were in Athens. But a different Athens from the humble city that he knew. It had wide streets and temples all of marble. There were exquisite sculpted pediments of Gods and heroes adorning the temples—Titans wrestling with Gods; ancient heroes wrestling with monsters. The girl was pointing to the splendid friezes, and Haris was looking at them with instant recognition, as though some prior cognizance were at work in him and he knew the monuments and what they represented. There were the Greeks and the Trojans on the battlefield of Troy and the Gods sitting atop Olympos, looking down on them. There was Achilles slaying Hektor. And Odys-*

207

seus sailing in his ship past the Sirens. And there, on another frieze, was the new hero that the blond barbarians had brought to Greece. Clad in sheepskins, a heavy club in his hand, the frieze showed Herakles setting out to perform his twelve labors.

Marvel after marvel, the girl led Haris through the magnificent art-filled streets. Presently they came to a place known as Kerameikos. Great crowds were gathered here. The city was celebrating the Panathenaia, the great holiday honoring its patron Goddess Athena, and all had gathered here to take part in the solemn procession to the Akropolis. Thousands were assembled: men, women, children, all richly dressed. There were handsome youths, the high-born sons of Athens's nobility, riding splendid horses. Behind them were great numbers of armed soldiers, the hoplites, with their shields and spears. There were men crowned with laurel wreaths. Some were riding in chariots, victors in the chariot races. Others were athletes, bards, and rhapsodists—all crowned victors in the Panathenaic competitions. Behind them came the high-born maidens of the city, carrying a filmy, magnificently embroidered robe, the sacred peplos of Athena. And bringing up the rear were the sacrifices—the bulls and sheep that were to be offered to the Goddess.

The girl took Haris's arm and they entered the procession. Solemnly the worshipers advanced along the sacred route. They passed the agora, approached the sacred Hill, and began to climb. The priests were chanting hymns. Haris and the girl followed, and when they finally reached the top and stood before the marble temple of Athena, Haris let out a shout. So loud it almost wakened him.

"The Parthenon," the girl smiled.

Haris stared. Never had he imagined such a temple. Such beauty! Such perfection! columns, metopes, cornices, all a miracle of grace. He looked and looked, and couldn't look enough. On its front pediment, facing east, was portrayed the birth of Athena. The marble frieze showed Hephaistos with his golden ax striking the forehead of the great God Zeus who was sitting majestically while Athena was springing fully armed from his head.

The maidens carrying the peplos approached the temple and went inside, into the shrine where the colossal statue of Athena stood. The Goddess, adorned in gold and ivory, towered in her tall helmet, her lance and shield in one hand, and Nike in the other.

The maidens bent and laid the sacred peplos with its thousand-fold embroidery at Athena's feet.

The bulls and sheep were slaughtered, the sacrifices offered, the meat divided among the people, and still Haris stood before the marble miracle, lost in wonder. The exquisite girl touched his shoulder. She was holding out a cup of wine to him, an enormous cup, larger than any wine cup he had seen.

"The Panathenaic cup," she explained. "Today everyone drinks from these cups."

Haris took a sip. He looked at all the wine and hesitated.

"Drink it all," the girl smiled. "Don't leave a drop. It opens the eyes of the mind."

Haris drank, and instantly he felt as though his eyes were opened, as though suddenly his mind had opened and the light of understanding entered. He looked curiously at the maiden. It seemed a glow was leaping from her solemn, lovely face, as from some goddess. Who was she?

"I'm Klio, one of the nine Muses," the girl smiled. "I'm the Muse of History." She put out her hand and touched his eyelids. "Waken!" she commanded softly.

Haris wakened with a start. Dawn was breaking over the waters. The sea was shimmering with morning light. He reached over the side of the ship and dipped his hands into the cool foamy waves. Across from the prow Theseus was standing at the helm, smiling down at him.

"Whatever you were dreaming must have been good," he laughed.

Haris splashed the refreshing water on his eyelids. "It was, my King!" he said, and his voice throbbed with emotion. "It was very good!"

43

Krino had climbed to the highest rock on the Akropolis and was looking out at the Saronic waters, watching for some sign of the Athenian ships. The days were passing, with no word from Crete, and she was sick with worry. How were the Athenians faring out there? What was happening to Theseus, and to her brother, and to her father?

Daidalos, too, had come to the sacred rock and was pacing back and forth before the Goddess's crude wooden temple.

209

"Ah, Masterbuilder," Krino moaned softly, "why don't you want to give us wings? I'd fly to Crete now and find out what's happened to them!"

"What could men do with wings?" answered Daidalos, shaking his head. "Let them become good first. Let them learn to love one another. With wings they'd only harm each other more easily." The old artisan stopped his pacing and turned to gaze across at beautiful Mount Pentelikos that was gleaming in the morning light. What marble it contained! What statues! what temples one could make with such material!

The sun rose higher. Out in the Saronic, where Salamis and Aigina were glistening in the sun-splashed waters, a lone white ship appeared. It approached, three-masted, with three white sails, and headed swiftly for the harbor.

The sun advanced. Noon arrived.

Krino rose. "I'm going down now," she said. "Are you coming, grandfather?"

But old Daidalos, engrossed in the future marble temples that his imagination was creating, could not yet tear himself away from the sacred rock. "I'll stay awhile," he murmured. "I'll come later."

Krino hurried down the hill. Shouts could be heard coming from below and the sound of galloping hooves. At the Palace a horseman was dismounting. People were clamoring about him, letting out joyous shouts.

Suddenly, men, women, children, were spilling from their houses, filling the streets. Cheering throngs were running to the orchards, gathering up olive branches, racing to the sea.

By sundown, the entire city had gathered at the harbor to wait for its victorious fleet.

Theseus, erect in his ship, was looking at the sandy beaches of Attica coming closer. The sacred rock of the Akropolis was shimmering in the last fiery rays of the setting sun. Lykabettos, across from it, was aglow with pines, and beyond, Hymettos was changing colors; from crimson it was turning violet, then deep blue. Theseus gazed at the indescribable sweetness and a profound calm quieted his soul. He could feel his heart mellowing, growing tame under the soothing harmony before him.

At the harbor, all Athens had turned out to welcome her heroes. Cheering, waving olive branches, the jubilant throngs lined the banks, watching their victorious fleet approaching. Ship after ship, the conquering vessels came, streaming toward the shore. Theseus's royal ship was coming first, with Captain Fox's three-masted vessel in the place of honor beside it. Behind them came the fleet, soldiers all erect on deck, striking their shields in triumph as they approached. The crowds cheered thunderously from the shore. Shields clashing, people cheering, the ships streamed in. And when the royal ship reached the shore, and Theseus, holding lance and shield aloft, leaped from the deck and roared his "Well met! I bring you Victory!" the air exploded with the people's cheers.

The men spilled from the ships, the crowds rushed to embrace them, and all Attica resounded from the trimphant din.

Athena's temple, adorned with olive and laurel branches, stood waiting, the statue of the Goddess shimmering softly in the silvery night. A full moon was looking down on the Akropolis when the jubilant city and its victorious army arrived to pay homage to the Goddess for their victory.

The soldiers laid the royal plunder on the temple steps, spread it on the ground, hung it from the columns—bronze Knossian spears, lances, helmets, sculpted swords, brazen bullheads with gilded horns. They laid out all the splendid treasures, the golden goblets, the earrings, the bracelets, the embroidered robes . . . until the humble temple glowed and the very stones appeared to laugh with joy. In the moonlight, many saw Athena smile, pleased.

Theseus approached the Goddess and touched her knees. "We have returned from battle, oh Goddess," his voice boomed in the night. "All that you commanded us to do, we did. We tore down the decaying Kingdom. We divided it among the barbarians. We infused its weakened veins with new blood. Now begins the work of peace." He lifted his arms to the Goddess. "Enlighten us, oh Athena, defender of the mind of man. Help us give just laws to our country, help us cultivate our land, help us use our bronze and our iron and our marble to create works of beauty, so that in time this entire city of yours may become a temple. Let peace settle in our country now, oh Goddess. War is good, but even better is peace."

"Peace! Peace!" the people chanted, lifting their arms to the Goddess.

Theseus stepped down from the temple, and the sacrificial bulls and sheep were brought forth. The animals were slaughtered, the sacrifices offered, and the crowds dispersed to celebrate the victory.

Haris and Krino went to sit on a rock nearby, with their father and old Daidalos. They had their arms around their father and he, too, was holding them close and looking down at them with tears of joy. A new road had opened to them. They would be living as human beings now. His heart was full. What he had wanted most in his life he had finally achieved—to live in freedom with his two children. He wouldn't be making knives and lances anymore. He'd be making hoes and plowshares. All that iron that he had brought back from Crete he would be turning into weapons of another sort now—tools for man to work the earth.

Old Daidalos was looking across at them and smiling. It had been a long time since they had seen the old master smile. For days now he had been coming up to the great hilltop, and they would watch him striding from one end of the rock to the other, examining, measuring, marking, sitting down, and gazing across at Mount Pentelikos.

"See that mountain?" he said, pointing to beautiful Pentelikos shimmering in the moonlight. "It's filled with marble. And what marble! Pure and white as snow. What statues one can make with such material! What temples! If only I were young, what work I'd do! I'd fill this Akropolis with such temples . . . such columns . . . such statues . . . that people would come from the ends of the world to admire it!"

Krino looked at old Daidalos and her eyes misted. *Some people should be immortal*, she was thinking, *. . . immortal to work and create forever. When this man died, he would take with him all the statues and temples that were in his head. . . .*

As though sensing the girl's thoughts, Daidalos smiled. "It's all right," he said. "I'm going to die, but others will come who will surpass me. They will do what I now ache to do. People die, but mankind lives immortal." His massive forehead was gleaming in

212

the silvery moonlight, and his eyes glowed with a new vision that was germinating in his head.

"I'm going to make a statue of Athena," he said, coming to sit beside the three friends. "I'm going to get marble from Pentelikos and make a statue of Athena." For a long while he was silent, gazing across at the mountain and pondering the vision that was taking shape within him. "I'll make her without a helmet," he murmured. "She'll have set it down, and she'll be holding Nike in her left hand."

"Nike with the great wings!" exclaimed Krino.

The old artisan shook his head. "No!" he said fiercely, "I'm going to cut off her wings! I'm going to make Nike without wings. . . ."

"So she can never fly again!" cried Haris, his eyes shining. "Yes, Master, make Nike without wings—so she can never fly away from Greece!"

TELOS

History

In the dim stretch of time before recorded history, before the emergence of the great Minoan palaces and the great Minoan kings, the island of Crete was inhabited by people who lived in caves. These early inhabitants were believed to have migrated from Asia Minor, and having found their way to Crete, lived there for thousands of years in stagnant and monotonous isolation from their neighbors. Stone axes and objects of bone were their tools, and female figurines among their unearthed artifacts suggest they worshipped a Mother Goddess.

In time, the Mother Goddess gave way in importance to a new male deity—the god Zeus. Among the lore of antiquity, where history and myth knew no distinction, there lived a legend that Rhea, fleeing her husband Kronos (who devoured his newborn sons lest they grow up and dethrone him), found haven in Crete where she gave birth to Zeus. There she hid him in a grotto and when he grew to manhood he dethroned his father, as decreed by an ancient oracle, and sired a son in Crete whom they called Minos, establishing the dynasty of Minoan Kings claiming divine ancestry to him.

Centuries before the worship of the god Zeus, and before the rule of the great Minoan kings, a wave of settlers, believed to be from Libya, invaded the island, bringing with them advanced skills and a knowledge of bronze-working. With the arrival of these tribes from the south, a new era dawned in Crete, marking the end of the primitive Neolithic way of life.

The start of this era (2800-2600 B.C.) ushered in a fresh vitality that gave impetus to shipbuilding and opened the way for trade between the island and other parts of the eastern Mediterranean. This active new exchange introduced the Cretans to the culture and art of the coastal populations of Egypt, Syria and Asia Minor, and eventually to the new god Zeus.

Sometime around 1900 B.C. the first of the great Cretan palaces began to appear. Huge, labyrinthean structures, they were built on the most fertile areas of the island—Knossos, Phaistos, Malia, and Zakros—where the power and wealth of Crete were increasingly concentrated. Around these structures revolved the political, social, economic, and religious life of the island where it is believed one powerful king ruled over all. This was a time of growth and prosperity for Crete. With its lush forests of pine and cypress, oak and ilex, its rivers and springs and fertile plains, the island provided amply for its people and a new creative energy burst forth, manifesting itself in decorative pottery and artifacts that for the first time the Cretans began exporting to markets abroad.

Around 1700 B.C., a natural disaster, believed to be a massive earthquake, struck the island and the three palaces were destroyed. Soon after, new palaces were built on the ruins of the old, this time bigger and grander, ushering in the island's "golden age." This was the age of Minoan *thalassocracy,* when Crete enjoyed her greatest power as mistress of the sea. With her impressive fleet she ruled the waters, aggressively pursuing wealth and conquest throughout the Aigean and Mediterranean. Freed of any need to fortify her great palaces (as no enemy could get past the "floating fortresses" that protected her shores), her people could enjoy in peace the fruits of her great prosperity. This is evident in the work of her artisans. Devoid of any warlike scenes, the exquisite art of the Minoans reflects a joyous spontaneity and carefreeness that suggests a happy and contented people.

In time, Crete's colonies and subject people began to challenge her rule over them. One by one, the conquered outposts began rising in revolt, vying with her for commerce with Egypt and other markets. By the mid-fifteenth Century, her naval supremacy no longer undisputed, the formidable power of Crete began to decline. Around 1450 the island suffered another series of earthquakes, believed to have come from the volcanic explosion on the neighboring island of Thera, and the great palaces were destroyed for the second and last time. Of the major centers, only the Palace of Knossos was rebuilt.

At the pinnacle of its power and influence, the Palace of Knossos was the largest and most magnificent of the three palaces. Rising four and five stories high in a dramatic setting between the Ida and Diktys Mountains, it contained some thirteen hundred rooms spread over an area of two and a half acres. One can imagine the impact on the foreign visitor setting startled eyes on the colossal edifice for the first time. Coming from lands, as did Theseus, where palaces were still humble structures, and houses no more than two rooms with a porch, what stories these visitors must have carried back with them! It is easy to see how in the telling and retelling of their tales, this gigantic complex with its maze of terraces and courtyards, its grand staircases, its vast rooms and corridors and mysterious winding passageways, lost the original definition of its name *Labyrinth,* which meant simply "House of the Double Ax," and took on the meaning of a bewildering maze.

No one knows exactly when this grandest of the great palaces was finally destroyed. It is believed some new disaster struck, perhaps fresh earthquakes or, as historians speculate, Crete was invaded by mainland Greeks revolting against their Minoan rulers. Archeologists date its sudden and violent end somewhere between 1400 and 1350 B.C.; but Homer, whose reliability as historian as well as poet has been gaining impressive credibility, describes Crete as still powerful and prosperous as late as the 12th Century when Idomeneus, a descendent of Minos, and now King of Crete, was able to equip a formidable fleet of eighty ships and sail off to join Agamemnon in the Trojan War.

With the collapse of the Palace at Knossos, Crete entered her final Minoan period. During this period, which lasted until 1000 B.C., new immigrants invaded the island—Mycenaeans from the mainland—who took over the Cretan *thalassocracy* and became rulers of the sea. Sometime after 1150 B.C. another wave descended on the island, this time the Dorians from Greece, and the brilliant Minoan culture that had flourished for one and a half thousand years came to an end.

In the thousand years that followed the Dorian invasion, Crete evolved through various stages, named by archeologists according to the art each stage produced. The years 900-725 were called the "Geometric Period," reflecting a geometric style in art. The "Orientalizing Period" (725-650) reflects the island's renewed links with the East. In the "Archaic Period" (650-500) important works in architecture, bronze and sculpture display a new vigorous style called the Daidalic style. The "Classical" (500-330) and "Hellenistic" (330-67) periods produced no works of great distinction.

For the next thousand years Crete underwent a series of occupations by foreign conquerors. From the Romans, who came in 67

217

B.C., to the Arab Saracens who followed in 824 A.D., to the Venetians in 1204, and the Turks in 1669, the island saw little respite. In 1898 Crete finally won her independence from Turkish rule and in 1913 became officially united with the motherland Greece.

Theodora Vasils
January, 1987
Chicago

ABOUT THE AUTHOR

Nikos Kazantzakis, one of the great European writers of the twentieth century, is best known in the United States as the author of the popular novel, *Zorba the Greek.*

His numerous works include novels, dramas, poetry, travel journals, translations, and essays. The most monumental of these is *The Odyssey: A Modern Sequel,* an epic poem of 33,333 lines which picks up the adventures of Odysseus where Homer left off and brings them into the modern age.

Nikos Kazantzakis was born in Crete in 1883, studied law at the University of Athens where he took a doctor of law degree, and continued his education in philosophy, literature, and art in Paris, Germany, and Italy. He traveled extensively throughout his lifetime and during brief intervals in his native Greece served as Greek minister of education and as president of the Greek Society of Men of Letters. In 1947–48 he was director of UNESCO's Department of Translations of the Classics.

His work earned him the highest international acclaim, including nomination for the Nobel Prize in 1951. He died in Germany in 1957.

ABOUT THE TRANSLATORS

Theodora Vasils has translated several works by Nikos Kazantzakis, among them, *Alexander The Great* (Ohio University Press, 1982); *Serpent and Lily* (University of California Press, 1980); *Journeying* (Little, Brown and Company, 1975), and *Symposium* (Thomas Y. Crowell Company, 1975); the latter two co-translated with Themi Vasils. Her work, for which she has received an honorary Doctor of Letters degree from Rosary College, is cited with co-translator Themi Vasils in the *Encyclopaedia Britannica,* Greece 363 (15th edition, 1986 printing). Among the translators' other works are short stories published in various literary journals, and a book of poetry, *In Another Light,* by Koralia Theotokas (Ikaros Publishing Company, Athens).